THE BUTTERFLY BOY

Tony Klinger

Andrew

First published worldwide by
Andrews UK Limited
The Hat Factory
Bute Street
Luton, LU1 2EY

www.andrewsuk.com

Cover photograph supplied by Tony Klinger

Contents

Acknowledgements

I would like to take this opportunity to thank the many people who have helped me whilst I was writing this book. As you know books don't spring forward out of a vacuum. This story is no different. It was inspired by the real struggles of the heroic and outstanding people who every day has to fight to overcome their disabilities.

On a personal level I couldn't have written this book without the constant encouragement over so many years of my darling wife, Avril, who has stood behind me when necessary and always at my side whether or not I have deserved such love and support, as have my daughter Georgia, her husband Matt, and my other children, Sarah and Daniel and his wife Doctor Sarah. You've all waited so long and patiently for me to be the writing man I was supposed to be.

In my short professional life as a novelist you need all the help and guidance you can get and again I have been singularly blessed. Therefore I want to publicly thank the lady who is my excellent and ever encouraging literary agent, editor and friend, Jenny Stanley-Clarke.

Without this reading like an award acceptance speech I also want to pay tribute to my remarkable parents who are both long since together in the after life. Lily and Michael Klinger were truly wonderful people and he was one of our finest film producers.

Many years ago, when I was seventeen my then agent, the late and lamented Greg Smith, told me I should be a novelist but I persisted with my career as a film maker. To prove his point he took one of my story outlines and procured an offer for me to write that story as my first book. I rather arrogantly and very stupidly turned down the very generous offer. I have enjoyed a successful and productive career making films and in academia but oh how right Greg was since I now know that I was meant to be a story teller. I live to write but life is full of mysterious circles and right now I am preparing that story as a film and as the book I should have written so long ago.

To all my family, friends and those that made this book possible, I love and thank you and appreciate your enormous patience and trust in me.

In the land of the blind, the one eyed man is king. Or put more beautifully and, I think hopefully, as the French poet Paul Claudel wrote: "For the flight of a single butterfly the entire sky is needed."

Tony Klinger
Northampton, England, 2013

THE BUTTERFLY BOY

Prologue

Nuremberg, Germany
1935

I'm not normally a pessimist but my situation is very bad, even by my standards. I am in a green walled interrogation room deep in the bowels of the Nuremberg Gestapo Headquarters. It is a lonely, intimidating place when you've been sitting, tied by tight ropes to a solitary wooden chair for what seems like an eternity. The room is damp, cold and I am very scared.

Forgive me, I should introduce myself, my name is Arnulf Hessel, but I've always been known as Arnie. When I'm frightened I draw up a mental inventory, pros and cons. I am scared so I am doing this now. I find this makes me see my life clearly, even if it doesn't solve my problems it does serve to take my mind off them for a little while. On the plus side is my age, I am 23, and I'm as fit as a butcher's dog. I have always been bigger than most men, not far short of 2 meters, or nearly 6' 6" in the other, English measure. This has always been an advantage for me, with both men and women. I wish I were in a warm bed with a hot woman right now. Back to the list, my eyes are blue and my hair is what I shall call dirty blonde, although my loving mother has always insisted it is the color of corn. Above these surface pluses I list my love of painting, and this love dominates my life, becoming a bit of an obsession, as I have grown better at it with time and patience.

As I look around at the depressing, claustrophobic little room I find more negative thoughts crowding my mind unbidden. Of course I do admit that I can be a bit obstinate sometimes, OK, all the time. Some see strongly held beliefs as a virtue but on this evil night I am forced to admit this trait has landed me on

1

this chair in this terrifying room. Being of mixed parentage I normally insist is an advantage but on this particular night I will admit that having a Jewish mother, however loving and kind, and a Christian father, who I don't really understand, is not a good thing for your health in Hitler's glorious Third Reich.

I can hear footsteps approaching in the corridor and I can't help but tense up in my chair. The heavy fall of booted feet on unforgiving concrete jars my nerves like a series of alarm bells. The noise ceases as they reach the door of my cell and a key is turned in the heavy lock of the metal door. I compose myself, trying to wipe the fear from my face, but you can't control the sweat that pops unbidden onto your brow, this mute traitor to my self-control.

Two men enter the room, one, Ratwerller, is dressed in a civilian suit, and he is thin, and reminds me of a hairless white rat, his head and face are pointed, unnaturally smooth and feral, but it is his eyes that I shall always remember, they are black lifeless pools, magnified horribly by metal framed spectacles. He is Rat, because that is how I can best describe him, preceding his bigger, fatter, uniformed colleague. Rat and I were renewing our long since moribund school connection. We had never been friends.

"Hello Arnie, you do remember me, don't you, we were friends at school?" the Rat asks me in what passes for his most pleasant tone, a high-pitched whine with a slight lisp. I instantly remember why I have never liked this man; in fact he has always repulsed me. "Call me what you want, you always did." I reply, perhaps too influenced by all the American tough guy gangster movies I watch. I am about to learn that in today's Germany such talk has a price.

"Naughty boy!" Rat hisses, he signals to his colleague who I shall call Fat Face who walks around my chair twice. I feel the hair on the back of my neck rise as he goes out of sight behind me. I am expecting something bad to happen when he is out of sight but there's nothing I can do except to tense myself waiting for the inevitable impact. Fat Face looks at me as he circles in front of me as if I am a particularly ugly specimen in a laboratory, a charming smile plays on his porcine face, which makes him look like an over ripe cherub. Fat Face stops pacing when he gets behind me for the third time whilst Rat walks in tiny mincing steps to the door where he stops and turns. "Teach our young friend some manners will you." he calls over his shoulder as he leaves the room. Fat Face begins to hum an unconvincing classic tune as he smiles and cracks his knuckles one by one out of my field of vision. "Wagner?" I ask, "Yes, Wagner's Ring Cycle," he responds, "It is a long composition" he adds with some conviction. "You have a nice voice" I tell him honestly, "Thank you." He answers, as he punches me hard, twice, in the kidneys. I try to cut off the howl of pain I feel, trying to stem it to stop him getting too much satisfaction. Just as I think I am managing the pain and the situation Fat Face slams his fist into my right ear, making my hearing go flat and the sounds in the room echo, my eyes are swimming with unbidden tears, now he hits me in the left ear, systematically jarring me so that the pain reverberates through my body, robbing me of coherent thought. Fat Face is still humming his tune in his pleasant voice, but now it is sounding a little strange because of my ears. I can feel the blood from them drip down onto my neck. He is still smiling as he walks in front of me to continue his work. He removes his the jacket and shirt of his uniform and pauses, he has a barrel chest, full of matted hair and sweating muscle. He follows my eyes to his torso and flexes his biceps.

"I have to keep in shape for this job." I nod my head; he is built like a powerful gorilla. He clearly enjoys his job, as his tongue licks at his sweating top lip as he starts to sing the Ride of The Valkyrie and he hits me with all his might in my stomach. I am unable to move because of the ropes holding me to the chair so I find myself straining into a fetal position. Now his humming and singing is beginning to really annoy me as Fat Face hits me squarely on my chin with an uppercut punch of such power that I hear my neck bones creak as my head snap back. "Stop!" I call, "Please stop!" I plead, Fat Face holds up his right forefinger for me to be silent. I smile in the hope he will accept my plea and stop hitting me. "I've learned my lesson, I will be polite, sir, I promise." I don't care if he knows I am a coward but I can't take much more of this beating without permanent damage. I hate pain, especially my own pain, and always have. Fat Face smiles, but there is no warmth reaching those cold eyes. He looks at his knuckles as if examining works of art and spotting some torn skin puts the damaged part of his hand inches from my mouth. ""Look what you did, go on, lick it better." I don't have a choice do I? I leaned forward and lick his knuckles. He sighs appreciatively and strokes the back of my head with his free hand. "Good boy," he says, "That's very nice." He removes both hands and then without pause he cups them both and cuffs me as hard as he can on both my ears. I howl in pain but as I do so he forearms me in the face twice. I feel two or three of my teeth being dislodged and I spit them out to avoid swallowing them.

Fat Face has resumed his singing and humming, all the time smiling. It is his obvious enjoyment of his sadistic beating that makes me lose my last vestige of self-control and fear. I lash out with my feet and kick the grinning bastard in his balls, he doesn't collapse, but subsides slowly to the floor, a balloon minus air, his eyes comically cross, holding himself and groaning, at least he isn't singing. He lies there groaning, prostrate at my feet. "I should kick your head in!" I roared, then my anger and humiliation get the better of me, and I kicked his head as hard as I can, knowing I have nothing to lose. I am panting with the effort. Now I get the feeling that there is another presence in the room. I look up and my skin crawls as I see it is Rat. He smiles, exposing his yellow, feral teeth, which are more like small pointed fangs.

"Don't you like the music Arnie?" Rat asks me. I don't like the look of the small leather object he extracts from his jacket pocket. His intent is obvious but there is nothing I can do as he raises the cosh high above his head and brings it crashing down on my head.

I'm somewhere in endless blackness, it's actually quite pleasant here. Like a big, warm dream. I don't feel anything. Memories of my life are swimming to the surface behind my eyes; I can hear something but can't make it out. Perhaps this is death, maybe I'm dead. I remember my parents, paintings, lovers, and friends. Someone is slapping my face, reality is coming back and with it pain and realization of my vulnerability.

My eyes open and I discover that I am back in my original cell with my friend, Hans. "How are you?" he asks gravely, "You don't look so great." "I'm OK." I answer, but I don't even convince myself. "You look bloody awful, like death warmed over." Hans continued, always the bloody realist, never discrete. "What did the bastards do this to you for?" he asks as he tries to clean me up with the aid of some spit on his dirty handkerchief. "I think it was because I simply don't like Wagner."

"Be serious will you," he rejoined, before continuing in a much louder voice, "These animals will be made to learn that they cannot get away with behavior like this in a modern society!" He speaks with exaggerated volume, hoping to scare the listeners we are both convinced lurk just outside our cell door.

"I would keep quiet if I were you Hansy," I warn him, "It really doesn't pay to upset the servants of the new order." Hans throws back his aristocratic Prussian head and hoots with laughter. "Don't tell me the little Corporal has frightened Arnie Hessel, I don't believe what I'm hearing. The little man is a bad joke, a momentary aberration. He came and he will go like a puff of smoke, poof he's here and poof he's gone, not a trace. You mustn't let these little bastards grind you down Arnie, it's not in your nature to give in." Hans claps me on the shoulder and I wince in pain as its one of the many places I have been damaged by the sadistic Fat Face, it gives me another jolt of pain to join the many others jostling for my urgent attention all over my body.

"Sometimes," I say to my friend, "you have to bend with the wind, before it becomes a storm and it snaps you in half, to adapt or you won't survive." Before I can complete my warning the door to our cell bursts open and in come Rat and Fat Face.

"Commendable sentiments Arnie," Rat says, happily smiling. He turns to Hans and continues, "You would do well to learn from your friends lesson," he says to Hans, "You don't scare me you lousy little bastard!" shouts Hans. Fat Face is on Hans before he can even draw breath, punching him to the ground. Rat pushes me out of the cell before I even realize what he's doing. I can hear that Hans is taking a beating but there's nothing I can do about it. I move down the corridor as Rat shoves me forward, using his boot to prompt my movements. I don't want to feel the weight of that cosh on my head again if I can avoid it.

"You're a lucky man Arnie," Rat breathes quietly to me as he marches me towards the gentlemen's toilet. "You're not a queer are you?" I ask, as he jostles me to a row of sinks opposite the urinals. "Very amusing," he laughs, and just for fun he hits me in the stomach which makes me bend over at the waist bringing my face down to the level of the washbasin. He holds my head down with one of his hands whilst turning the cold-water tap on with the other. Rat begins to wash my face with a strange intimacy and attention that is even more unsettling than his previous brutality. He continues to talk as he does so. "You're a very lucky young man, if I had my way we would strictly impose the laws dealing with defectives like you and that would be an end to you and your line like you. It's what comes when you take good Aryan stock and dilute it with sub human blood. But as it is your very nice mummy and daddy have come to get you; what are you going to say about our hospitality?"

I decide to play along with his obvious concern, "I shall tell them how kind you were throughout this misunderstanding." I try to pour all the scorn and irony I can into these words, but I don't want to upset the applecart so close to my possibly getting out of this place. He clearly doesn't like my line in sarcasm as he pushes the bar of soap into my mouth before I can finish. Rat resumes the conversation as I gag on the foul tasting carbolic taste.

"I thought you had really learned your lesson but perhaps I shall leave you alone with my colleagues for another session, he tells me that there are still one or two things he would dearly love to discuss with you." I shake my head as Rat pushes my face into the water and holds it there for what seems like an eternity, I think I'm drowning he holds me down for such a long time, I nearly lose consciousness before he lets me up for a gulp of air. "So Arnie, for the record, how are you going to say we treated you?" he asked me with the oily solicitude of a latter day Uriah Heep.

"You have treated me with courtesy at all time." I answer, having had enough of his courtesy to last me a good long while. I just want to be somewhere that Rat is not, far from his clutches. I might not understand why this stinking functionary of a hated regime should be so concerned about my parents, after all my father is only a middle ranking bureaucrat himself, and my mother, that most questionable citizen of the Reich, a Jewess.

I don't arrive at any conclusive answer to this interesting question as the cleansing process is concluded without further incident. Rat dries me off with brisk efficiency, although his every gesture is permeated with loathing. He finally unties my bindings, which had, of course, been totally unnecessary in my particular circumstances. My wounds are now patched up and are largely concealed under a fresh change of clothes supplied by Fat Face who gently helps to dress me. I catch my reflection in the mirror and am amazed at how normal I appear.

Rat ushers me into the hall with elaborate courtesy as if he is leading some visiting potentate on a tour of his station house. During the walk towards the public part of the building Rat becomes ever more unctuous. "Now we can all forget that little bit of unpleasantness can't we Mister Hessel?" I smile in response, I just can't believe or understand the reason for this total transformation. "What about my friend?" I ask, sensing now is the time to do deals. "He has already been released, while we were cleaning you up after your, accident." He answers as he stands before a large wooden door and hesitates, "It goes like this, our story, you got involved in a unfortunate brawl, you were arrested, you took your punishment like a true son of the Fatherland, no hard feelings?" He holds out his hand to shake mine, forgetting my problem for a moment. Of course I ignore his small discomfort.

"Why shouldn't I say the truth, that your brown shirted thugs attacked me and my friends while we were having an innocent drink in our favorite beer hall for no reason. Then we were arrested and beaten up, again for no reason, then I am let out, again without an explanation that makes any sense, and now what do you want, a bloody thank you note?"

The little rodent of a man controls himself, barely, and I think that whatever strings my parents have pulled are seemingly too strong for this bastard to do anything about them. "In any event, I do hope we meet again in more fortunate circumstances, perhaps we can discuss our time at school together?" Rat says all of this as if it might even be true, with a sickly smile playing on his face, but never quite reaching his dead eyes.

"At your funeral perhaps." I respond with more sincerity. He opens the door. I push past him and the first thing I see is my lovely mother, it's only a year since we last saw each other but the time has somehow diminished her, she's more frail, but when she smiles the room is still lit up. I follow her eyes, which nervously indicate some warning to me, I don't know what until I turn to my left and see my father. My mouth drops open in shock, he is dressed in the full black uniform of a Gestapo officer. My word is falling apart, my father now a member of the Nazi elite, my mother a Jew. I find myself saying hello as if I am a puppet, my father responds with the words, "Heil Hitler!"

Chapter One

Darmstadt, Germany
1910

"I simply will not marry you in a church," said Bertha loudly. "And I will not change my religion for you or your family!" retorted Bertie Hessel, with even more volume. They stood, toe to toe, in the wood paneled drawing room glaring at one another. Someone would have to give in, but whom, thought Bertha. "Why should I always be expected to give in, just because I'm a woman?" "No" he answered carefully and with his usual precision, "Because you're the woman who loves me." She melted, her resolve dripping away like hot wax, "What about my parents, they could never even set foot in a church?"

He looked at her for a long moment before answering, "then they shall not attend our wedding, which will be a pity, but not something we cannot overcome." He intoned coldly, totally without passion. Her anger returned in a rush, "Then we won't get married at all!" She shouted at him.

He looked at her with a mixture of contempt and longing, at times like this she was like a magnificent wild animal, when she was angry her nostrils flared, her heavy bosom heaved and even her coal black hair, currently tied in a granny knot on top of her handsome head, seemed charged with electricity. He didn't agree with her one iota, but he wanted her more than ever.

"It is possible that we could marry in a civil ceremony, by the Magistrate in Frankfurt." He said speculatively. She thought about this compromise but knew it would also result in a set of new problems.

"If we did that it would make everyone miserable, and why Frankfurt, who comes from Frankfurt, not your people or mine, why not here in Darmstadt, where we're all from, it's our town, we've done nothing to be ashamed of, after all we do love each other don't we?" Bertie looked at his woman and smiled, and said the words that were to seal their fate. "It might be the twentieth century but it is a man's duty to make the important decisions, and I say we will get married by civil ceremony here in Darmstadt next week, and if our parents care for us as much as they say then they will be there to share our joy."

Bertha was amazed, this was the longest speech she had ever heard from Bertie, normally so quiet and taciturn, even by the standards of a restrained polite society such as provincial Germany in 1910. She rushed into his arms and kissed him boldly, full on the lips. Her mother's warnings about men in general and Gentile men in particular, made her pull back when her body's impulse was to commit the ultimate sin, sex outside marriage. She would never admit this to a single living person, but she had felt something stir in her heart, and her loins when she was kissing her man. Wasn't this proof of love, particularly as she had felt him harden briefly before she had pulled back.

"We can wait, it's only a few more days." She breathed. His breath was ragged, "Yes we can, and we can wait just a little bit longer." He agreed. The few days were to seem like forever for the young couple.

Despite many heated arguments, pleading, shouting and eventually begging, Bertha's family would have nothing to do with either the wedding or Bertie. On the day of the ceremony Bertha came down the stairs of her affluent family's mansion to find all the mirrors in the house covered in black cloth, which at first she didn't understand. Upon entering the drawing room she found her parents and two brothers sitting on a row of low chairs, the men unshaven and wearing their skull caps, ready for prayer, her mother was veiled and weeping. "Daddy, what is it, what's happened, has someone died in the night?" Bertha asked her father, who didn't even look up. It was as if she hadn't spoken. Bertha moved to stand in front of her father, so he couldn't avoid her, still not fully comprehending the situation, "Papa, why are you doing this?" Receiving no reply she knelt in front of him, with her face inches from his, "You're sitting Shiva for me aren't you?" He raised his eyes to meet hers, he was crying, gently rocking back and forth on his low uncomfortable wooden chair.

"My daughter, Bertha, she passed away today, it was sudden." He said this in a dull monotone, which did nothing to conceal the sobs in his voice. His daughter stood up, fury briefly replacing her misery on her beautiful face. "Are you all mad, I am here and I am alive, look at me, I am your daughter, the daughter you love and who loves you, how can you mourn me like I'm dead?" She shouted at the man she had always adored and who loved her without question until this moment. "David" she said, turning to her handsome older brother, "Speak to our parents, they've gone mad, and you must make them understand!" David looked at his sister, his large eyes swam with tears as he shrugged his shoulders expressively, "What can I say Bertha, what can I do?'

Bertha turned toward the rest of her family, "Mama, Jonathon, please, stop this madness, you can't punish me for loving the wrong man!" But her younger brother and mother turned away from her. She softly placed her hands on each of her mother's cheeks and forced her to meet her direct gaze, "If you let me walk out of that door like this I shall never come back." She snapped these words like whiplashes across the family. Trying to force them to reconsider, to inflict pain on them like they were doing to her.

Bertha saw that her words were having no effect so she turned on her heel and strode out of the door. Her father watched her retreating back. "Don't worry, she will come back one day" Mama said to Father, "How can she come back, she's dead." He replied.

That afternoon, at three in the afternoon, the wedding took place just as Bertie had planned. It was a lonely, cold union witnessed by a pink old woman who usually served as the tea lady and cleaner for the Magistrates. Nevertheless she smiled almost coquettishly as the young couple exchanged their vows. It reminded her of the day, many years before when she had her moment of glory so many years before. Bertie placed the ring on his bride's finger and the couple kissed almost chastely. After cursory thanks to the Magistrate Bertie collected the marriage certificate and led his young bride out of the baroque building into the crisp autumnal air.

When, later, Bertha had the chance to look back at the start of her married life, she would often muse that this was the day that the sun ceased to shine in her life. The light went out of her passion like a candle guttering by the cold practical winds of matrimony. Yes, certainly their house was elegant and grand thanks to Bertie's inheritance from his paternal grandparents but it also never felt warm. She felt the cold creep into her very substance, but there seemed like there was nothing she could do about it. The grounds were extensive and well manicured to a peak of almost unnatural perfection, nevertheless Bertha still enjoyed long walks among the fine trees lining their section of the secluded, narrow river that steered a gentle, curving path through the bottom section of their land and on into the undulating pastureland beyond.

In other circumstances this might, in fact should have been an ideal start to their married life together, but both soon realized that they had committed an awful mistake. Being young, headstrong, and above all obstinate people they were determined not to admit failure to each other or, more importantly, to themselves. The shame would have been unbearable. Bertha's life was lonely and vacuous, her eyes, previously sparkling, vivacious and intelligent had taken on a far away and wandering look. Her appetite vanished; she yearned for the closeness of her family and friends all of whom had abandoned her. Her once voluptuous body became thin, the skin slack and sallow. But Bertha had no one but the mirror to tell her what she looked like, and she had long since abandoned peering at her reflection.

Perhaps she wouldn't have noticed the changes in herself over that first year, as they were so slow and gradual that they might have been imperceptible.

Bertie now lived an almost entirely separate life. He and Bertha had drifted apart, a small night disturbance due to his having influenza in the second month of their marriage had resulted in him kindly offering to temporarily move into the guest bedroom so that he wouldn't disturb Bertha's sleep with his sneezing. That had somehow stretched into a permanent arrangement. When he needed sexual release, which was not too often, he had taken to frequenting a tired but clean old whore in the city centre. He never kissed or caressed the woman, who was unfailingly polite, if a little brisk and antiseptic, but he was able to gain release in her. His work as a petty local government bureaucrat in the administration office for forestry was dull, repetitive and unfulfilling. He found fulfillment, both physical and mental, with the local militia, in which he soon reached officer status. He enjoyed giving orders and found the respect he got most stimulating, and of course, the uniform, he loved dressing up in the uniform. As Bertha spent less time in front of her mirror her husband more than compensated as he preened himself in front of his bedroom mirror in his full dress uniform.

Chapter Two

Saarbrucken and Darmstadt
November 1911

Bertie and his paramilitary unit were posted in the countryside for a large-scale exercise hard by the French border near a town called Saarbrucken on the River Saar. The day started uneventfully with a perfunctory goodbye kiss on Bertha's sleeping cheek at 05.00 hours on a Saturday morning.

The train ride with his men had been quiet, everyone lulled to sleep by the click-clack hypnotic rhythm of the slow train. He reported to the officer in charge of the depot, a bucolic bewhiskered man in his late fifties called Muller. He had an oddly insulting smell of cheap stale whisky on his breath, which was evident as he leaned close to Bertie's face whilst directing him towards the maneuvers on the nearby river.

Bertie led his men, who were soon huffing and puffing to the war games. He soon discovered that their assignment was to assist the engineers as they built a temporary pontoon bridge across the narrowest part of the fast flowing river in order that the impatient cavalry section could cross the threatening water. The heavy thump of the blank artillery shells made even the shouted orders hard to hear, and how Bertie longed for such action, such chaos in reality. If he ever had the chance to go at the French he would show them just what his Germany could do. He continued to scream his orders to his men and barely noticed the rain as it beat down harder and faster on him and his men. Soon the men's footholds on the riverbank became a muddy quagmire despite their antlike scurrying to lay the heavy timbers into the cloying mud. Muller re-appeared at his shoulder, nodding down from the horse he was perched on.

"This is all a bit realistic don't you think?" Bertie nodded in agreement, "That is precisely the reason for us undertaking such an exercise." He responded curtly, not caring or noticing that Muller was disturbed by his abrupt response. Muller thought the man an awful snob and bore, and he wished he were in a tavern drinking something warm. Bertie watched his normally disciplined men rapidly turn into a disorganized muddy rabble unwilling to help the struggling engineers secure the first pontoon to the second which even now was being positioned with great difficulty against the raging frothing tide of water.

A sergeant on the second barge bellowed to Bertie for his team's assistance, and although Bertie couldn't hear the man's words over the noise of the howling wind he did understand the man's frantic hand gestures as he signaled for immediate assistance. Bertie was unable to gather more than a small handful of his men, maybe five out of fifty for the urgent task of securing the second floating pontoon to the first. He realized he couldn't delay as this would result in the engineers working on board being swept away. Bertie led the way, climbing aboard the first pontoon with his small group of men and almost instantly he regretted his decision. The craft was too fragile and delicate for its task and the wooden slats were already cracking and groaning loudly in protest against their securing ropes which snapped dangerously taut to their three safety posts driven into the riverbank. Pointing towards the stricken craft Bertie screamed orders to his now terrified men, never allowing them to see his own fear.

"Quickly men, catch their line before it's too late!" Bertie shouted. One of the men, a young Corporal rushed forward, he was a man of limited intelligence but great courage thought Bertie. The younger man reached for the rope in the heaving, tempestuous water, seemingly unaware of the danger as the swirling current heaved the two flat bottomed boats together with a horrific grinding noise, trapping the Corporal between them. He screamed for help as both his hands were trapped for a horrible instant until the contrary, capricious river parted the boats. Bertie was the first man to reach his corporal who was staring in shocked disbelief at his arms that had both been amputated at the elbows with almost surgical precision. "My hands, where are my hands?" he screamed at Bertie. He didn't know how to answer the frantic young man who was in the first stages of hysteria. Bertie slapped his face hard, "You must keep calm, and do you understand me, calm!" The corporal nodded mutely as Bertie undid his own belt and braces and wrapped them tightly on his junior's arms, forming a crude but effective tourniquet to stem the heavy pumping flow of arterial blood gushing from both his arms, turning the swirling water red around their feet.

Bertie turned to another young soldier who was paralyzed in shock by the accident. "Get this man back to the first aid tent immediately!" The soldier managed to gather his wits when confronted with his officer taking charge with such certainty. "At once sir!" he responded instantly. He lifted the Corporal over his shoulder as the man was passing out. Staggering under the load he made his way to shore where several of his mates helped take the load of their friend.

Bertie's attention was immediately drawn back to the original problem as the two boats crashed together again. One of his men bravely reached for the rope now thrown by the second boat's sergeant. The brave man over reached, lost his balance and fell into the water. Although Bertie rushed to help he was too late. By the time he had traversed the small vessel the man had already been swallowed by the roaring torrent of water. Bertie knew that his duty was to jump in after his man and attempt a rescue, but as he looked at the slate grey wall of water he knew that he didn't have the guts to face his own death on this day. He looked away, as much to see who was watching him as to seek help and saw two of his men staring at him, in that instant an understanding passed between them all, let's all keep quiet and survive.

"Come on boys, we've got to secure these pontoons before anyone else is hurt. Come on be quick!" Bertie called to the men. They all made their way forward with great care, now visibility was reduced to near zero, the rain whipping almost horizontally into their faces across the river. They were unable to see the sergeant on the other boat when Bertie called to the man. "Throw us that rope Sergeant!" the other man didn't respond, "Throw us the rope!" Bertie shouted as loudly as he could.

As if from nowhere the rope flew into view, landing neatly at Bertie's feet. Bertie immediately grabbed it, and working with his men they hooked it through the steel hoop at the blunt prow of the boat and pulled it taut. Within moments the second boat was securely tied to its sister craft. The grateful sergeant and his men jumped quickly onto Bertie's boat and followed him and his men to the safety of the shore.

The rest of the day became a happy, glazed memory for Bertie. His bravery was assumed and accepted by all, his initiative went unquestioned, his cowardice unknown except by his two silent accomplices. He would have to deal with that later, but for now, all was good.

The biggest honour was to be personally congratulated by General Erwin Kessel in his command tent over a liberal, warmed tot of brandy. One drink with the General turned into two, then some more, a lot more in the officer's mess later. By the time Bertie arrived back at his house in Darmstadt he was very pleasantly drunk, too drunk to find the key hole, so he called out, "Bertha, let me in woman, Bertha let me in, the wandering hero returns to his little woman, it's Bertie the hero of the river Saar!"

Within a few moments Bertha opened the door for her husband, she was wearing a flannel nightgown and a dressing gown tightly closed by a chord at her waist. In her hand she held an oil lamp. "Be quiet, you're drunk, too drunk to even use your key!" He waved aside her protests and pushed her aside as he stumbled in. "Don't be such a shrew woman."

"I'm going to bed, you disgust me when you're like this." But before she could take a step he grabbed her roughly by the upper part of her arm. "Don't you even want to know why I'm drunk?"

"Let me go, you're hurting me!" she answered, but instead of complying he shoved her into the drawing room and took the oil lamp from her hand and placed it carefully on the table. He poured them both a large brandy and handed her a glass.

"Don't you think you've had enough Bertie?" she asked.

"Always with the clever tongue, well now I've done something even you can be proud of, and you'll toast me or I'll pour it down your throat by force."

"You don't scare me you drunken oaf."

"We'll see about that!" he jumped at her, grabbing her long hair he forced her head back until she was teetering off balance. Laughing at her he poured the brandy into her open, protesting, spluttering mouth forcing her to gag. "How do you like that bitch, not so high and mighty now are you?" He poured more brandy down her throat, "I should have done this to you a long time ago, shown you who is the master in this house, and now I am going to have you on this floor, right now!"

Still holding her head back he threw the glass to the wall and reached inside her gown and roughly fondled her breasts. Hating her body for its submission and weakness they both felt her nipples instantly harden and she felt the moistness betraying her between her tightly clenched thighs. He reached into her and smiled wickedly when he felt her.

"So, you like it rough eh bitch, I should have known." He pulled her face up and kissed her roughly full on the mouth. She bit him as hard as she could on the lip and it forced him to momentarily back away, she slapped him with all her strength on his face, he grabbed her by the collar of her gown and pulled with all his strength, the cloth of her nightgown ripped from shoulder to flank, and she stood almost naked before him in the flickering light. There was a pause as he looked at her, his eyes registering his animal lust, she started to back away but he simply walked after her.

"Please don't, not like this." She implored, but he was beyond listening, beyond reason he unbuttoned his trousers, releasing his rampant manhood. He reached behind her, pulling them both to the floor and ramming his knee between her thighs, forcing her legs apart and thrust himself into her as they rutted on the floor.

"Tell me you don't want this." He whispered hoarsely into her ear as he thrust into her repeatedly, in and out, "I can feel how much you want this, go on tell me you love it bitch. Despite herself her passion was engorge, she hated him but loved it, involuntarily her hips began to buck to meet his thrusts, her arms now around his neck, "I hate you monster!" she shrieked as her body began to convulse, "Do it harder, do it harder!" she breathed through racking sobs, she felt herself melting to him as his thrusts roughly hammered her, pinning her to the floor, her breasts heaving with each thrust, she felt him start to jerk and then, for the first time in her life she experienced an orgasm.

A policeman found the missing soldier, drowned, far up river, several days later. No one but Bertie and a couple of others would ever know how he had died, and he was sure that they were going to remain silent. Such things were best left unsaid.

Chapter Three

Darmstadt
1912

Listed in the Social and Personal column of the Darmstadt Chronicle of September 23rd. 1912 there was the following announcement:

> HESSEL: The family Hessel of 12 Kaiserstrasse, Darmstadt are proud to announce the birth of their first born son, Arnulf Bertram; Mother and Child are well and happy to receive guests."

Bertha had carefully worded the announcement in the forlorn hope of enticing someone from her family to make contact. Still, she thought, she did have the consolation of her beautiful son. Arnie was a golden baby, big, handsome, chubby, smiling and everything a baby should be. She called the little chap Arnie, despite, maybe because Bertie really didn't want her to. Bertha thought deeply about the way their son had been conceived in violent, degenerate, drunken sex but had arrived at the conclusion that despite this she would always treasure her son, perhaps more so, because out of bad had come good. Her hate for her husband deepened into something cold and hard, like a gut of steel deep within her, never truly dissipated, but churning at her like acid.

Soon Arnie was bringing light to the darker corners of her mind and even her dour husband began to take some pleasure in their son, proudly joining them as they walked the baby in his pram through the local park. Other young mothers were drawn to Bertha by her radiance and it wasn't long before she began to make some new friends. Bertie noticed the change in her, the newly reasserted confidence, the rekindled sparkle in her eyes and was grateful to Arnie for giving him back the wife he had fallen in love with in the first place.

It was shortly before Christmas and as usual Bertie and Bertha were arguing about what to do, and perhaps of more importance, what not to do about the Christian festival in their mixed home. As ever he wanted the whole ornate, particularly Germanic Christmas festivities that had its origins, as she was fond of reminding him, in pagan mid winter celebrations. Bertha, although never having been an orthodox Jew herself when she had been single found herself progressively more uncomfortable trying to be a hostess presiding over a wholly Christian gathering.

"No, I simply won't do it, I shall not be a hypocrite." She stamped her foot with a flash of temper which Bertie hadn't witnessed since Arnie was born. "Remember this is my house, and in my house we shall do things my way." He replied with some finality, hoping that the silly row would not spoil their hard won recent equanimity. "If you suddenly want to become religious you can do it without me or your son." She pointed towards the unknowing little bundle wrapped snugly in the swaddling cloth in his pram, "And by what divine right do you hold sway over our son's upbringing?" he asked. They both realized they had arrived at the nub of their argument, it wasn't for them, this discussion of religious trivia, but the future of their son which was at stake. The unstated problem always buried deep and unseen had suddenly surfaced with explosive impact.

"We agreed our children would be taught about both our traditions and religions and could make up their own minds about what they want to be when they're older." She stated with cold anger.

"My son is a German boy, and he must learn German ways first." Bertie stated his argument as if it were simply a recitation of fact. "What, I'm not a German?" she asked with incredulity, "My family traces its lineage in this country for more than five hundred years, can your people trace their heritage that far back?"

The volume of their argument had risen until it disturbed the baby's slumbers. He started to cry and Bertha went to Arnie and hugged him to her breast, soon he was comfortable and quiet in her comforting warmth. Bertie couldn't help himself, his resolve to be severe crumbled as he watched his child begin to search for his wife's breast. "Let us agree to disagree," he said whilst stoking his son's head, "Because I know you would never do anything to harm me or the little chap." How little he knows me, thought Bertha as she opened her blouse to suckle their infant. "Was it Voltaire who said I might disagree with every word you say, but I shall fight to the death for your right to say them?" Bertie smiled indulgently as he continued to be enchanted by the image his wife and son presented.

"It was the beginning of the end of civilization when they allowed women an education." He said, "And who knows or cares if it were Voltaire or some other Latin effeminate, is it pleasurable?" he asked Bertha as she shifted Arnie to suck from her other breast. She looked up sharply, worried where the conversation was potentially leading, "Feeding our son is wonderful, fulfilling, why?"

"And why do your people answer a question with another question?" he responded sharply, "What like you?" she asked with equal alacrity and with a smile playing on her pretty face, her head tilted slightly to one side in the attitude people so often adopt when waiting for a reply. "What is it you really want to know, do you want to know if Arnie sucking my breast arouses me?" Bertie shifted in his seat uncomfortably, clearly she understood him only too well. "Don't squirm like a boy, after all you're my husband, you're not a stranger; yes it's sensual, but it's not the feeling you can give me, that's a type of love to, but our sex is different altogether. You know there are all kinds of different things that happen between consenting adults that would surprise a stranger. Why, are you becoming jealous of your son, do you want some of my milk?" Bertie's face went red, the woman was a witch, how did she know everything about him, with the baby at her right breast she held the free one in her other hand out towards him, "I don't mind, I won't tell anyone."

Bertie found himself drawn to the rose tipped globe like a magnet, he sank to his knees and gently, as if a baby himself, sucked at his woman's breast, Bertha stroked his head as he fed. He put an arm protectively around Arnie not realizing what an improbably but beautiful tableaux he and his family would appear to the world. She smiled as she thought that she finally understood her man and herself.

Winter turned to spring and the talk in the town was of the changing nature of their lives. Who would have ever dreamt that their sleepy backwater was to grow such a size and become so industrialized so fast? Factories were springing up at a pace unparalleled in the nation's modern history. Farm workers from the surrounding countryside were abandoning ancient rural lifestyles to pour into the city's mushrooming tenements and tiny houses erected for them like sentinels guarding the giant chimney stacks, iron foundries, steel works and railway construction yards. Bertie saw all this because it was his function to issue these new concerns with the necessary permits. This he did with his usual stolid efficiency, unable or unwilling to spot or use the many chances for personal advancement and gain all around him.

Another thing Bertie seemed to totally miss as he withdraw ever deeper into himself was the growing up of his son. Nurtured lovingly by his mother, Arnie had taken his first steps and uttered his first word, which naturally enough was, "Mama."

Bertha found herself habitually walking past her family mansion, which was situated next to the park. She never allowed herself the luxury of hope, she realized she was dead to them but she still cherished the hope of catching a glimpse of one of her relatives and she nevertheless derived some comfort form the thought of their sheer physical proximity.

Arnie delighted in taking faltering steps on the grassy carpet of the park opposite his unknown grandparents' house. Bertha would spread a rug under the protective branches of an ancient oak tree and sit contentedly watching the boy gambol about punctuating his many falls with the exclamation, "Bumps a daisy!" until the little fellow started to say it to himself which would result in them both laughing as if they shared some wonderful joke. Arnie was a boy who was in love with the world though all of his senses, every blade of grass a universe of wonder to him. Whilst he was thus absorbed in everything he could see, touch, feel and smell his mother was transported by her love bordering on devotion of him.

Arnie handed his mother a daisy he had picked especially for her with due solemnity. She patted her son's head in a mixture of maternal love and gratitude for uncomplicated adoration of her, something we all need on occasion, in moments of vulnerability, she thought. Her son was a boy who gave and took love with a true spontaneity he'd inherited from his mother. Being cuddled by her was as necessary to his well being as eating or breathing particularly so since recently he felt a distance from his father who, for some reason his immature mind couldn't understand, pushed him away when he tried to get close. His daddy seemed an impossibly distant giant and forbidding figure, too busy to play, but not too busy to scold. A gulf in Bertie's emotional intelligence had rapidly become a yawning chasm.

Arnie was quick to grasp the rudiments of the three R's and art by his British nanny, Brigitte, who he called Birdy because her English sounding name was too hard for him to pronounce. But the jolly, well rounded and comfortably proportioned young woman didn't mind anything her young charge called her, she plainly adored him almost as much as his own mother. Birdy had once harbored artistic ambitions herself but had only demonstrated enough talent to realize her potential was limited by a lack of personal passion and commitment. Instead of seeking to become an artist Birdy had sublimated her creativity and channeled her energies into the teaching of others. Very quickly she discerned the raw talent in Arnie's raw unstructured daubings, a talent she had never witnessed in others before. Birdy soon started to bring this undoubted talent to Bertha's attention. His mother was unsure how to react initially, in the Jewish tradition it was almost unheard of for anyone of the age to paint or draw at all. It was considered a sin to render anything in the image of God and as man was himself God's creation art was, to the more orthodox Jew, a no go area. But Bertha was a modern woman and was thrilled when Birdy came rushing over to her one day to show the proud mother her son's latest painting, "He has it in him this boy, God's gift to show us the world a special way, through his eyes that have magic in them." She said to Bertha, and anyone else that would listen. Any casual observer could see that this tiny boy had a finely observant eye for detail in one so young and his enjoyment was a joy when he daubed a multitude of colors all over the paper his mother so liberally supplied, and it was hard for either of the women to remember that he was not yet three years old.

Despite their enthusiasm Bertie was singularly unimpressed by any discussion regarding art, his son's. , Or anyone else's. He thought all art was a decadent waste of time and the only music he could bear to listen to was Wagner. In fact he was totally disinterested in his son's progress, and even the small regard he had for the boy was diluted in direct proportion to the world's worsening crisis reported with such apparent relish in each day's newspaper.

Each morning Bertie would sit at the table in the bright and airy breakfast room ignoring his family's chatter and the convivial yellow floral decorations while he buried his head in that morning's journal.

The morning Bertha was destined to remember started with the normal pattern. The routine mutterings and grumbles from

Bertie suddenly erupted as he read the front page which read, Archduke Ferdinand Assassinated in Sarajevo. "This means war!" he said, and then looked his wife in the eye, "A war we will win within six months."

Bertie was right about the war but not the time it would take out of his life. He had the distinction of being the first volunteer to join the army of the Fatherland in the town of Darmstadt that promising spring of 1914. His farewell to his wife and son were perfunctory as he had mentally already left for the front, such was the eagerness of Bertie to prove himself the only way certain men can, in uniform, holding a gun.

Chapter Four

Darmstadt
1917

Certain funny little things fascinate most small boys, usually tadpoles or puddles, something wet and messy will do but green slimy muddy places and objects are by far the best. But Arnie Hessel was an unusual little boy. Seven years old and big for his age he loved to look at the world around him and marvel at the shape, color and texture of the things around him. He seemed unaware how disconcerting it could be for an adult if a small boy decided to stare at the bump on the end of your nose or the swell of your bosom, but he did know, with the certainty only possessed by a seven year old that he wanted to look and look he would.

The day promised much excitement for Arnie. He was so excited that he was awake far earlier than normal when his mother came into his room to rouse him from bed. They both loved their shared morning ritual of her first kiss on his smooth warm cheek as he lay bundled comfortably in the snuggled up, body warmed eiderdown. Every morning she would kiss him and every morning he would feign sleep and suddenly reach out with both arms to hug his adored mother around the neck. He loved the way she looked, smelt and felt. She just loved her son, without thought as most mothers love their sons. Bertha was still an unconventionally beautiful luminescent woman, her raven hair totally at odds with Arnie's almost white blond and curly locks. What struck people first when they met Frau Bertha Hessel was an overall impression of beauty rather than noticing one particular feature. Her eyes were also blue, but of a different, deeper hue than Arnie's, hers giving a distinct echo of the Mediterranean whilst his were of the cold blue northern skies on a cold clear winter's day.

Bertha has promised to take him for a special outing to his favorite place, on the river, if he was good the previous day, and of course he had been exceptionally good. So they set off in the little horse and buggy before nine with all the necessary accoutrements, including a bulging picnic hamper from which Arnie had already artfully purloined a piece of his mother's special honey bread to supplement his meager, rushed breakfast which he had been too excited to eat. As ever the drive into the countryside was full of pleasure for them both. They sang songs and Arnie continually pointed out all the small things of boyish interest that Bertha might not have seen despite the fact that they had driven this particular route on many previous occasions and he always pointed out the self same objects of interest. If his mother didn't turn to look where he pointed he would gently place his hands on either side of her cheeks and direct her face where he desperately needed her to look. It had become a game for them both, for Arnie to embellish and give new, richer, ever more elaborate descriptions of every interesting tree, or bird and today a hedgehog, which received minutes of rapturous and detailed story telling by Arne that made it appear as if the boy imagined the small prickly animal was in fact one of the lesser known survivors of Hannibal's attack on Rome. Such rich nonsense was terminated by their arrival at the riverbank.

Arnie didn't wait for his mother, but simply leapt to the ground, and from there reached up to grab his painting kit from the seat next to the one he had just vacated. "Be careful" Bertha called after him, a chuckle of pleasure in her throat, "Yes Mama!" he shouted back over his retreating shoulder as he ran towards a field some distance away that he had been impatiently waiting to paint for weeks.

Bertha set out their traveling rug by the river and on it placed the picnic hamper. She started to take out their settings and in the distance she saw that her son had already set up his small easel and was preparing to paint.

Arnie watched a butterfly perched on a hedge; the boy was transfixed by the insect's beauty and grace. Arnie sat poised, with his paintbrush over the blanks piece of paper, unsure where to begin, at first his strokes had been crude and unfocused, even to his own young eyes, but now he was beginning to be able to translate his awe and wonder onto to the canvas. His brush traced the shape and color of the wings with surprising sureness of touch and strength of purpose. The beautiful object slowly became a painting of almost equal beauty. Arnie's fierce concentration was finally interrupted by Bertha calling to him from the distance. "Come on Arnie, it's time for some lunch." Arnie reluctantly looked up from his unfinished work but smiled when he saw his mother waving to him; "Mother, just a little bit longer and I'll be finished," he pleaded. Bertha laughed, she had heard all of this before from Arnie, and minutes could soon turn into hours if she let him have his way. Arnie laughed also, he was a bit hungry after all; he knew when to give in gracefully. He ran over to her, happy to exercise his stiff body. She patted the blanket next to her where he gratefully plopped himself down. They settled down to eat without too many words, extremely comfortable in their silence as they both appreciated everything around them.

Immediately after he had eaten the last bite Arnie pulled his mother to her feet despite her giggling protestations. Bertha walked along the riverbank whilst Arnie skipped and cart wheeled with the seemingly boundless energy and impish good spirits that nature reserves for the very young.

Arnie spotted an irresistibly inviting tree, which arched out over the river. The challenge was daunting but Arnie immediately accepted and was soon clambering precariously out on the protruding limb, swinging by his legs upside down: "Look mummy, I'm a fruit bat!" he called to Bertha. "Be careful up there!" she responded with maternal care.

The boy was about to respond but heard something, he turned from looking at his mother, to the branch from where he'd heard a loud cracking sound, He turned to his mother anxiously and she immediately realized his predicament and rushed to help. "Arnie get down now!" she shouted but it was too late. The branch snapped before she could get reach him, "Arnie!" she screamed as her son and the broken branch he was still holding plunged into the river far below.

Without thought for herself she dived into the river after her son. Initially she couldn't find him as he didn't surface, and she was treading water and looking wildly about as she repeatedly called his name, "Arnie, Arnie, where are you Arnie!" she shouted in desperation, looking around the deserted countryside for someone to help them, but the place was empty. Then suddenly there he was, his head bursting to the surface, like a cork in water, he spluttered for a moment and then seeing his mother swimming towards him in her summer frock made him laugh, and he swallowed a great lung full of the brackish river water and it seemed to reach out and re-claim the boy who vanished under the water again.

"Arnie, stop playing, where are you Arnie?" Bertha called to her son, but he had vanished. She swam to where he had last surfaced and searched for her son with growing desperation, fumbling about as she tried to penetrate the almost total blackness of the river water. For an instant she saw her son's hand surface but it vanished below the water so fast she wasn't quite sure if she had seen it at all. "Arnie!" she screamed again and again, her own breath coming in ragged gasps as she looked for him with growing panic. She dived below the surface but it was hard to see just a few feet in the murky water, then she saw a shape, a white shape, rolling and gliding, inert, as it moved sluggishly in the slow and lazy current, she instinctively pushed toward it. As she got closer she realized it was her Arnie, she reached him and lifted his inert head and shoulders out of the water as if were weightless.

With strength born from a mother's love she surged with him to the shore. It was almost impossible to make her way out of the slippery and steep bank but somehow she struggled up its side, carrying her boy like a woman possessed. Al the time she was stroking his head, not sure what to do, but understanding he had to breathe or die. He seemed to be dead there was no sign of his small chest heaving, no expression on his face, nothing. She somehow managed to conquer her rising hysteria knowing instinctively that if she gave in to it he would have no chance. She laid his inert form on the bank, her iron resolve wavering as panic bubbled near the surface. For a moment she forgot her long held distance from any celestial being as she looked from her boy up to any empty sky, "Oh God, don't take my boy away, please don't take him!" she wailed to the seemingly uncaring deity above.

Not knowing what to do next she instinctively kissed her son on his lips and then tried to breathe live into him. She thought she saw a slight rise in his chest, but there was no other sign of life. She hammered on his chest with her fists, "Come on Arnie fight you have to fight, you are not allowed to die, do you hear me, you are not allowed to die, come on breathe, you have to breathe or mummy is going to get very angry!" she shouted as loud as she could into his ears. But there was still no flicker of life from him, she pounded him repeatedly on his small chest, "Breathe!" she begged him, "you have to breathe, listen to mummy, you must breathe." But his face showed no reaction, no indication of life and it was turning a deathly blue; Bertha screamed incoherently in fear and rage. Now losing her sanity momentarily she flipped her boy over onto his front, and pushed down with all her weight onto his back, "Got to get the water out of him!" she said to herself, unaware that she was speaking her thoughts out loud to any empty, uncaring world.

Miraculously Arnie mouth opened involuntarily in a short forced exhalation, the foul water held so long in his tortured lungs spewed out in a small torrent. Bertha realized that there was suddenly hope where previously there was just despair, she rolled him over again, as he spluttered and spewed, she cradled his head to her chest, searching for more signs of life, an inwards breath, anything, "Arnie, that's a good boy, come on now, breathe again, that's right." She felt his body tense as he struggled for breath, "Arnie live, you have to live for mama, come on another breath, you want to finish your lovely picture don't you, you haven't finished your lovely picture yet." With these words Arnie took a great big breath, his eyelids fluttered and the sickly pallor of his skin began to return to a more normal color.

"That's right'" Bertha coaxed her son, "Come on now, for mama, another big breath, you'll feel better." But it wasn't necessary as he was already spluttering through semi-consciousness as if he were waking from a particularly bad nightmare. Suddenly his eyes opened and focused on Bertha; "I'll be all right now mama," he said and smiled brilliantly, "I promise I shall breathe."

Bertha exhaled herself, realizing how terrified she had been all along. Now everything was going to be all right, her Arnie was alive, smiling and whole again, everything was going to be just fine. She kissed her son until he pushed her away with ill concealed embarrassment, "I could kill you for scaring me like that." She said, but contrary to her words her actions were those of a doting mother brought too close to the edge of a terrible precipice.

Chapter Five

A few weeks in 1917

The next week was normal in every respect except, perhaps, that Bertha was even more watchful of Arnie than ever before. Normal that is, until the morning of the eighth day, when Arnie woke feeling feverish and stiff.

Initially Bertha simply felt his brow and declared it a simple head cold, he did feel slightly hot and clammy, but even after she had washed him with damp cloths he still complained of being wobbly and nauseous, so although not really believing that her Arnie was too ill she decided to keep him in bed for the day. She saw him smile at that thought, and her mind tempted her toward the thought that somehow he was playing some small boy's trick to avoid a day at school. He wasn't too keen on lessons when the weather outside was temptingly nice for painting or playing. She announced she was going to summon Doctor Springer. "We all know what doctor Springer does to little boys who are malingering don't we Arnie, he holds them by the nose with one hand and gives them a big dose of cod liver oil with the other!" Arnie didn't even seem too concerned at her humorous threat and that worried his mother.

The doctor, actually a very kindly man in his mid sixties, came quickly after being summoned by the downstairs maid. Methodically the doctor examined his young patient, feeling, probing and measuring in the mysterious ways some doctors have of appearing like initiates in some secret magic rites. During this Bertha kept herself occupied by fussing around the room, unsuccessfully trying to be inconspicuous as she straightened the bedroom for the fourth time as Springer stood up and patted his young patient on the cheek. Bertha couldn't conceal her anxiety when she noticed the doctor's grave expression, "Chin up little man, like a good soldier for the Fatherland." He said to Arnie, who responded enthusiastically, "Will I miss lessons this week doctor?" The doctor smiled indulgently, "Yes you will young Master Hessel, now I must speak for a little while with your mother." But before he could speak to Bertha the boy had another quick question for him, "All week?" The doctor smiled again, "I should think at least that long, and as much jelly and ice cream as you can eat!"

Arnie smiled towards his mother, this was the best doctor ever he thought as his mother and the medical man left the room. "Don't you worry young man, I shall arrange for them to send you plenty of work from school so that you don't fall too far behind." He sighed theatrically as Bertha and the doctor as they left the room and she led him on to the drawing room, out of earshot of Arnie. "Now, Herr doctor, what is it, some kind of flu he's caught?" The doctor shook his head and paused before continuing, "How long has Arnie had this temperature?" still the enigmatic medical man, "It began last night." She replied, "Any other symptoms?" he continued his questioning, "Symptoms?" she asked, feeling a little stupid, what did the doctor mean, wasn't it obvious the boy has flu she thought, why was he worrying her like this?

"Yes, symptoms," he continued, "Has he been listless, restless, irritable has he vomited?" She smiled, "Other than the vomiting he is always running around like a toy solider, he has incredible energy."

Arnie had been watching the exchange like a spectator at a tennis match, but he was losing interest in the boring adult conversation which seemed to be of no interest to him as the nice old doctor with the cold hands and his mother were now using very long words that he didn't think anyone else could possibly understand. "He did have some tummy trouble as well," she said, and the doctor was interested in this, "Has he had many episodes of diarrhea?"

"We will run some tests. It's probably nothing serious" the doctor added when he saw that the boy's mother was reacting badly to the stress of her son's illness. Arnie, who had become progressively more bored by the whole affair was upset when he saw his mother becoming emotional. "What's wrong mummy?" he asked her, she shushed him with a rush of words. "I'm talking to the doctor, and he's telling me that you have a cold in your tummy, probably from when you fell in the river last week."

The doctor interrupted her immediately he heard this, "Did he swallow much water?"

"Yes" she answered, "but he's been perfectly well for more than a week since then so the two incidents are clearly not linked at all. He's been absolutely fine all week" The doctor's demeanor, already serious, became even more concerned, Suddenly, the outward appearance of calm in the room was shattered as Arnie's small body went into convulsion, his head snapping back as if pulled by a giant, unseen puppeteer. Bertha and the doctor moved over to Arnie immediately. They both noticed another symptom as the young boy's eyes had gone out of focus. "What's wrong with my son?" she asked, searching the doctor's concerned face for an answer. She now cradled her boy in her arms as the spasm gradually subsided.

Doctor Springer turned away from the bed and Bertha's penetrating stare. "Your husband is still away at the front?" he asked her. "Yes doctor, but tell me what's wrong with our son," She replied. "You are going to have to be very strong my dear, I know your people tend to the emotional outburst but now you must be stoic and rise to the challenge, like a good German woman." She looked at him dumbly, insulted but more concerned to know the truth about her son than to deal with his attitude. "Doctor don't patronize me, what is wrong with my son, I want you to tell me immediately?"

The doctor was not used to dealing with assertive, modern women like Bertha, and although she was very attractive in a Mediterranean, sultry slightly sluttish manner, he certainly did not like her uppity manner. He was used to handling the relatives of patients in what he considered a dignified manner which both he and his mostly middle aged bourgeois clientele, because he thought of them that way, rather than as merely patients or relatives of patients, "Frau Hessel you should understand presently I can only make what amounts to a preliminary prognosis, as it is we have many tests to conduct, results to gather, to collate, to assess." She was now plainly furious with him, "Stop waffling for God's sake, just tell me what is wrong with my son!"

The doctor was not used to being addressed like this, he started to pack his medical bag all the while huffing with indignation. "Perhaps madam would be best suited to seeking a second opinion, there is Doctor Meyer, who is, I am given to understand, a perfectly adequate doctor of the Hebrew persuasion, with whom madam might well feel more of an affinity." Bertha could barely contain her anger, "Stop being a pompous oaf and tell me what is wrong with my son or I shall take this knife and geld you!" Bertha picked up a dull bladed fruit knife that was on the table next to her son and brandished it at the doctor. He gulped in surprise, this was not the way most ladies would behave.

"Young Arnie has a particularly virulent form of polio, do you know what that is Frau Hessel?" Bertha nodded, for a moment mute with shock, "It can't be polio, there must be something wrong with this, my boy can't have polio, what can I do?" She pleaded. "There are several things you must and must not do," he answered, "You mainly catch Polio through contact with stools from an infected person. This can happen in one of several ways, including: Eating food or drinking liquids that are contaminated with poliovirus. Poliovirus is commonly found in sewage water. I strongly suspect that the water in the river where Arnie fell in was contaminated and that would have been enough to start the infection." He paused to see whether the woman was digesting the information. Then he continued;

"I really don't think it was caused by his touching surfaces or objects contaminated with poliovirus then putting his contaminated hand to his mouth. As from now neither you nor anyone else can share foods or eating utensils with Arnie. Do you understand me, it is vital we contain this outbreak or it can spread like wildfire. As a precaution we are also going to quarantine your house until Arnie is no longer in danger of being infectious." Bertha was shaking her head as he concluded. She was simply too horrified to accept what he was saying.

"I'll get a second opinion as you suggested, I don't think this is possible, Doctor Mayer will tell me a different story, perhaps you enjoy telling me such things because you don't like Jews?" she accused, he shook his head sadly. "I don't confuse my personal attitudes with my professional diagnosis, your son is very sick, and now I will have to report this fact to the medical authorities of our town so that they may protect the other citizens from contagion."

He rose to leave, but before he could do so Bertha grabbed his sleeve. "There must be a cure, there is always a cure, just tell me what to do, where to go, I don't care how much it costs, we'll pay whatever is necessary." He shook her hand free from his sleeve, "Madam, remember your dignity." These foreign people, he thought, under that thin veneer of German manners they were still more comfortable in some Byzantine bazaar. Best be direct, he thought, before she became even more hysterical. "Your son has acute poliomyelitis." She mutely shook her head in denial that the doctor misunderstood to be lack of understanding. "The boy has polio."

Bertha still said nothing, she was too horrified to speak, and she had prepared herself for some bad news, but not this, never this. Nothing could have given her the strength to face this new trial.

"There is a cure, nowadays there is always a cure?" she asked rhetorically. The doctor recognized some inner strength in the woman, and found some sympathy for her. He shook his head sadly, "There is no cure that we know of, but we might well be able to mitigate the resultant paralysis on some occasions; put another way, if we're lucky the crippling aspects can be minimized." Bertha was staring deep into the eyes of the doctor, and he found it very unsettling, that intense personal scrutiny. She interrupted him again, "No," she shook her head, "my son will never be a cripple, never, not as long as I draw breath."

Bertha tried to listen as the doctor patiently explained the medical regime she would now have to follow with Arnie. "Your son will have a high temperature, that might well become very high indeed, he will appear not to want anyone, even you near to him, touching him, he will suffer some great pain, but what you must watch for after a day or so is an inability to use one or more limbs properly, if at all. You must then summon me at once to examine him and I can try to limit the paralysis. For your part, you must use every effort to make him move those limbs. We shall wrap his spine in cotton wool and mustard plaster as the latest thinking is that this will ease the effects of the onset of the polio." The doctor turned to go, but Bertha made him pause by placing her hand on his sleeve.

"There is nothing more I can say or do presently, except suggest that you pray to your God for his help for your son's safety as he travels through hell." She walked after him as he moved towards the door, "Should Arnie be place in a hospital?" The doctor shook his head, "The hospitals' are already full of our injured soldiers and the very seriously ill and dying, there is no further room Frau Stegmann, but perhaps we could find you a nurse to help you here? He offered,

"No." she replied, "I shall take care of my son."

The next few days were a confused nightmare for both mother and son. Bertha religiously followed the doctor's strict and specific guidelines, even when they appeared distinctly odd to her keen mind. She felt the boy's pulse, measured his temperature and closely examined his arms and legs. She noted even the most minor variation in a book she headed "Arnie's Road to Recovery" in bold black letters on its blue front cover.

However, instead of recovering, his condition continued to deteriorate with every passing day. All Bertha's thoughts and energies were concentrated on the boy as she blotted out anything extraneous to this all-consuming mission. She didn't leave his side except to grab food or visit the toilet. She noticed her reflection in the mirror as she scurried past and it gave her pause as she realized she had not washed or combed her usually lustrous hair in days, and thought nothing of it. Bertha left unanswered Bertie's letters from the Front of the War as he was relegated to another, far less important plateau.

The decline of Arnie reached crisis point some four days later when he was unable to move either his arms or legs. Bertha refused to panic. "Sit up Arnie." She instructed her son. The boy strained to comply, but the effort was hopeless, "I can't move mama, I can't even cry, what's happening to me?" he whined with self-pity. Bertha slapped him across his face; the shock stopped his tears. He found it hard to catch his breath for a few moments. Bertha grabbed him by both his shoulders and stared into his eyes. "You are to be brave, do you understand me, you are a soldier for the fatherland, and this is your battle, and brave German soldiers do not cry in a fight, do you understand, you must be brave?"

The small boy's fear evaporated hearing his mother's patriotic call to arms, her courage shamed him, he smiled bravely through his drying tears, "I will try mama, I shall try my hardest."

The improvement in his condition was very slow and extremely painful, but Arnie did not cry for himself ever again. He found the courage to deal with the very slow progress; so slow that it was Bertha alone who noticed the infinitesimal signs of improvement.

The doctor had tried on many occasions to persuade the woman to accept her son's total paralysis. In fact the doctor thought, these people were, at least, stubborn in their resolve, almost donkey like in not giving in easily. How was it that they were described in the good book, they were indeed a stiff-necked people. The woman hovered over the boy endlessly, constantly feeding him the prescribed diet of warm milk and cod liver oil with extract of malt. With increasing vigor she massaged his lifeless arms and legs.

"Move your arms, move your legs." She ordered him every time she massaged his tortured body, but despite the small lad's tremendous efforts he was unable to do so. "I can't do it mama, I just can't." He was worn out from the fruitless, unremitting and ultimately exhausting effort. "Your toes, you can try to wriggle your toes for mama," she said this as if his inability was the most ridiculous thing in the world. "I can't do it mama, I really can't do it." He repeated in desperation, his voice a testament for pity, for release from his mother's constant bullying. "Then you must simply try harder." She commanded, he tried but was again unsuccessful, but something snapped inside him with this final mighty exertion. "Mama!" he shouted, and before she could angry at the boy shout directly at her she realized what had made him scream. Tears had formed in his previously dry eyes, and now were coursing down his soft cheeks; she stared at his face in disbelief. "You're crying Arnie, you're crying!"

"I'm sorry mama, I'm trying to stop it but it won't" she stroked his confused face, "these are good tears Arnie, these are wonderful tears, you keep crying, it is simply perfect!"

Arnie's face battled between the tears that were now streaming from his eyes and the huge grin on his face that contradicted them, "I can cry again mama, real tears." They both cried, great tears of happiness, she hugged him to her, "Does this mean I am going to get all better?" she regained her composure and stood back, she shook her head.

"Arnulf Hessel, we're over the worst, and if we work even harder we will win more than we lose, do you hear me, we will win."

It was around this time that Bertha reached the fateful decision that she was not going to tell her husband about my illness. She convinced herself that she could nurse me back to full health, despite all the medical evidence pointing to the opposite result. She was determined that nothing was going to spoil her man's triumphant return from his ultimate victory at the front.

Bertha's hope in this regard was misplaced, as, despite all her best efforts at nursing I was never going to regain the use of my arms, and it was to take months, many months, pain filled and seemingly endless, before I could even walk again, but with mother's constant support walk I did.

Chapter Six

Darmstadt, Germany
1918

Bertha showed me an envelope marked army mail service and began to read to me in her low, warm and melodious voice.

"Dear Arnulf, All is well with my comrades and myself. We continue to carry the fight to the Tommies and it shall not be too much longer before they surrender. We have given them a terrible hammering. I am at Ypres; in France that mother will show you on the big atlas I sent you last Christmas. You will see exactly where we are, and I shall look at my atlas, and we can think of each other. When we fire out big guns the whole earth shakes as if God himself were stamping his feet in anger. I'm sure if I were a Tommy I would give up and go home to England. Soon we'll be together again and you'll show me all the fine pictures mama tells me you're now painting. I can't wait. Much love, your father."

Bertha put down the letter and I noticed for the first time that she was quietly crying. "Are you all right mama, are those good or bad tears?" she wasn't able to reply through the tears, "what is it mama?" I asked again, and buried my head in her lap. I guess I was seeking to give her some warmth from the only human contact I could give. Mother smoothed my hair and this calmed her. "Now mama is OK, you go and play outside, I have lots of things to do."

I obediently left the room, instantly finding other new things that were much more interesting to a small boy. Like most adventurous children I was always fascinated by what might be around the next corner. I didn't see my much-loved mother reading a second letter from father.

This one spoke guardedly but at length, in distressing detail, of the privations, the ferocity, the horrendous loss of life, trench foot, mustard gas, disease, men drowning in the flooded trenches, unworthy and unrecorded bravery, and acts of cowardice, that Bertie despised but Bertha sympathized with. How she wished that her own father had not been so heroic, as only two days earlier she had read in the Darmstadt Chronicle that he had given his life for the fatherland. How she wished that they had the one last chance to say how they loved each other, how she regretted their estrangement, which all seemed so petty and futile now.

Bertha questioned herself again, why hadn't she told her husband about their son's illness and disability, and now it might be too late. Arnie only knew one thing, however stern and solemn and distant his father might be, he was still his daddy and he would soon be home as a hero.

As time drifted on it felt like forever to Arnie. He waited with growing impatience and skepticism for the soldiers to return home. The only men who did come back were too wounded or ill to be able to continue with their soldierly duty. To Arnie they seemed particularly useless, and oddly frightening. He had seen men without limbs, and even one man without a face. He had nightmares about the man but he felt even more sympathy for the men who were blinded. Imagine not being able to see the world he thought. Now Arnie began to fervently regret praying to God for him to bring his daddy back immediately, especially if the price he would have to pay was some kind of terrible injury. He could stay away a little longer if his coming home meant he would have to return as a cripple, like himself.

Time passed with molasses like slowness for all of Germany. First the tide seemed as though it might turn their way when the Russian army mutinied and returned to the East, but this was made much worse when the Americans came in their huge numbers and riches. The initial myths of imminent victory had long since vanished and were replaced by a grudging acceptance of harsh, unpleasant, unpalatable realities. "Perhaps" they muttered in their beer halls, churches and homes, "Perhaps it was just a matter of a little more time, perhaps another year or two would see the job done." But the belief in final, total victory, remained absolute with the German people.

It was during this period that I remember my mother-sought reconciliation with her parents. But it was not to be. Her mother exchanged messages with her, but the word came back that her father stipulated that it would be impossible for him to meet with a dead woman, and since when had the dead given birth to children. Therefore, to him, and his fellow orthodox Jews I could never exist.

Bertha and Arnie didn't much care who won the war anymore; they just wanted Bertie home. Neither of them could remember what the war was about any more, or why they were fighting. In fact it was Bertha who wanted Bertie back, Arnie could barely remember who his father was, he was just a distant hazy memory. Bertha had begun the process of mythologizing her husband, who she had not loved so dearly when he was with her. Now she ached for him in every way, for his companionship, for his touch, and even for someone just to talk with who was not a child. It hurt her just to think about how much she yearned for her man.

Arnie was less concerned about his father since he cared much more for the wonders of the magical world that crowded around and encircled him with a rich wondrous embrace. All he wanted was to touch this world with his paintbrush as he spent endless hours working on the difficult technique of holding the paint brush in his mouth and perfecting his brush strokes.

He became ever closer to Bertha; she was his mother, father, teacher and nurse to him. News of the endless military stalemate was of far less interest to him than the shape, color and texture of a tree, not because he was uncaring about his father and his millions of fellow soldiers but simply owing to the fact that they were entirely absent from his experience and life. He wasn't aware of what he didn't see. Letters still arrived from his father via his mother but even this slight channel of communication began to shrivel and die since Arnie simply didn't see the need to respond despite mama's constant nagging for him to do so. Scribbled notes were as much as she could drag from him addressed to the ghost like figure of his father, now just a wraith like memory. It was so difficult to use a pencil in your mouth to write anyway, what was the point?

The final war years drifted for Arnie and Germany as the country gradually bled its resources into the ground of Western Europe. This process was a lingering torture for people everywhere but like most small boys Arnie simply delighted in watching men from the army march through his town, celebrating whatever marching armies celebrate, victories, real or imagined. Still it was exciting to follow the marching band and play at being a soldier, but when he said, "I want to be a soldier, just like my daddy!" she burst into tears, at once both thankful that this could never be the case, but regretful that he could never enjoy that choice. Arnie rushed away from mama, unable to bear her tears, so he suffered in grand childish isolation unable to understand his misdemeanor but confidant that the entire world was conspiring against him. Soon his mother recovered sufficiently to come and seek him out to cuddle him. He didn't need or understand the explanation offered, content with the feel of his mother's closeness, calmed by her clean soapy smell. He loved the warmth and softness of her femininity. He asked her if she wanted to have a kick about of his favorite football, and there was no greater compliment he could give, she sometimes would kick the ball back and forth, and for a girl she was really quite good he thought, but today, for reasons beyond him, she declined. Arnie kept badgering her and she smiled as he stood before her facing her directly so that he could talk into her eyes without her being distracted. Suddenly he smiled brightly, "I'm a chatterbox aren't I?"

They both laughed and she ruffled his mop of unruly blond hair about which he always tried to be fastidious, if he could get mama to comb it for him. "Are you my little man Arnie?" she asked playfully, but perhaps tinged with just a tinge of seriousness. "I am mama, I'm your little man, and I will never go away and leave you on your own, I promise." They both paused for a moment, the implied rebuke of his father left in the air to float between them in silent conspiracy.

One morning, not long after this, mama spent more time than was usual preparing herself for the day. When questioned by Arnie she smiled enigmatically and said she had a very wonderful surprise present for Arnie and it would be arriving that very morning on the train at the central station in the town. Not bowing to her son's persistent interrogation she finally allowed her frayed patience a bit of freedom, "don't be so tiresome Arnie, what have I told you about behaving like a turgid parrot with verbal diarrhea. Be quiet and all your questions will be answered."

Naturally his mother's vocal annoyance embarrassed and upset the small boy who still idolized his mother. He managed, just about, to keep silent as they traveled to the train station on the new electric trolley bus and although the mood of the town was grey and somber, the station itself was packed and happy, full of excited, loud women with their even noisier children. In the bustling crowd of grown ups Arnie became scared and overwhelmed by the people all around him, the inadvertent knocks into his unprotected body. What is all this? He thought, who are these people, what do they all want, what are they doing here, what did it have to do with him and his mama?" his questions were answered soon enough.

A big man with mutton chop whiskers and a Prussian style moustache came over and hugged his mother, then to Arnie's utter amazement the man kissed mama full on her lips; the stranger then reached down and picked Arnie up to hug him. The small boy struggled to break free. "Don't you recognize me

Arnie?" the man asked, clearly concerned. Arnie shook his head, quiet and disturbed, scared by the man who gently set the boy down on his feet.

Bertha knelt next to her son, "This is your father Arnie, this is daddy, and he is now home for good." Said Bertha. Arnie looked back and forth between his parents, and, after a long pause, he kissed the man on the mouth. Bertie pulled away from his son, wiping his mouth with the back of his sleeve as he did so. "We don't kiss like that Arnie, we kiss like this." He pecked Arnie on the cheek with the absolute minimum of contact with his lips. Arnie stared seriously at his father. Neither was sure how to react to the other.

Bertie turned to his wife, "What's wrong with the boy?" Bertie asked her above the noise of the crowd, moving back from his son as if might be contagious, "There's something not right with him." Bertha saw the confusion and pain on her sensitive son's face.

"Our son has been very ill, but now he's better, he had polio." Bertie's face turned to a look of thunder, "what do you mean, had polio? He clearly cannot use his arms, he is still ill?"

"It sounds ridiculous now, but I was trying to protect you, you had matters of life and death to deal with every day. I'm sorry I always meant to tell you, but there never seemed to be a right time." Bertie became silent, looked between mother and son and then turned on his heel, visibly rejecting them both. Bertha followed him as she pulled their son after them. Arnie would always remember his father's terrible silence and the anger he could feel from the man's back. His father gave no other visible sign of a reaction; Arnie tired to stop his mother dragging him after his father but was powerless. He tried not to cry but tears forced their way through his clenched lashes and eyelids as his felt completely humiliated. He believed every eye in the station must be on him but the truth was that hardly anyone was aware of this small human drama being played out in their midst. Bertha pushed and forced him to follow in his father's wake through the crowded station until they joined this man, who was clearly pretending to be his father, in the suddenly claustrophobic hansom cab.

The ride home was silent other than for the clip clop of the horses' hooves and the solitary breathing of each of the people in the small space. Somehow, it was clear to Arnie, that every exhalation was an accusation from his father. It said, "who are you, what did you do with my healthy son you cripple?"

Days became weeks and they flowed sluggishly into months for Arnie as he discovered what his father had become. This was a miserable experience for the small boy whose fantasies of a loving father were being supplanted by a much harsher realty. Bertie had transformed himself into a military martinet during his service for the Kaiser. He was determined to stamp out anything in Arnie that he deemed soft, effeminate and weak, and this certainly included painting. He directed his anger at art, but really his hatred was for Arnie's handicap, which he blamed on Bertha's bad mothering and the boy's own self-destructiveness.

In effect Bertie instructed his son to get better, and this meant Arnie needed to find a way to make his arms work again. To that end Bertie brought in a fitness instructor from the spa in the town, and every day this young man worked on developing the upper body strength of the tortured little boy. But nothing worked, since nothing could work, it wasn't humanly possible, despite everything the boy did to make his father hate him less.

Initially Bertha allowed all of this pressure because she was a wise woman, clever in her understanding of men, and their frailties. She understood that her husband found it difficult to readjust to civilized life after spending so long fighting and living like a savage in the mud and squalor. But even her saintly patience became exhausted as her kindness and smiles were rejected and answered by scowls and anger. Now a mother's instinct to protect her young took over from her wish to placate an unreasonably angry man who, instead of loving her as he had once done, now took her brutally in the dead of night as if she were his whore. All thought of finding a reconciliation were fast fading as she moved her husband's things back to the guest bedroom and found the key to lock her bedroom.

Next, summoning her courage, she confronted her husband about the way he had been treating their son over the last months. One morning over breakfast she waited until they were alone and, although he was still engrossed in his newspaper she spoke, "Of course you know there is nothing wrong with the love of art Bertie." He put down his journal and stared at her for a moment with a look of pure contempt, "It is a cosmopolitan weakness and is not to be encouraged in our son, do you hear me, and I will not countenance this." Bertha considered this for a moment as he resumed reading. "I have an equal right to decide how our son shall be raised Bertie." She stated, with her voice raised, and quivering a bit more than she wanted with anger.

He put down his newspaper and smiled. "What nonsense is this, you are my woman, and you and the boy will both do my bidding or I will take my belt to both of you, do you understand?" She knew he meant it, but this was too important for her to be intimidated. "My parents were right about you, you're a bully, and if you can't win an argument you resort to violence." He laughed at her, "Are these the parents that love you so much that they pretend you're dead?" Despite herself she found herself crying, and hated her weakness. "When did you become so evil, I loved you, and now you've become so horrible."

He looked at her closely, as if she were an exhibit in a display. "Is this the moment when you cry and I am supposed to become sympathetic? It is not going to work this time, I assure you. This is far too important; it is about the well being of our son.

Chapter Seven

Darmstadt
1920 - 1927

The only value of being a child without the use of their arms is that if you survive you will only do so by becoming harder, stronger and more determined than any of your peers. So it was with Arnie, without realizing it he slowly became a much stronger person in many ways, he was forced to build an emotional wall to keep out the hurt and keep in the dreams.

The day that his father had returned to the lives of Arnie and his mother was burned into the mind of the small boy and in his heart, but he wasn't to realize this for a very long time. Bertie was angry with the boy for being infirm as if it were the boy's fault. Mostly he was angry with himself for the inadequacy he felt when failing to know how to deal with the situation of his son.

Arnie tried to block out the pain by activity. He almost managed not to notice the pitying glances of his father but sometimes the perceptive little boy couldn't avoid noticing the disdainful reaction of his father to his disability. The child buried this growing pile of hurts under an even bigger mound of happier accomplishments. Simple triumphs of any small boy became magnified into huge semi imagined accomplishments. Nevertheless certain small hurts couldn't be avoided. The way Bertie ignored his son was compounded by the older man's silences, by the way he refused to respond to the boy's happy chatter, which quickly echoed into sad little silences. The home gradually settled into a house, just a place where the family Hessel lived. Before too long Arnie grew to hate his father with all his growing strength. Arnie convinced himself that this miserable man was an imposter, sent to replace the real Bertie, who must have died a hero's death on the Front.

But small boys can be determined and Arnie tried in his childish way to ingratiate himself with his father. He instinctively realized that the man respected hard work, discipline and application so he tried to excel in everything he did. When he saw his father admiring other boys play sports Arnie spent countless hours re-learning how to run. He didn't have a mirror to see how ungainly he looked as he began this huge effort, and he wouldn't have cared. Just the feel of the wind in his face and hair as he ran felt so wonderful. In his mind he was running like a big cat, but to look at he was simply hobbling fast, his arms flapping lifelessly at his sides like some kind of demented mobile windmill. But Arnie was not satisfied, now he wanted to play football like all the other boys he saw playing in the park. He had no friends to play with. He didn't understand that his friends avoided him out of their being uncomfortable and embarrassed rather than because of their casual cruelty.

Arnie solved this problem of his being solitary when he realized he could kick his football against the walls in his family's secluded rose garden. It still proved difficult because when he kicked the ball with his left foot he repeatedly fell to the ground helplessly because his right leg was still weak and insecure. He kicked the ball against the wall times without number. Thousands of times he pounded the ball until he became better. He could hit the ball high or low, right, left or middle, fast, slow or in high bouncy arcs. In his young mind he was the king, the absolute master of those old red bricks and that piece of inflated leather. Finally he was so confident in his ability he asked his mother to invite two of his old best friends, Tomas and Otto over for tea on the next Sunday. He also begged her to make certain that his father would also be present. Although his mother wasn't sure Bertie's presence was such a good idea she was delighted that her son wanted to meet people again, so she happily complied.

Sunday arrived and so did Arnie's friends. He greeted the reluctant but inquisitive visitors with caution, his sense of self worth remaining very delicate. "Hello", he said, watching their equally wary eyes examine him for some monstrous infirmity. "Hello", they chorused in reply. Tomas noticed the ball lying on the grass unattended, unsure what else to do he turned to Otto, a shy boy always eager to follow his lead. "Let's play football!" Tomas shouted to Otto as he ran across the grass.

Arnie turned when he heard his father approaching. "Good morning boys, good to see you, its been too long." The boys were nervous of the man, but were soon distracted by kicking the ball to one another. Bertie turned to his son, "mother told me there was something you wished me to see?" Arnie smiled nervously, he was proud of his accomplishments with the ball, so hard won, but his nervousness around his father stuck his tongue to the roof of his mouth. He found himself unable to speak, his mouth opening and closing with no sound coming from it. "Don't stand there like a bloody fish!" roared Bertie. Arnie noticed his friends, who were pretending not to hear, look up and snigger at this, "You have no doubt got something silly to show me, so get on with it, I don't have all day to waste."

Arnie was determined to show he wasn't as worthless as his father thought, and bravely held back the tears that were pressing the back of his eyes, clamoring to roll down his cheeks. "Tomas!" he called, "Give me a kick." Tomas looked at Arnie in surprise as he ran onto the grass. Tomas looked to Otto and Bertie unsure of what to do.

"Go on, kick him the ball and let's see what he'll do with it." Said Bertie, a spark of interest quickening within his cynical heart. Tomas put his foot on the ball and rolled it backward, quickly managing a tricky maneuver that enabled him to get his foot under the ball so that he scooped it up into the air and onto his knee, there Tomas kept it bouncing as if he were a magician, "I say, bravo Tomas." Bertie said, clapping his hands together in appreciation. Tomas always played to the gallery, and at that moment Arnie hated him. His friend kicked the ball into the air and then sent it in a lazy airborne trajectory toward him without it ever touching the ground.

Arnie knew at the moment the ball blotted out the sun on its way to him that all his efforts and practice were going to be inadequate when compared to his friend's football tour de force. The ball came toward his right leg, he tried to turn so that he could carry his weight more comfortably on his stronger left leg, to trap the ball, but he was too slow and ponderous. The football hit him on his right arm just as he was at his most unbalanced and he stumbled backwards, landing hard and clumsily on his bum on the grass. The shame, the ignominy as Tomas then Otto, but worst of all, his own father burst into uncontrollable laughter at Arnie's collapse. No one moved to his assistance as he tried to get to his feet, their cruel laughter was to echo in Arnie's mind for years to come.

It was at that moment that Bertha appeared at her son's side. But she recognized the need for him to get to his own feet without her help. All she could do was smile in his direction, and nod, as if by these mute signals they would share the information, Arnie get up!

Arnie focused all his attention on that task and used his legs to propel himself back towards an oak tree, which he reached after a huge effort, having rubbed his bottom raw. He used the sturdy bough of the tree as a support for his back and working his legs like pistons he forced himself up the tree until he was standing upright. Perspiring with the effort and feeling distinctly wobbly after over taxing his weary leg muscles Arnie kept his eyes focused on the ball at his feet, scared to look up into mocking eyes. Reaching for the ball he knew that just kicking it would not remedy his embarrassment. But Arnie was nothing if not determined, and he decided to try the trick he'd been rehearsing so hard for so long. Failure didn't cross his mind as he summoned up the willpower to overcome his adversity. He put his left foot on the ball and gently rolled it back a few centimeters, quickly locking it between his heels and in one glorious motion that he'd practiced endlessly he jumped and whilst in the air he jackknifed the bottom half of his legs sending the now released ball high in the air and over his head. Before it could touch the ground he volleyed it back over his head and turned in time to witness it land perfectly at Otto's feet. Both the boys watching Arnie were amazed at their friends athletic triumph, too amazed to speak, their smirks of condescension replaced by quickly found boyish approval.

Satisfied with this Arnie looked away from his friends to seek a similar reaction from his father, but Bertie had already turned his back to march off toward the house. He had given up on the small boy before witnessing his achievement. "Papa!" shouted Arnie, his voice a mixture in equal parts of anger and self-pity. The man stopped and turned to face the boy. "Perhaps you should realize your limitations and try something less difficult next time." Before Arnie could summon a response Bertie marched into the house. His back seemed like a giant accusing wall shouting no to his son. "But papa, you missed my trick!" He called over his shoulder, without looking back, "Don't waste my time." He entered the house, Arnie's devastation would have been total but at the moment of his deepest hurt and depression Tomas and Otto appeared at either side of him, both of them smiling broadly. "Can you show me how to do that trick?" Otto asked him. His approval was a wonderful, if temporary, substitute for his father's total lack of interest and support.

Over the following months Arnie didn't speak with his father except at the behest of his mother who did all she could to mend the rift between the two men in her life. Arnie's interest in and love for painting became an obsession as Brigittete and Bertha worked with him to seek methods to perfect the way he could hold a brush in his mouth instead of continually mourning the fact that he couldn't use his hands. The major difficulty of holding the brush this way was that it brought Arnie's eyes too close to the canvas on which he was painting. He couldn't see the overall look of the painting as he worked. He tried working with longer stemmed paintbrushes but soon discovered that these were almost impossible to control with any accuracy. Often Arnie came close to despair as he saw the results of his painstaking work were nowhere near the same level he had achieved with so little effort before his accident and infirmity. His mouth ached from clenching the brush too hard between his teeth for so many hours but still his paintings didn't come near to the levels he had set himself. He didn't want to be a good disabled artist, he wanted to be just a good painter.

One day he finished trying to paint a portrait of his mother who had patiently sat for him as his model for two entire afternoons. The light diminished so Arnie let the brush drop onto the palette on the chair and stood back from his labors. He looked up at the canvas and sighed, despairing of his lost ability. The line of the work was uncertain, unsteady and disgustingly weak. Bertha looked at the painting and said nothing for a long while. Brigittete, always uncomfortable in such silences, looked at the painting; "it's lovely Arnie" she said kindly, the boy could sense her insincerity, and despised himself for being weak enough to want to believe the woman.

"No," said his mother grimly, "there must be some other way for you to paint or you will never amount to anything at all. This simply is not good enough." Arnie tried to summon up the will to argue, but knew she was simply telling him the truth.

Bertha set about using her inventive and elastic mind to discover some method to enable her son to unleash the talent she knew lay within him, undiminished by his physical impairment. The trio tried everything for day after day, but still they were no nearer to a solution. They began to despair after the days became weeks and they became months, still without success. Arnie couldn't bear the repeated failure and he begged them to leave him alone. "You think I'm some kind of game don't you?" he cruelly asked his mother, who loved him without reservation. He was mortified when he saw the tears welling up in his adored mother's eyes, "I don't mean that mama, its just that you'll soon have me standing on my head painting with my feet!"

Brigittete laughed but Arnie saw his mother with that familiar glint in her eye. She had an idea. Within the hour she had her son experimenting with various types of brushes clenched between his toes. Initially Arnie couldn't reach the canvas comfortably so it was raised, lowered and adjusted at the same time, as was the chair. A process of elimination had the women place cushions strategically behind him, under him and to his side, until, they made the idea functional even if Arnie was not secure on his perch. This seemed to worry no one except Arnie as he labored hard to clench the brush firmly between the first and second toes of his left foot. However hard he tried the brush was impossible for him to control. "This is hopeless, just hopeless!" he called out, "I'm useless, just a useless cripple." His mother, always his unquestioning support and anchor looked at her son long and hard, "I agree, we really shouldn't waste any more time on you, you're twelve years old now, no longer a baby to be mollycoddled and cajoled. You haven't even managed to equal the paintings you did when you were seven yet, I am going to give all your painting equipment to the people at the orphanage, they'll appreciate it." She started to pack away all his precious brushes and paints. Arnie didn't know whether to get angry or cry, he decided on the former. "That's not fair!" he roared, "I wasn't crippled then, its not my fault I can't paint as well as I could then." But his mother continued to pack away his artists tools as if he weren't talking, "Mother why won't you listen to me," he turned his head towards Brigittete, "Tell her she's being unfair." Instead of answering him the teacher began to help Bertha to pack away his paints in a brown canvas bag, "Why are you both being so wicked to me, it isn't fair, I try to paint, I just can't do it any better, it's not my fault I can't do it." His mother paused in her work and looked at him.

"Fair?" she said scornfully, "what does fair have to do with anything? You keep repeating I'm not fair, the world's not fair, why do you expect fairness from the world? It's time you realized that no one owes you anything. If you want to live like a lump feeling sorry for yourself that's how the world will value you. But while you're working this out for yourself I expect life will simply pass you by. You will be one of those people who could have been something, could have been, might have been. You will meet many people who tell you that they have a great notion for a book that they will write if only they have the time, but they never will find that time. We all have ideas and many people have talent but talent without application is nothing at all. To achieve anything worthwhile takes a person with talent thousands of hours of hard work; then one day, hopefully, other people might recognize this. Talent without application is like a sail without wind, useless, like you, and I'm your mother and I love you, or I simply wouldn't bother with this truth. You are handsome and will be a charming diversion for people passing by in their busy lives, but you'll be one of those bitter people who could have been somebody, but settled for being a nobody. Don't worry though, your father, would probably think I was simply stating the obvious and thinks all this effort is cruel on my part, he has already made provision for you so that you'll always have a roof over your head and food on your table. Me, I just thought you'd prefer to do this for yourself than settle for being a self pitying lump, I was wrong." She swept from the room without looking back and Brigittete, now shaking her head and quietly wiping a tear from her apple cheeked face followed her out.

Arnie bowed his head in shame. Was he really how his mother had described him he wondered? He sat there, alone for hours, until the light from the sun dimmed, and he was in the darkness without the ability or will to do anything about it. He examined and weighed the evidence of his mother's words and his own beliefs and arrived at the same conclusions. This made him even more miserable, to the point of desolation and despair. He had degenerated into being simply a burden on others, especially those that loved him, always expecting someone else to do anything difficult or irksome whilst he had grown accustomed to his using his infirmity as a shield from hard work. The unpalatable truth was that he had become accustomed to starting everything in a half hearted fashion anticipating certain failure, a pat on the head and then assistance, quickly followed by platitudes that would excuse him. He instinctively knew that his mother was forcing him to face up to himself for his own good.

The next day Arnie woke with newly discovered iron determination. He didn't speak of the hard truths spoken by his mother, but she was quietly thrilled to see her son begin to flower from his own efforts. He even managed to gratify his general studies home tutor, Professor Epstein. He was a small bantam cock of a man, bespectacled, with a halo of white frizzy hair and sparkling, dancing chocolate brown eyes. No one could ever guess the man's age, "He was probably born looking just like that, permanently middle aged!" joked Bertha. The Professor was a hard man to satisfy and Arnie suspicion that his mother had chosen the man to tutor him because he was a tough taskmaster was correct. He had also been her tutor when she was a girl and she enjoyed this tenuous link to the otherwise totally severed ties with her family. When she looked at Epstein she saw faint echoes of the men in her father's family, now becoming just ghosts in her memory.

Epstein regarded anything less than total accuracy, objectivity and honesty as failures beyond redemption. He saw something in the blossoming young man that he considered worthwhile. After her son's first lesson with the Professor Bertha too Epstein for a small walk to a chair in her garden. As Epstein swatted away the summer insects with his fussy little hands he listened attentively to the woman he had known since childhood. "It is good to rekindle our acquaintance Herr Professor." Her smile was reinforced by his own, "Where are my manners, would you care for a drink, coffee, tea, a piece of strudel, perhaps a schnapps?" Epstein consulted his watch and shook his head, "I'm afraid I no longer have time between lessons I am so busy these days." She hesitated, "Do you still see my family?" she inquired, "Only at synagogue on the High Holy Days." Recognizing her discomfort he spoke again before she could, "They looked well, your family." She smiled before he continued, ".... and they would have good reason to be proud of their grandson, I like the cut of the boy, he has something about him, he is going to be a fine young man." Bertha also smiled, "You see something of promise?" The Professor took off his glasses and polished them on his large linen handkerchief given to him by the mother of another grateful student. "If he continues how he has begun he will be a credit to you, his family and his country; and perhaps we could try a nibble a little of that cake with just the one cup of tea perhaps?"

Of course Arnie knew nothing of this conversation or the extra care and diligence of the Professor's seemingly harsh and austere learning regime. All the growing boy recognized was the mental gymnastics that Herr Epstein put him through on his way to the school he worked in, for precisely thirty minutes, and for another ninety minutes on his way home. Epstein then evaluated Arnie's daily work and set him extra studies for the evening, which he would then ask him questions about the following morning.

During one of these morning visits, when the Professor was pushing his student especially hard, the pupil turned to the teacher and demanded, "why do you push me this hard?" Epstein took his timepiece out of his waistcoat pocket and looked at it meaningfully, "The brain is like a sponge, the more you work it the better it will respond, perhaps a better metaphor is that its like a muscle, and it gets bigger and stronger the more you exercise it, and unfortunately your brain needs extra work to catch up with where it could be, or perhaps, where it should be. Does this answer your question?"

Arnie thought about this for a while and then smiled and it was like the sun coming over the horizon, "Professor, have you never heard the expression, all work and no play makes Jack a dull boy?" Epstein laughed, a rare occasion for so thoughtful and careful a man, but after a moment's consideration he studied the young boy next to him in the study, "Everything in life is a balance Arnie, too much one way and it all falls over, and too far the other way, then you have the same result, everything in moderation except learning, of that you can never have too much. Life will provide you with many opportunities to indulge yourself, and no doubt, you will seize them. Now can we continue with your studies?"

The Professor's regime emphasized literature, mathematics, philosophy, science, history and geography. The man's priceless gift to Arnie was to open his eyes to all the aspects of the world around him. Through Epstein the boy mentally traveled to the high Andes, and the bottoms of the deepest oceans, he took his mind to the vast steppes of the Russian Empire and introduced the boy to Kings and peasants, presidents and prime ministers, farm laborers. Arnie was amazed by the words of Shakespeare and soon realized that his father's totally negative opinion of all things English was obviously an error. No nation that could deliver such eloquence and erudition could be entirely evil.

Armed with this newly discovered knowledge Arnie tried to question his father about his undiluted hatred for the people that he simply called, "the enemy!" almost spitting on the ground as he did so. But now, despite his father's apparent indifference, Arnie's mind was alive with a million questions as his imagination took flight with the careful prodding of the Professor and Bertha, always ready with a prompt or a question. She was delighted to see this flowering of her son, she wasn't sure what route this journey might take, but she was excited by how alive his eyes were now, every day sucking up information as if it was food for the mind.

The time rolled by with increasing swiftness and as it did so Bertha couldn't help noticing that her son was maturing into a handsome young man of fifteen. The Professor had warned

Bertha that they wouldn't be able to meet all the intellectual and artistic challenges this highly intelligent and articulate boy would generate.

On his birthday Bertha had arranged for his friends Tomas and Otto to visit. The drinks and cakes had become almost obligatory, as had their uncomfortable little silences, the stilted conversation and forced smiles. Arnie realized that they weren't bad friends; it was simply that they had grown apart as they had no shared points of reference except for Professor Epstein who also taught them at the Gymnasium. But Arnie had never set foot in the place so it was no surprise to him that he and his friends were unable to make conversation. Arnie tried, he spoke of the terrible inflation and unemployment affecting their country but they appeared to either not knowing or caring about this. They offered no opinion on any subject and I had no idea of what to do next. Now that we were eating our tea they couldn't seem to tear their eyes away from the spectacle of my mother feeding me, but what could I do, a fellow has to eat! Between mouthfuls I tried another conversational tactic, and asked, "Tomas, how's that sister of yours?" He smiled mischievously, "You fancy Marlene? " he asked me, I felt the redness shoot up my face in boyish embarrassment, "I haven't seen her in years, she must be all grown up now." Tomas was now embarrassed as Otto made an exaggerated hourglass shape with his hands, and leered outrageously, forgetting my mother was in silent attendance, I tried to cough and direct him with my eyes in her direction, but he clearly hadn't picked up on my signals as he continued, "She's all grown up all right." Tomas elbowed Otto in the side and pointed at my mother who was pretending not to hear anything as she concentrated on her embroidery.

"Oh, I am sorry Mrs. Hessel." It was Otto's turn to turn red as he realized his gaffe, mama looked up, as if she knew nothing at all, "Sorry for what Otto?" she said, pretending not to have heard him. I was so proud of my mother at that moment, for making it possible for me and my pals to share the moment, for making us all comfortable.

The morning passed in meaningless chatter which had the result of making me realize that although insulated from the world by my handicap I still knew more about it than both my liberated friends put together who simply didn't understand the wonderful gift of their freedom.

Before venturing outside the boys both ceremoniously handed their presents to mama for her to unwrap for me. The two unveiled packages were soon revealed to be books. From Otto a novel that was instantly forgettable and Tomas had given me a wonderful thick and oversize book entitled "Renaissance Art of Italy". He flicked the large colorful pages containing beautiful prints for me. I found it difficult to restrain my enthusiasm for the wonderful book. It was the best present I had ever received.

Later we played some football on the lawn but I could see that my friends felt they were humoring me. Both boys were now in the school team and told Arnie vivid if implausible tales of their heroic exploits. Arnie couldn't help but notice that Otto kept looking at his fob watch and indicating to Tomas that it was time to go. Arnie could sense their boredom but had no idea what to do about it. Tomas was more generous with his time and himself, but Otto was the natural leader of the two. Arnie took it upon himself to end their mutual misery; "I have a study period now, so you two had best push off." Otto smiled and half pushed Tomas toward the door as soon as he heard this. "It's been smashing to see you Arnie." He said disingenuously, "Yes, goodbye," said Tomas, "Perhaps next week I could come over with Marlene, she often asks after you?" I didn't need a second to think about that offer, "that would be wonderful." I responded with alacrity. After a brief look of incredulity flashed from Otto to our mutual friend, they left. I was alone in the garden, with no lesson planned, but with time to think about Marlene. Arnie's imagination overflowed with the exotic images and possibilities of a girl all grown up as only the mind of a pubescent boy can.

The following week passed by in a flash but Arnie neither saw nor heard anything from Tomas. He reconciled himself to the probability that his friend was just being kind when he told him that his sister had any interest in him. Why should any girl have any interest in a person like him? The best thing he could do was keep his head down, not get in anyone's way and scrape up some kind of living in the future. As ever no one except mother seemed to be aware of Arnie's deep disappointment but even she couldn't do anything about this, his first adult hurt.

Another few days passed without incident and Arnie was kicking his football against the wall of the house in the bracing air that foretells of snow soon to fall. He saw someone watching him from the trees in the middle distance. Now that he had an audience he began to perform his full repertoire of tricks and flicks. Out of the corner of his eye Arnie could see that the person watching him from the trees was a girl of about his own age. She made no move to come out from her semi-concealed position as he continued to hit the ball against the wall. Being a boy he didn't realize that his ball control would be the very last thing that might impress any girl. Convinced she was spellbound by his virtuosity with the ball he now kicked the ball ever higher on the wall, turning with alternate bounces, moving further from the wall, readying himself theatrically to kick the ball over his shoulder with a flying airborne kick which he thought he could achieve whilst landing on his feet. Unfortunately Arnie's ambition outweighed the realities of gravity and he landed with a bone-jarring thwack in an inglorious and humiliating heap on his ass. He heard the girl laugh before he opened his eyes. As he did so he saw her approach in a halo of sunlight, realizing that she was more of a young woman than a girl, but her laughter was delightfully girlish and unrestrained by the conventions of the mature.

"Would you like me to help you up?" she asked solicitously, but still giggling. "No" Arnie replied, "Marlene, you are Marlene aren't you?" he continued, "How did you know?" she asked him, impressed by his powers of deduction. Arnie managed to stand up with as much grace as he could muster, "Just a lucky guess." He responded, she moved slightly closer. It was at this moment Arnie was to remember, that he fell hopelessly, totally and forever in love with her. In his eyes everything about Marlene was perfect from the rich cascade of her blond hair to the tiny feet encased in her sensible lace up boots. Her dress, although properly modest served to emphasize the promising curves of her slim body rather than conceal them, but it was her face that truly captured his heart. Open, honest and happy, with a slightly pointed chin, wide set frank powder blue eyes, a button nose atop a cupid's bow naturally red lipped mouth always slightly parted in her warm and engaging smile revealing even perfect teeth. Marlene was Arnie vision of an angel and he silently swore to himself that she would be his partner for life whatever else would happen.

He bowed slightly from his waist, "How do you do?" he asked, "My word, you sound like a gentleman from a previous century." She said, laughing gaily, her voice surprisingly and pleasingly husky and mature. Marlene seemed totally unaware that Arnie was in awe of her. She reached down and placed his lifeless hand in her own two hands, she squeezed it before gently releasing her grip. "It's good to meet you at last," she said, "Would you care to sit down?" Arnie asked, "I only have a short time'" she answered, after just a moment's hesitation, Arnie hooked his foot under the leg of a chair and pulled it towards her, "Please then, for a little time."

Marlene and Arnie sat down. "How is your family, I expect Tomas to call?" Arnie said this, rather than the words he would like to have said if he dared, wanting desperately to tell the girl how he loved her and wanted to kiss her beautiful lips. Instead of which he nodded politely as she responded to his question,

"Everyone is well, Tomas sends his regards but couldn't come himself because he has to revise for his end of term examinations, if he fails them again this time father will tan his hide!"

Arnie smiled at the delightful girl, he found conversing with her progressively easier. "How are you doing at the school, you are at senior school yes?" he said this trying to discern her age. Marlene smiled, immediately realizing his ploy. "Yes, of course, I'm almost the same age as you Arnie, my birthday is in March. Actually I am nearly top of my class," then revealing her youth, she continued, "there's only Greta Wirtmuller ahead of me and she just memorizes everything like a parrot." She finished the petulant little outburst with an alluring, entirely feminine pout. "I don't see Tomas so much anymore." Arnie said, Marlene quickly changed the subject, "how is your family, tell me about what you do all day?"

Arnie smiled again, he wasn't used to the social niceties, "My mother still nags me and my father still ignores me with ever growing passion, he hates me almost as much as he detests anything not German, especially the English, the French and especially the bloody Yanks!"

It was Marlene's turn to smile somewhat nervously, she hadn't anticipated such as direct, no nonsense answer to her innocently asked question. "Oh I think you're exaggerating, your own father couldn't possibly hate his own son like that." She reprimanded him.

"I know what you're thinking'" he added hastily, "he doesn't hate me just for being a cripple these days, I don't even think that enters into his thinking. No, it's my politics, that makes me the spawn of the devil, especially as I disagree with his disgusting views." She tried to lighten his mood, "I don't know anything about politics, and don't care to do so, but this only provoked Arnie to become even more heated, "What!" he exploded in outrage, "You don't care how your life is to be run and by whom?"

Marlene recoiled in her seat slightly, "I didn't say that exactly, besides which I know who runs my life almost entirely, mother, father and the school." Arnie, forgetting how much he wanted to be connected to this wondrous girl continued his attack, "It is everyone's duty to be involved." She paused, allowing him time to calm down, "OK," she said, "Tell me what you believe in, and convince me." Arnie was thrilled with this invitation, no one ever listened to him discuss politics, not even his mother.

"I'm an international socialist." Arnie solemnly explained, "What's that," she asked, "Some kind of super Communist, or a follower of Trotsky?" now it was his turn to recoil, outraged at the suggestions she had put forward, "I am beginning to suspect you might know a bit more about politics than you said." He volunteered. "I didn't say I was a Communist, I believe in both a world without borders and ownership of the means of production and distribution by the proletariat." Arnie began to feel that this conversation was slipping a bit out of his control, "that sounds impossibly grand, international socialism," she rolled the term across her tongue experimentally, "But what will it mean exactly, to you and me, in our lives, now and in the future?"

Arnie was becoming ever more defensive, his well rehearsed arguments being questioned and prodded by this girl who admitted no political knowledge. It wasn't right. "Now you're sounding rather like my father, I would appreciate your not patronizing me as if I was an idiot, my arms don't work but my brain does thank you young madam!" he regretted his words almost the instant he said them, "I'm sorry I didn't mean to upset you, that was entirely inappropriate." She flushed with quick anger of her own, "stop apologizing!" she ordered him, "What's said is said." She stood, ready to leave, but before she could take a step Arnie also stood and on impulse he planted a kiss full on her mouth. It cut off her protests, and, after a long moment she stepped away from Arnie. He could see from the high color on her flushed red cheeks that she was as confused and aroused as he was. He smiled tentatively, but couldn't decipher the expression on her appealing face, he didn't know if he would be kissed or smacked in return, this was new, grown up territory for both of them. "I believe what's mine is yours and what's yours is mine, but my mind, that's mine." Marlene laughed which somewhat eased the tension, she touched her lips with her tongue, "You shouldn't have done that." She said, "Your mouth is saying one thing, but you mean something else, I have read that women say one thing and mean another, and I never understood it until now," he answered.

She smiled again, "I'm not any other woman, I'm not even a woman yet, I'm just a girl and you're not a man, just a boy, we have plenty of time for growing up."

Now it was his turn to smile, "do you really believe that, I don't think so, I think you liked it as much as me?" Marlene didn't answer but her blush deepened as she thought about what he said, then the fates took a hand in events and a cold wind whipped through the garden and broke the spell between them. It was as if Marlene and Arnie were wakened from a trance, "I had better make tracks for home, and my parents must be wondering where I've got to."

Arnie wanted to believe she would have stayed were she able, but understood that the conventions demanded that she leave. But he was nothing if not persistent and determined.

"Are you afraid to be left alone with me, after all what can I possibly do to you, just a crippled boy without the use of his arms, what harm could I do to a strong young lady like you?" she examined his face, looking for the hint of mockery she knew lurked behind his feigned innocence. "I imagine you could do quite a lot of harm actually." They both paused for a moment and then they burst into laughter, recognizing both the mischief and sexual chemistry hidden just below the surface between them. "You're impossible!" she said, "Worse than all the other boys I know put together."

He bent one knee to the ground and looked up at her, "Truly I'm just a lonely boy, your being here brings me my only ray of sunshine, I just have one wish...." He left the thought unsaid, teasing Marlene, "You can't stop there, what is it, what do you wish for?" he shook his head, "No I can't ask it of you." "Tell me." She insisted,

"I need to see a woman's body, desperately." Marlene was truly outraged, "This time you have gone too far, how could you say such a thing to me, and do you think I'm a complete trollop?"

Arnie quickly stood up and shook his head, "No, you misunderstand me, this is for art, I am an artist." He pleaded, "Now I've heard everything, you take me for an idiot. What art could you do, you have no arms!"

"I'll show you." Arnie said, turning towards the rose garden down the incline of the lawn. He was relieved to see that she followed him to the charming little clearing. "This is beautiful." Pleased with the discovery, she was enchanted by the spot. Then she saw Arnie's easel set up in the middle of the lawn and she walked to the canvas and stopped, she stood staring at the painting. It was a simple enough study of a rose bush, one of the best Arnie had managed to that point, but nothing he was particularly proud of, but Marlene was clearly more impressed.

"It's wonderful, who painted it?" she asked him. There was a pause, where he wondered, is she mocking me, and she pondered on this strange, unique boy man. He laughed, "Why are you laughing at me?" she asked, "You think it's impossible for me to be the artist don't you." He accused, "How could you paint?"

She paused in consideration, "nothing is impossible, but I don't know how it's possible." He shrugged expressively, "that I can show you." He walked over to the easel and picked up a fine brush from the water cup with his mouth. He dipped it into the pallet and using his mouth as he had done for long years of private practice he started to paint. His technique was now fairly assured, his hold of the brush strong enough and his touch particularly deft for this special audience. Out of the corner of his eye he saw Marlene's look shift from cynicism to pity to something between admiration and awe. "It's a miracle," she said at last, Arnie smiled at the praise, he forgot that the brush was still in his mouth.

"It's a mmmmm". He mumbled before Marlene kindly took the brush out of his mouth, "It's not a miracle but it does stop me talking and ......"

"And what?" she asked,

"And kissing." I completed. Again Arnie covered her mouth with his, this time there was no resistance although eventually, and reluctantly, she stood back. Their eyes locked as they stood a couple of feet apart, both slightly breathless. Very slowly she began to unbutton her dress, moments later she stood before him completely naked. Arnie couldn't believe such female perfection existed and was standing so close, if only he could touch her. He didn't know what to do. He coughed, suddenly he was a small boy again, a boy facing a woman, she angled her head in a question.

"I don't have another canvas to paint you on here," he said to cover his embarrassment, "I don't want you to paint me silly boy." She said this with a meaning that Arnie couldn't misunderstand. He slowly moved closer to her, closing the gap careful not to spoil the magical moment or startle her. He was now standing just inches away from her naked flesh so close that he could he feel her heat. "You'll have to help me." He said, and she did, until he needed no more assistance. They made love and were to remain in love for the rest of their lives.

Chapter Eight

Darmstadt High School
1927

Time seemed to drift by on a cloud for Arnie following his first intimate encounter with Marlene. He was dreaming of her whilst his mother soaked him in the bath with distressing results. "I'm sorry mama." But there was little he could do to conceal his tumescence from her as she smiled understandingly, "It's entirely natural for a young man, there's nothing one can do about such things." But this did nothing to stop him feeling total humiliation with this predicament in front of his own mother who carefully avoided his very obviously aroused penis as she washed her son as she had done so many times before. "These things happen." Marlene said, "I wish you could stop talking about it!" he replied.

His mother set about distracting him by making him sit up as she washed his back with a painfully hard bristle brush. It soon took him mind off of his other problem.

"Have you thought any more about your going to the art academy?" she enquired, "Mother," he said, always being more formal when she annoyed him, "how many more times must we discuss the same, dead issues?" Arnie knew he must sound inflexible and obstinate, but he couldn't cope with his mother in this mood, and found himself becoming more childish the more mature she wanted him to be. "I'll keep discussing this particular issue until you admit I'm right." She insisted, "Mother, you love me so you're blind to the fact that I'm simply not good enough to be in the academy." She made a harrumph noise, "Nonsense, of course you are, you're simply scared to go in case the other students are better."

Marlene knew her son too well, he nodded, "All right, I admit I'm scared, but I'm also not qualified." She made that noise again, like a horse whinnying, this time a bit louder, "Who is it that says you're not qualified, they would just have to use their eyes when they look at your paintings and they would have to know you're more qualified than any of the rest of them." Arnie felt his conviction wavering but although he would like to believe that passion and wanting could get a person anything they really wanted, the logical part of him dictated the truth and this stated that there would be no places in the art academy for those who had not matriculated the school. Then, if you had done particularly well in the conventional subjects, would a student's artwork, which demonstrated outstanding talent you would be considered, but as Arnie reminded his mother, "I haven't even been to school since before I was...for such a long time, so the whole idea is just a fantasy." Arnie had avoided the use of the word crippled, not because it upset him, but since he knew it made his mother so angry. She couldn't bear to hear him admit any defeat, however small, ever. There were no permissible excuses, since they did not, could not exist except to be overcome. "Professor Epstein, who is the most qualified tutor in Darmstadt says that you are very bright, brighter than almost anyone your age at the school." She stopped massaging Arnie's legs but her obsession was beginning to make Arnie angry.

"Herr Epstein's opinion doesn't count for much when measured against a matriculation!" She looked at her son with that special look that spelled trouble, "Yes, you're right, that you'll now have to do for yourself. Now let's get you out of here so we can dry you off." Bertha helped Arnie pull himself upright so that he could step out of the bath. She began to dry him as though his total lack of privacy and dignity, still so like a baby, should be of no concern to him. "I would have to be in the school to even be allowed to enter for the examination, it's forbidden otherwise."

71

She paused in her drying, "So you will go to school, like everyone else." Marlene said this as if unaware of any difficulty." "I can't" he replied, "You mean you don't want to because you're scared the other students will laugh at you. Isn't that the truth?"

She was right of course, as she almost always was, but Arnie hadn't even admitted this to himself, and certainly wasn't ready to do so with anyone else,

"Look at me mother, I can't even wipe my own ass!" he spat out at her. Her slap stung more than hurt him, they stood staring at one another; it was many years she had hit him at all, she didn't believe in it, and she instantly regretted the impulse. She kissed him on the cheek she had hit. "Don't talk to me like that again, I don't demand too much do I, but mutual respect is the least we must share or we lose everything civilized." Arnie was deeply disturbed that he had caused his beloved mother to lose her temper; theirs was a mutual devotion.

"I'm sorry, truly sorry, but you don't understand what it is to be different from all those around you." Bertha looked at him as if he were a fool. "Your mother is a Jew in Germany." She said this as if it responded to him directly, but Arnie didn't agree, "Please mama, we're living in modern Germany, serious persecution is a thing of the past, who cares about your religion except you, why should they, but I'm a cripple, I can't decide not to be a cripple, and everyone can see I'm a cripple every single day. Don't you get it, your son is a cripple."

She stood back on pace and let his towel drop to the ground. She stared at her son with something bordering on contempt. "You're pathetic," she said coldly, Arnie simply had no response left to give, "If you're going to worry what other people think about your outside you'll never let them inside to find what a wonderful person and marvelous artist there is to discover. Inside is something strong and pure and talented, and if you're not prepared to share your talent with the world because of your fear you disgust me! She finished and then stomped out of the room leaving him alone as she slammed the door.

"Are you going to leave me to wander the world naked?" he called after her, but she didn't answer. "I'm not going to be the school freak!" he yelled at the door, but his defiance was wearing thin as he felt the air begin to chill his skin. "All right, you win, I'll go to the damned school but for God's sake please come here and put on my underpants before I shrivel up and die." His mother, who had been waiting just outside entered the room, her face a picture of radiant happiness.

Chapter Nine

Darmstadt High School
1927 -1928

The weekend prior to Arnie's first day of high school started most unusually. The family was eating breakfast in the dining room when Brigittete, who had now taken up permanent residence, entered the room looking extremely agitated. There was a hasty whispered conversation between her and Bertha, which Bertie studiously ignored whilst Arnie strained to hear the women unsuccessfully.

Bertha bustled to the front door with Brigitte and the latter soon returned. "Arnie your mother wants you right now." Arnie reluctantly got to his feet and obediently followed her.

When he got to the drawing room a thin young man, with a small, meticulous but sparse goatee beard stood talking to his mother. He was immensely tall, cadaverously thin and white enough to qualify as a zombie drained of all blood. However when he turned to Arnie the boy could see how alive the young man's eyes were. His manner was like that of an ostrich; he pecked at his words, his Adam's apple bobbled sympathetically. "Hello Arnie, pleased to meet you, my name is Herr Rosen, I'm a journalist with the Frankfurt newspapers, and I'm very pleased to make your acquaintance at last."

His head appeared to bob up and down in sympathy with his words and his throat at each breath. Arnie found it hard not to laugh. "Say hello Arnie, where are your manners?" said Bertha, "Hello Herr Rosen." he responded, "Yes, well, as I was saying, I am an arts correspondent, Brigitte was kind enough to send me one of your smaller works together with a letter explaining your indisposition. To be frank I didn't, no couldn't believe such a thing was possible. Your work fascinates me and that's why I'm here."

Arnie was too dumbfounded to respond coherently, so he remained silent. "Have you any other canvases that I could see?" he enquired, "What for?" was Arnie's response, "I beg your pardon." Said the correspondent, nonplussed by the boy's negative reaction. "Why do you really want to see my paintings, perhaps you want to compare me to the chimpanzees having tea at the zoo, an amusing distraction, but not to be invited into polite society. The truth is that you've come here to see the freak, isn't that the truth mister Rosen?" The room was momentarily silent, but Rosen wasn't someone easily blown from his chosen course. "Certainly not, but perhaps if you let me look over all your work I could offer some constructive criticism. I promise if I think your work is good enough I shall review it and say so in my column, without mention of your disability. If your work isn't yet good enough I shall put away my typewriter until the day that you are ready, fair enough?"

Not being an entire moron, Arnie nodded his head with alacrity. The pursuant viewing was an unqualified success. Rosen loved Arnie's work almost without reservation. Brigitte suggested that Rosen be allowed to borrow three of his favorite canvases, although Arnie was loath to release them from his sight but he was just too excited to refuse.

The following Monday morning began with some excitement as Bertha dressed her son in his new unfamiliar school uniform. He felt most uncomfortable but when he looked in the mirror he was pleasantly surprised by how good he looked. They went down to breakfast together and found Bertie, his head already buried in the newspaper, as usual, managed a monosyllabic grunt in reply to their chorus of Good morning. They all settled down to their toast and marmalade when a roar of anger and outrage from Bertie suddenly interrupted the peace and quiet. "My God!" he jumped to his feet upsetting his coffee in the process. Bertie held up the newspaper as if it had attacked him.

"What is it, what's wrong?" asked Bertha of her husband. He threw his newspaper onto the table and then his wife picked it up, and she started to read aloud from the offending page, "The heading on the arts page - Darmstadt's crippled art prodigy, Arnulf Hessel." She paused and looked toward her son, "Do you want me to continue?" Arnie nodded, unable to bring himself to speak.

"Today I was privileged to see evidence of the remarkable artistic gifts of a handicapped fifteen year old youth in the ancient town of Darmstadt. This crippled prodigy, without the use of his arms since contracting Polio at the age of seven has taught himself to paint using, instead of his hands, his mouth and feet. The youth's name is Arnulf Hessel. We all need to take special note of that name after seeing Master Hessel's wonderful and original work. Arnulf is proof that our German youth can and does overcome any adversity. I have no hesitation in calling upon our National Academy of Arts to provide Herr Hessel an exhibition so that everyone could share this sublime talent."

Arnie's Mother paused to smile at her son who now had his mouth half open in astonishment, "He broke his promise, he promised not to mention my handicap." Tears of self-pity were forcing their way past his long eyelashes, he hated his weakness and ran from the room determined not to be the subject of anyone's pity. "Why do you raise that boy's expectations when you know he will ultimately fail?" asked Bertie.

Later Bertha was able to reconcile Arnie to the meaning of a journalist's promise being like ice on a very hot day; only kept if circumstances allowed. This was a lesson he always remembered. Arnie soon managed to convince himself that no one outside a small and obscure number of folk in the rarified world of high art would ever know about Rosen's article. It helped that Arnie noticed that although the journalist hadn't kept his word he had praised the young man's artistic abilities to the heavens and one place such comments wouldn't go unnoticed was the Art Academy.

Feeling much better after reaching this conclusion Arnie walked to the school. It was a golden day, when the warm breath met the cold air and signaled your path like a steam train and the cold frost in the paving stones quietly attacks the soles of the feet right through the soles of your shoes. Autumn had been sent cowering by its more severe and pernicious big brother, winter. The shock of the newspaper article had been replaced by Arnie finding himself a schoolboy for the first time he could remember at the age of fifteen. Any normal boy would be rightfully nervous but he felt a knot of sheer terror at the pit of his stomach. Would his peers realize he was normal in all respects bar one, or would they, as he dreaded, use his handicap as a weapon to beat him with?

He approached the large red brick building hesitantly. He saw a group of youths and smaller children gathered in little huddles. For Arnie they all seemed to be staring at him alone, their eyes like the turrets of a thousand guns, trained mercilessly at him.

Arnie, with much relief, saw his friends Tomas and Otto in the center of a crowd of about ten other boys of similar age all huddled near to the door of the building. He approached with a smile on his face but as he did so the group all pointedly turned their backs toward him, except for Tomas who, alone smiled at Arnie and walked the few steps between them. "Good morning and welcome!" he boomed, loud enough for anyone and everyone to hear, "Good morning Tomas, and thank you."

One or two more of the group sneaked a quick look in their direction but made no move to break ranks.

"I shall always be here to stand right next to you Arnie." Tomas said, again so that everyone should hear. The ringing of a bell by a young man with a feral face and sly smile interrupted the slight warm glow Arnie felt. "That's Ratwerller, " said Tomas quietly to Arnie, "We call him Rat, and watch out for him, he's Head Boy."

The boys and girls lined up in classes and entered the school in orderly ranks. Arnie was left alone, not knowing where to go. Ratwerller came over to Arnie and regarded the new student scornfully. "You must be the new boy, they told me about you, follow me."

Rat led Arnie through a maize of innumerable corridors past seemingly identical frosted glass paneled doors concealing their quiet classrooms. Arnie was convinced that he would never be able to navigate these interminable routes without assistance. Everywhere the head boy and his charge went they were stared at by all the other students and teachers. Arnie was trying hard not to be totally intimidated by the experience. They eventually arrived at a room, which had large double doors with a sign stating, STAFF ONLY. Ratwerller knocked politely twice and then hearing someone call "Enter" led Arnie inside. The sole occupant was Professor Epstein, his normally avuncular private tutor. Arnie didn't notice Head Boy Ratwerller's departure such was his relief at finding the Professor smiling in his direction. At last, another friendly face. "Welcome" he looked at the big clock standing by the wall and noticed it was now two minutes past the hour. He made a tutting noise, shook his head and said, "Follow me, it doesn't do to be tardy." As he led Arnie out of the staff room he turned at the door as he opened it for him, "We'll soon settle you in."

The professor led Arnie down yet more endless corridors. After what appeared to be an endless trek they arrived at a classroom marked "4A". They entered and were met by a sea of staring, distinctly hostile faces, this wasn't Arnie's paranoia, nor, he would later discover, much to do with his handicap, but the class did appear to dislike him on sight. After all the group had been together since they were small children, and now they felt they were being invaded by this strange and different newcomer.

Arnie was very relieved to see Marlene in the class, and she smiled to him, without any thought of hiding her pleasure at seeing him. The Professor indicated an empty chair for Arnie, which he took as quickly as he could doing everything to blend in to these strange new surroundings, a difficult achievement when you're the biggest person in the room. The Professor spoke, "Good morning class," They responded by rote, "Good morning Herr professor."

"I want to introduce a new colleague to you, some of you no doubt already know Master Arnulf Hessel, he's an unusual young man..." before Epstein could finish the thought Otto called out from the back of the room, "Yes only a half of him works!"

The Professor's face turned thunderous, and Arnie noticed that although some of the class joined in the cruel laughter, many did not. Arnie couldn't understand the cruelty of a boy he had thought of as a friend, but he was learning fast that morning of the realities of the rough and tumble of school and the mercury like fluidity of some of the relationships found there. Arnie felt some of his naiveté peeling from him like the skin from an onion. Before the oafish laughter of Otto and his group died away Marlene turned to him.

"At least *his* brain works." Now the class laughed at Otto rather than with him. Epstein banged his hand on the lectern; the loud noise silenced the interruptions.

"Any further interruptions and the culprit will be sent to the principal for corporal punishment, does everyone understand, Otto and Marlene?" The class settled down as the professor continued, "as I was saying, Arnulf Hessel is unusual in that he is an extremely gifted individual. His ability in all matters scholastic is, as you will soon discover, equal to or exceeds that of any of you now present. But his unique gift is to be found in the arts. His one disability he has managed to transcend by sheer hard work allied to a wonderful ability. It is his hard work that is a trait you could all do well to duplicate. Now, without further ado, let us proceed with today's work."

It seemed to Arnie that that the more he tried to become less noticeable the more others sought to point him out. Realizing, as he did, that his mentors only meant well did nothing to lessen his acute embarrassment at being so lavishly lauded for his gifts, as such a paragon of scholarly virtues, that it to set him apart from the very people he would have to get along with.

During the rest of his time at the school Arnie was to discover the alternatives others held in store for him. It confirmed that he either evoked total love or total hate; very few people were to remain neutral on the question of Arnie Hessel.

But the first painful day of his schooling was not yet complete. At 11.30 the bells sounded for the morning break. This was a chance for everyone to stretch their legs, have a snack and play in the big spaces of grass surrounding the school. Arnie soon found himself surrounded outside by Otto and his group of friends. "Unusual gifts. Is this something the old Jew spots in the crippled Jew? Otto laughed again, but hadn't seen Marlene appear close to his left. She was holding a string bag containing an apple. "That's enough Otto." She said quietly, "I can deal with him" interjected Arnie, "What is Arnie, does the big girl have to look after the little boy?"

"What have I done to make you so angry Otto? I thought we were friends." Otto sneered at Arnie, "Friends with you, you must be joking." Arnie felt the tears well up behind his eyes at this hurt, but he couldn't allow this emotion to be seen, as he instinctively knew that the group surrounding him would regard this as a terrible weakness.

"I knew you were stupid Otto, but a bully also?" said Marlene. He was furious at being made to look small, but convention forbade him from attacking the girl, "If you were a boy I would hit you for that." He snarled, "and if you were a gentleman I think you'd know how to behave better." She replied.

Otto wasn't finished, he needed to vent his anger physically, he shoved Arnie to try and force him back, but Arnie was bigger and solidly built, he stood his ground. "Think you're tough do you?" Otto said to him loudly, as if Arnie was the aggressor. Otto started to rifle through Arnie's pockets, "What do we have here?" He took out Arnie's money and after showing this around theatrically put it in his own pocket.

"Put that back now." Marlene told him. "Why?" he replied, "is anyone here going to stop me?" Arnie didn't know what to do, but was nearing the point of breaking down in frustration and anger. Otto spat in his eye. The filthy muck started to dribble down Arnie's face.

Without warning Marlene swung her bag at Otto's head smashing him on the nose with the apple at the end of the bag. There was a spontaneous burst of bright red blood as he staggered back from the impact. He was so infuriated that his natural instincts took over and he aimed a fist in the direction of Marlene's unprotected face. Before he could hit her Arnie threw his bulk between them, taking the blow on his shoulder. Taken by surprise Otto wasn't ready for the well-aimed kick Arnie took at his groin. Otto sank to his knees much to the astonishment of both him and his cronies.

"How does that feel bully boy, put on your knees by a cripple and a girl!" she said. Before he could recover Arnie kicked him in the chin with devastating effect, sending him sprawling onto his back as some of his teeth and blood flew from his torn mouth. Two other boys grabbed Arnie from behind, and after seeing this Marlene disappeared in the melee. Other boys helped Otto back to his feet. He surveyed Arnie with murderous intent, spat out a tooth and some blood, and slowly removed his jacket, his every move calculated to menace. He wiped his hand across his mouth and then looked at the blood on his hand, he paused.

"So, the cripple is a tough guy eh, now we'll see if you can take it as well as give it." He hit Arnie as hard as he could in the stomach and as the bigger boy doubled up in pain he hit him again, this time in the face. He kept pounding Arnie until he thought he was going to knock him unconscious, but Arnie was determined not to give an inch, he kept getting back up to take more punishment. Otto's frenzy knew no bounds as Arnie's stolid refusal to ask for mercy enraged him, making him feel powerless to impose his will. Now the only sounds were Arnie's sharp intake of breath when Otto hit him in the belly and the latter's exhalation of breath with the sheer effort of his blows. The other boys began to drift away, there was no joy in a massacre, and Otto's cruelty became their own if they watched. Arnie only remained on his feet due to his sheer bloody mindedness. Tomas broke into the circle with Marlene. They interposed themselves between Otto and Arnie.

"What are you doing Otto have you gone crazy?"

But the more powerful Otto pushed Tomas out of his path, "This is between him and me, you stay out of it or you'll get the same." Otto said to him. Two of his cronies pulled Tomas out of the way, but Marlene stood her ground.

She stood, her hands on her hips, defiant, facing Otto and the rest of the boys, "So, do you want to follow beating a handicapped boy with hitting a girl, is that how you prove how tough you are?"

Otto perfunctorily pushed her aside, ignoring her jibe as he looked up into Arnie's face. "You had enough cripple?"

Arnie was too weak to do anything but laugh unconvincingly, "It has been like being hit by a butterfly.

"I'll show you!" Otto leaped on to him, incoherent with rage. A whistle blew and instantaneously Otto stopped his attack and the rest of the crowd miraculously melted away, leaving only Arnie and Otto to face Head Boy Ratwerller. Even though everyone had already obeyed his whistle he blew it again, three times, until he was standing right next to the combatants, blowing it directly into their ears.

"What do we have here?" he demanded of them. Neither responded. Ratwerller turned his attention so that he focused on Arnie, "You, tell me what you two have been up to."

Arnie turned from the Head Boy to Otto and shook his head, refusing to answer. Ratwerller continued, "Not a very impressive first day. You're clearly a disruptive element Mister Hessel, you'd best watch your step around here in future or I'll see to it that you're expelled. Understood?" The small and skinny head boy had not cowed Arnie. "I am sorry to have bled so inconveniently all over your play area Herr Rat, I shall try not to leak in the future." Ratwerller lifted his hand as if to strike Arnie but restrained himself when Otto stepped in between them.

"I wouldn't do that Ratwerller." His voice was full of threat and menace. Ratwerller backed off, clearly intimidated by the physical presence of Otto whose reputation as a brawler clearly preceded him. "Cross me again and you two will regret it." Said Ratwerller, before whirling away with pseudo military precision and marching away. Otto looked at Arnie hesitantly, who took a couple of deep breaths before speaking, "OK," said Arnie, "We're alone now, are you ready for more or do you surrender?" Otto's face broke into a smile, and Arnie found himself grinning stupidly. Soon both boys were laughing loudly. Otto grabbed Arnie in a bear hug of an embrace, tears of laughter now rolling down both their faces. "You're alright you are," He said, "Even without your arms you are twice the man that Rat bastard will ever be. No one has ever put him down like that and got away with it."

Chapter Ten

Darmstadt
1928

Otto and Arnie were never to fight again, and, although they never became firm friends there was a guarded and mutual respect. Word soon passed around the school of the fight that they had, and it assumed almost mythic proportion. No longer isolated, Arnie was now treated as something of a cult celebrity by the rest of his class. In fact if anyone ever contemplated picking a fight with him they would first have to deal with Otto, who had now made himself Arnie's unofficial champion.

Most of the rest of the year's schooling passed without further major incident. A succession of lessons punctuated with all the usual tests, evaluations and examinations.

In Arnie's final year at the school, as he was approaching the matriculation examinations he had his first solo gallery exhibition. Although excited by the event at the time he was to recall very little about the momentous event except the musty smell of the small grimy well-worn shop in which it was held. Arnie adamantly rejected the idea of his own attendance at the event, convinced he would simply be regarded as the freak. He did visit the shop prior to the big day to make certain that his paintings were hung in a manner he thought correct. He also refused an invitation for another interview, a follow up feature with the journalist Rosen. Arnie suspected it was him that had been instrumental in persuading the elderly gallery proprietor, Bernd Shuster, to host the show.

Much to Arnie's surprise the weeklong event resulted in the sale of all twenty-one of his exhibited works and orders for another nine. His mother, Bertha, opened a bank account on his behalf and told him that he had earned more than his father had in the previous year. This fact would have upset him greatly, had he taken any interest whatsoever and therefore known about it. Bertie remained capable of totally blocking anything bothersome or that simply displeased him and Arnie fell within that category.

Arnie was now mentioned in numerous newspapers, which invariably drew attention to his handicap, age and art in that order. But Bertie never seemed to read or know about any of them. Arnie was worried he might not get a good series of results for his matriculation as he was desperate to do anything to find an exit to his home, to get out into the world under his own steam. The atmosphere at home was at a poisonous low trough between his parents.

It was at this time that Bertie received an invitation from Arnie's headmaster to a meeting. Bertie replied affirmatively, and a date was set, despite his foreboding. He anticipated more bad news to blight his already depressing recent life. Nothing had been as it should have been, could have been, since the Great War. He wasn't living up to his own expectations, let alone those of his peers. He felt their snorts of derision, although these were imagined. Now more plump and grey he nevertheless visualized himself as the dashing young officer he had once been. His abiding preoccupation was the Fatherland, although no one knew in which direction this wonderful country, the beating heart, brain and brawn at the centre of Europe would go as nothing seemed to work as it should. Order needed to be restored.

Bertie entered the cluttered office of the headmaster knowing that anything to do with his son would, from bitter experience, lead to pain, aggravation and disappointment. He looked across the dusty desk and through the piles of books that served as a frame for the aged Professor Schiller, the headmaster. He reminded Bertie of an old tortoise, his head disproportionately small on his chubby body which struggled to fit into an overly capacious and scruffy academic cape. No, thought Bertie, he's more like a peanut set on top of an orange. This impression was soon dispelled by the headmaster's voice, which was gruff and guttural. "Would we care for a schnapps Herr Hessel?" he asked Bertie before he'd managed to settle into his chair. "No thank you Professor, it's a little early for me." The Professor shook his head, "We don't think it's ever too early for a good schnapps. Are we sure we don't want a little comforter?" he chuckled, but Bertie bristled in annoyance. "I never drink before sundown, you asked me here to discuss my son, are his studies unsatisfactory, I wouldn't be too surprised, I did warn your Professor Epstein he was taking a bit of a risk on the boy?" he tapped his forehead with the back of his hand, "It wouldn't surprise me too much to discover if he was a little touched up here, it's his mother who is always pushing the boy. You know how they are."

The Professor looked at Bertie in some surprise and then took his schnapps in one long gulp. Schiller shook his head after coughing as the fiery liquid found its way down his throat. He clasped his hands together making a cathedral of his fingers. "I've met Mrs. Hessel several times, a charming lady. No we're not dissatisfied with anyone in your family. We're more than satisfied with your son. In fact we'd say he had done remarkably well. In fact we could wish all our other students were to show such application and talent."

Bertie shifted uneasily in his seat, uncertain how to deal with this unanticipated praise for his son when he was more used to pity or pretence. "That's good to hear, of course. But you asked me here as a matter of urgency?"

Nothing appeared to hurry the older man. He shuffled over to the other side of the large room and seemed surprised to discover a large cabinet. Delighted he opened a tall mahogany cabinet and in it was a large array of bottles containing every type of drink known. The professor was delighted, and turning again to Bertie said, "We think we better have another, for the joints. Are you sure you don't want to join us?"

Bertie didn't bother to respond, resigning himself to a further wait as the headmaster imbibed yet again, seemingly unaware of the other man's growing impatience. He turned suddenly, invigorated by the blended whisky he was consuming with such relish, "Your son Herr Hessel, how would you be seeing his future?" It was not a subject Bertie had spent any time exercising his brain upon.

"What future can there be for a person with such an infirmity? I shall do my best to secure him a comfortable existence, of course, that is my duty." The headmaster nodded sagely, "Just so, as we thought." Schiller ruminated further as he took yet another pleasure filled swallow of his treasured Scottish import. He turned to look out of his window and saw Arnie and a group of his friends happily playing soccer. The professor turned to face Arnie's grim and austere father.

"We believe your son has an outstanding future as an artiste, outstanding, he has truly exceptional talent." He watched Bertie closely for a positive reaction but it was in vain.

Bertie replied, "What you mean is that Arnie has exceptional talent for an artist who paints with his feet and his mouth."

"Certainly not. " replied Schiller, who was clearly angered and less inhibited than might have been the case had he not been steadily drinking through the afternoon. He calmed down and continued, "Personally we have a scientific and mathematical background but anyone, anyone with even half an eye can attest to the fact that your son has a talent that is both unique and wonderful. How he does what he does is immaterial to the result, which is wonderful. Don't you understand Herr Hessel, your son, Arnie is a genius!"

Bertie was shocked by such a blatant affirmation of Arnie's talent by a learned professor, even one who drank so liberally, Bertie respected authority absolutely, and Schiller represented it. "Arnie a genius, my son is a genius?" Bertie was unable to mask his sudden pride and genuine surprise.

"Surely you cannot be surprised Herr Hessel, you have seen his paintings, you are an intelligent and educated man, you must have known his work is very special?"

Schiller was bemused by Bertie who averted his eyes from the professor's steady gaze, " I think we should talk more about this perhaps?" the old man said quietly, trying to probe for the answers as gently and circumspectly as he could. Bertie's iron self discipline began to unwound like the gas from a cylinder, quietly and steadily. "I have never looked at one of his paintings." He said this almost inaudibly whispering the admission, ashamed of himself. Silence ensued, hanging between the two men like a safety net, "Perhaps I could join you in that schnapps now Herr Schiller?"

There were several more drinks and a long conversation between the academic and the military martinet. Bertie derived a special kind of comfort that a more religious man might find from a kind priest in a confession. He found the experience and cathartic and almost spiritual. He listened carefully to the professor's advise before returning home to discover his son.

Arnie and Marlene were in the Hessel family pantry examining a large piece of rock clamped securely onto a workbench. A head was taking shape from the stone, although it was, as yet, impossible to discern whose face it would be when it was eventually completed. "Why do you do this, to punish yourself?" she asked. Arnie smiled enigmatically. He always did this, as if he knew something that someone else didn't. Usually his smile actually meant that he didn't know the answer to the question. "Don't be my judge and jury," he said, "Give me the mouthpiece," he asked, she laughed as she placed the device in his mouth. "At least this will shut you up."

It was a fairly comfortable device designed by Arnie and Brigittete that she had manufactured by a local dentist. Arnie had the idea for it after watching a film of a boxing match he saw at a cinema. It was between Germany's superhero Max Schmelling who had fought a two-round exhibition with the American World Heavyweight champion Jack Dempsey in 1925 in the city of Cologne. The type of gum shield they wore formed the basis of the design. After repeated use he had become proficient with this contrivance but his jaws still ached, sometimes for days afterwards. He nodded to Marlene and she put the medium weight chisel into his mouth and he clamped down on it.

The veins and muscles of his neck stood out, as they were small steel chords beneath his skin. Arnie studied the piece of rock as if it were both enemy and friend, he willed himself to summon up the power and strength to finish his task. Nothing would stand in the way he decided. Suddenly he closed his eyes, his head reared back on his neck then with all the energy he could summon he lunged forward forcing the chisel to bite into the rock. Again and again his head snapped back then forward like a fist with eyes on the rock. Nothing deters or distracts Arnie's almost manic focus and concentration.

He became only dimly aware of Marlene watching his self-inflicted torture at first, but then even she faded from the periphery of his mind as he was swallowed in his intense involvement with the unforgiving piece of stone. His eyes danced with both pleasure and pain as he battled with this, the hardest artistic discipline he imposed on himself. Now it was just him and the stone, and nothing else mattered.

He hammered his head back and forth, no feeling the sharp pain in his mouth and jaw with each terrible impact. He was only aware of shards of stone splintering off as I cajoled a shape into the rock. He ignored the chippings flying around his face as he unconsciously accelerated the rhythm of his work when he sensed his creation was becoming a living, vibrant face.

Unknown to Arnie his father had quietly entered the room. Marlene saw Bertie who signaled for her not to disturb Arnie's work. She smiled to him and nodded her compliance. Bertie was stunned by his son's manic devotion to his task. To his untrained eye it looked as if his offspring was torturing himself with an obscure but wonderful rite of masculine passage. Hardly daring to breathe the older man went deeper into the room and circled behind his son.

When he reached a position beside Marlene Bertie saw the shape of the face that Arnie had hacked out of the rock; it was a bust of him. Arnie had lovingly fashioned his father's face.

Bertie was struck dumb when the realization struck him what love his son must have for him, and what sublime talent he had used to express this love.

Marlene turned to Bertie and saw the tears running down his cheek; with a tender entirely feminine gesture she wiped the tears away with her handkerchief and then kissed his cheek with her healing lips. "I didn't know" he whispered to her, "I understand." She said, and, after looking between the two Hessel men she left the room.

Arnie felt the currents of air shift as she departed and turned just in time to see Marlene leave. It was at the same instant that he saw his father.

Bertie was still clearly transfixed by the bust; it was so powerful, so full of love, at once primitive and dignified, a magnificent raw piece of imagery.

Their eyes locked, "I didn't know, I never realized." Said the father to the son. Arnie spat out the chisel and then the mouthpiece and stood up. He didn't lower his guard; nothing was permitted to pierce his protective carapace of self-protection. He had been hurt too many times by this man.

"Hello father, what, you didn't know I could sculpt?"

"No, that you cared for me enough to do that." He pointed to the statue. "You like it?" Arnie asked incredulously. "One doesn't merely like such art, I am engulfed by it, it's not enough to simply appreciate it, it's not enough to talk about such things, I love it, I am proud of it, of you, I love you, I am so sorry."

Bertie suddenly rushed forward and embraced Arnie who had not felt any affection or physical contact from his father in all their years together. Their tears ran and mingled, their joining together a signal of a genuine newly discovered closeness. Something drew Arnie's eyes back to the work that had served as a bridge across the yawning emotional chasm between them. The face he had created had, for him, a malevolent cast to it, which he knew he had engraved into the jaw line, mouth and eyes. Which was the true face, the one he had sculpted and known for a lifetime, or this new and suddenly loving father. He prayed to heaven that he was wrong, that it was the latter.

Chapter Eleven

The excitement of the drive to Frankfurt was only marred for Arnie by his having to say farewell to Marlene. But youth is the great healer; youth and distance can certainly help deaden such adolescent pain. Arnie's acceptance as a student at the Academy of Arts in Frankfurt had been the culmination of so much effort over such a long period that he could scarcely believe the actual day of his enrolment had arrived.

The journey by road from Arnie's home to Frankfurt was quite short in terms of distance but millions of miles by any other form of measurement. Unlike the slightly claustrophobic atmosphere of his town this new town had streets that were broad and straight, the buildings taller and more imposing, the citizens milled busily about, and there were huge numbers of them. Arnie would treasure and measure of his own anonymity amid the louder, more rombustious. Everything was more, and Arnie loved its brash lusty arrogance.

Bertie and Bertha spoke to their son almost continuously on the drive but he barely heard a word they said. He sat in the back of the car hypnotized by the sights and sounds of this seemingly endless city. Finally the car pulled to a halt outside an imposing edifice, which he was soon to discover was the Academy. Bertie helped Arnie out of the car as his mother waited awkwardly. She was not used to her husbands newly found consideration for their son, and still couldn't quite place her faith in it lasting.

The small group of three found themselves unsure of how to navigate the correct rituals for saying farewell. They had not been apart like this before and Arnie felt a combination of fear and trepidation for an unknown future and a wish to rush headlong into its embrace. As ever it was Bertha who found the words first, "I'm certain that all the arrangements promised for you will be in place, your father did write to them and explain the situation comprehensively, didn't you father?" Bertie smiled patiently, he had reassured his wife on this issue several times. As ever his preparations had been methodical and meticulous. "Of course, they confirmed all the arrangements, remember, I showed you their letter."

Bertha nodded her head, somewhat at a loss with nothing to worry about for every minute of every day. Arnie turned to her and also smiled reassuringly at his adored mother, "I'll be fine mother, and you really don't have a thing to worry about."

Bertie spoke again, more hesitantly than normally when he was so certain of everything. "Son, if you want anything, anything whatsoever, just get in touch with me, and if it's within the scope of our pockets we will arrange for it immediately, understood?" Money was not an issue that Bertie ever spoke openly about, and certainly never in front of his family. Arnie was immediately concerned, especially when he saw the same emotion flitter briefly on his mother's face. "Is business that bad father?" Bertie avoided looking back directly at his son, pretending to look at the busy street traffic.

"It's not good for anyone in Germany right now Arnie." His mother answered for his father. "I shouldn't be here if we can't afford it." Arnie said, appealing to their common sense, "Don't you worry Arnie, you enjoy your time here, you will be living out our dreams for you." She smiled radiantly at her son as she said this to him.

Bertie felt his son's stare, "All we can ask is that you do your best, perhaps when Herr Hitler reaches his rightful position all our businesses will improve."

Arnie bristled, "If Hitler comes to power then..." but before Arnie could conclude this thought his mother interjected, "No politics you two, you promised me today would be just about

Arnie coming to the Academy." Bertha had, as usual, managed to find a way to paper over the cracks.

A handsome young man, about Arnie's height, with dark hair, but thinner, dressed immaculately in a perfect simulation of the clothes of an English country squire, a habit he would never break, whatever the circumstance. He bowed to Arnie's mother with elaborate and courtly courtesy then saluted Bertie who liked him on site and returned the formal military greeting, everyone's face were wreathed in smiles.

"You must be Helmut Von Thyssen?" said Bertie to the young man, "and you must be the Hessel family, welcome to Frankfurt and hello Arnulf," He replied, turning toward Arnie. "You must call me Hynie, all my friends do and I will be distraught if not to be counted amongst your friends."

Helmut shook hands with both Bertha and Bertie and as he did so Arnie took the opportunity to study his newfound friend. This charming, handsome young man appeared to have it all. Everything about him was engaging from his smile revealing perfect white and even teeth that for Arnie, appeared to twinkle with abnormal whiteness. Helmut was all Arnie could have ever aspired to, all he had ever wished to be. Helmut clapped Arnie heartily on the shoulder, a gesture he would learn to tolerate as a small price of his friendship over the years to come. Arnie and Helmut liked each other immediately, both appreciating the other's apparent openness and candor.

"Hello," said Arnie, quietly and with some timidity, "You must call me Arnie."

"Arnie it is then," he replied happily. "We'll leave it to you chaps then" Bertie said. "We'll be just fine I promise you. It has been a pleasure to make your acquaintance, however brief. Don't worry about Arnie. I'll see to it that he doesn't get in too much trouble."

More handshakes were exchanged between Helmut and Arnie's parents who then both hugged their son much to his embarrassment. Helmut picked up Arnie's bags as if they were weightless and led him toward the building's impressive main entrance. Arnie turned to look at his parents as they trudged the few steps back to their car, they seemed to have suddenly aged. It was a very sad moment for them all, somehow so terribly final.

Bertie and his wife watched their son disappear into the academy after Helmut. Bertha cried into her pretty lace handkerchief and blew her nose; Bertie self-consciously placed a protective arm around her shoulders. "Don't worry Bertha, our son is man to be proud of." He put the car into gear and slowly drove away. Bertha looked back to the building as it diminished behind them.

"I'm simply being selfish, I won't have anyone to look after anymore." She said, "You can look after me." He replied.

Helmut led Arnie up to their room up a broad and deserted staircase. The interior of the academy's sleeping quarters was intimidating. Everything was of such epic proportions and magnificent works of art hung everywhere. Helmut pointed out facets of the places that he thought might interest Arnie.

After the grandeur of the public section of the academy Arnie was not prepared for the comparative squalor of the quarters that Arnie and Helmut were to share. The room was tiny and shabby, and clearly Helmut was not the most tidy of people, his clothes, books, sketches and unfinished projects spilled everywhere. "Be it ever so humble," said Helmut, as ever without any sense of irony. Arnie was to find his ever-ready smile and unfailing good cheer impossible to resist. Arnie smiled as Helmut randomly unpacked and placed his cases carelessly tossing the contents into any available spaces he could find in the already crowded wardrobes and drawers.

"You shouldn't feel you always have to do things for me, I'm quite self reliant," said Arnie, "I'm sure you are, and believe me I wouldn't dream of doing everything for you, but my mother would love to see me doing something for someone else for a change, it might do good for my immortal soul or such like."

"I could pay you perhaps, or hire a nurse or such like," Arnie suggested, although where the funds would come from for such extravagance he had no idea. Helmut laughed, "Pay me. You must be joking, my family own about half of Bavaria and if you were to hire a nurse that could cost my family a fortune." Helmut saw the bemused expression on his new friend's face, "I would feel honor bound to impregnate any nurse you might engage, it's a family tradition, matter of honor, family motto, if it moves nail it, might have been referring to something else, result, knock up all the serfs, then parents would feel there was no alternative but to pay exorbitant rates to some back street doctor to relieve her of such a burden, so, result is, best leave matters as they are old chap."

Arnie laughed at Helmut's tortured and somewhat idiosyncratic logic. "I simply don't understand why you're being so decent to me." "Decent I ain't," Helmut leered comically, "I'm selfish as all hell, but you're a widely celebrated artiste Herr Hessel, quite the coming thing, your fame precedes and spreads before you like a magical cloak with which I might also enfold myself for warmth, comfort and transportation since your reflected glory won't hurt this very mediocre wielder of the brush, if not with the august academy then at least with the young ladies."

"Me, help you with the ladies?" roared Arnie incredulously, "The sympathy angle dear chap, the sympathy angle never fails, and that's if my charm, good looks, talent and vast fortune fail to entice."

Arnie found himself laughing yet again, as Helmut collapsed on his bed and lay prostrate with his hands locked behind his head. "Now, before I adjourn for my vital afternoon siesta is there anything the maestro requires, pick your nose, scratch your back, light a cigar, I dare say I could even find a young lady, or chap if that's your preference, after all we are broad minded artistes, to pull your plonker for a bit?" The more the laughter bubbled out of Arnie the more encouraged Helmut was to continue, but as he finished it was as if his energy was all used up.

"Must admit been burning the candle at both ends and middle..." before the last words were out of his mouth Helmut was breathing deeply and he began to snore with some determination. Arnie felt he had found a new best friend.

The next day, a Monday, found the pair in a large rectangular brilliantly white room that was to serve as their studio and classroom. It was lit by natural light that flooded in from the vast glass roof, which would serve to fry its inhabitants during the summer and freeze them during the winter. The place was only truly comfortable for about two months of the year, and unfortunately, six of these eight weeks were exactly when the students were to be on holiday. There were twelve other students arranged behind their easels and they all waited anxiously for the professor to appear.

The sole exception to this was Helmut, who had spotted two pretty girls who were seated close by. Arnie noticed that both the girls were very attractive, one a blond, the other a redhead and both giggled at Helmut's outrageously lascivious attempts to attract them. Arnie soon found himself led down the same path as he copied the style of his new friend, with nods, winks and Helmut spoke to Arnie out of the corner of his mouth, "I don't fancy yours much my friend, mine's not too bad, and I could easily a arrange a paper bag for your young lady to wear." Arnie made a loud kissing noise at just the moment a pocket sized little man marched into the room. His eyes seemed to bore holes into each student in the room, paying particular attention to Arnie and Helmut.

"My name is Schindler, Professor Schindler, and when I enter a class all students will stand and be ready for their work, this is not a kindergarten and you are no longer babies. Anyone arriving late will miss the class."

Something about this over zealous little Prussian with artistic pretensions seemed hilarious to both Arnie and Helmut. They both began to giggle and it was infectious and within moments the entire class could no longer contain themselves and were soon all laughing.

"I amuse you Hessel?" Schindler demanded.

"I'm sorry sir," Arnie said, but no power on earth could stop his giggling.

"Perhaps you would be better suited to a job as a fun fair attraction, the no handed artist, what will they send me next, a blind painter, now that is funny!"

Arnie and the rest of the class all became quiet and shifted uncomfortably in their seats. Helmut stood.

"Forgive me Professor, the fault was entirely mine."

"I don't need martyrs, I need talent allied to discipline, now sit Von Thyssen and we will see if any of you possess these attributes.

This proved to be a skirmish that set the tone for the next two years of artistic drudgery. Schindler seemed to take particular and malicious pleasure in persecuting Arnie above all the other students; this despite Arnie working ever harder to improve his techniques and knowledge, the professor likened him to an average pavement artist. The man never appeared satisfied with anything the young man did and it became Arnie's obsession to prove the teacher wrong in the only way he knew, with his paintbrush.

It was the summer, a hot day in early July. Arnie felt he was getting nowhere and his ambitions to be a respected professional artist were never going to be realized. He had just finished a line sketch of a nude young woman. Two years earlier and he would have been pleased with the result but such was his uncertainty that now he didn't know if it had any merit.

Schindler glanced at it and shook his head. He told Arnie to stay late after the rest of the class. Arnie waited as instructed, expecting another torrent of abuse and debasement. Schindler walked slowly to a position behind Arnie and studied his drawing at some length, eventually he spoke. "This is adequate, quite adequate Hessel." Schindler then smiled and Arnie couldn't believe his eyes as no one had ever seen a genuine smile on the professor's usually taciturn face, "In fact your best work so far, in fact your recent work is quite excellent and I am proud to be your teacher."

This praise was so totally unexpected that Arnie couldn't believe this was not the precursor to some cruel jibe but the professor went on to say more, "You are our star pupil you know and it has been my duty to keep your feet firmly planted on the ground. We needed to push you to the limits of your ability so that you didn't backslide into excuses and second best gimmickry, the comfortable cushion of easy praise you will have experienced for merely possessing a somewhat freakish ability to hold a brush in your mouth."

Arnie felt like an abused woman who was pathetically grateful to a bullying husband for the moment he stopped beating her. Arnie instantly turned from hating and fearing the professor to become his biggest fan. Arnie rushed out to tell Helmut the good news. It was Helmut who brought things back into focus with a cold splash of logic. "You could always paint like an angel, all this means is that Schindler has finally had to admit to this as well, now, at last he will lay off of you, that's worth getting drunk for anyway."

We walked across the grass square behind the academy and joined two young ladies, Martha and Putsy, two girls of the town who modeled for our class. They were easy to please the boys in any way they chose in return. It was a happy arrangement for all concerned.

They went to the nearby bar; a small Italian owned establishment called Marco's. It was small, dark noisy and full of smoke from the millions of cigarettes puffed happily in the grimy slightly damp atmosphere. It was a battle weary serious drinking establishment that once had better pretensions. The students from the academy often paid for their sometimes-unaffordable drinking habits by lavishing their talents on his black walls in lieu of payment.

The foursome sat at a long trestle table amongst the other revelers, a mixed bag of students and working men all packed together in joyful revelry. They all drunk beer, Arnie through a straw supplied by Helmut.

Helmut drunk with his usual gusto and soon finished several flagons, he held his most recent stein aloft in salute. "The toast is Arnie Hessel." Helmut swallowed a huge gulp of beer as the others struggled to keep pace with him. He bowed toward Arnie who returned the bow from his seat as the others called for him to make a speech in response to the toast. Helmut overcame Arnie's shyness by hauling Arnie to his feet. "Professor Schindler!" he called, "No!" responded Helmut, but Arnie was determined, "To Professor Schindler who forced me, with all his bullying to be a better artist and a more determined man, to Professor Schindler, the greatest man in Germany."

Arnie became aware of Helmut looking over his shoulder to something behind him.

It was at this moment that I became me, the rascal you might recognize. I turned to see four brown shirted Nazi young men, about my own age, clearly drunk and eyeing us, particularly me with clear threatening intent. The biggest of the brown shirts turned to the man on his right.

"Did that cripple say he likes to be bullied?" the second fellow laughed as if this was the finest joke he had ever heard, "We could help him there couldn't we, yes?" the big one continued as he led his group towards us. Other patrons of the bar melted away, wanting no part of this. I was still standing, aware that I was a big target. I spoke to my friends in a voice that I hoped didn't shake with the fear that I felt, "Some people, like myself, have physical infirmities, whilst others..." I looked directly at the first Nazi thug, "are mentally inadequate."

My calculated insult that I felt might shame the Nazis into retreat had the reverse effect. They approached even more closely and looked even angrier. I remember the smell of bratwurst on the breath of the bastard. Helmut interposed himself between me and their leader, who spoke directly into Helmut's face.

"Tell your friend," he said, "That the toast is Adolf Hitler, our glorious leader!"

Helmut nodded in my direction, hoping for my discretion. "Of course," I answered, "I am happy to toast Adolf Hitler since we have something in common, Hitler and I, painting. The difference being that he couldn't paint a wall properly with both his hands, whilst I can perform artistic miracles with my mouth and feet." Helmut and the girls laughed loyally at precisely the same moment the Nazis attacked us.

We tried our best, a handicapped man with big boots, one man and two slim girls against four big brutes with hate in their heart, but the odds were too heavy for us. I managed a couple of crafty well-aimed kicks and one well delivered head butt before succumbing to the frenzied attack. No one came to our aid. The last thing I remember before loosing consciousness was worrying what would happen to my college work.

I awoke, as you will remember, in that cell under the Frankfurt Police Headquarters, being brutally re-introduced to my old chum, Ratwerller, more appropriately known as the Rat.

Chapter Twelve

Darmstadt
New Year's Eve 1933

No amount of drunken revelry could reconcile me to the New Order. I had never fitted within our society before, but now I was considered a cancer not to be pitied but to be eliminated. I guess the only thing between elimination and me was my father, the Nazi. He stood for everything I despised. I tried to reconcile his ideology with his being married to a Jewish woman and being the father of a Jewish man. He never responded.

The cobbled square was packed tight that night; the crowd was enthusiastic and happy. Nazi flags hung from every window overlooking the huge throng. Men and boys in various smart uniforms lined the steps of the town hall. On the building's central balcony a man was haranguing the crowd, he was flanked by a large group of men and women. My father Bertie had made us attend this rally, and he was entranced by the speaker's words, throwing his head back and roaring "Heil Hitler!" with the rest of the mob. I noticed that my mother kept her head down and never raised her face or her arm in the obligatory Sieg Heil salute. As the crowed spontaneously began to sing the national anthem of our country father led us into the building, showing our tickets to the guards.

I stood uncomfortably next to Marlene, now a fine young woman and wondered how we had allowed ourselves to arrive here, at this point, as if we were blind, with white sticks and no sense. Marlene was accompanied by a friend, who was a handsome young lady with jet-black hair, pale skin and sparkling, challenging eyes. Her body was more athletic than

Marlene's which I had always adored for its curvaceous and luscious appeal.

As the anthems and shouting stopped the band segued into conventional party music and we danced. I usually felt self conscious when I danced since I couldn't use my arms to embrace my partner, but in this heaving crowd no one noticed that despite my intimacy with Marlene my arms staid resolutely by my side.

I whispered to her and she giggled and moved slightly back from me. "You're incorrigible Arnie, don't you ever think about anything else?" We both smiled as I looked over to her friend who was observing everyone from the side of the ballroom. "What's your friend's name, are you seeking to protect her from me for the entire evening?"

The tune ended and we walked towards her friend as Marlene responded, "I have already warned my friend all about you and your seeming disability and how you always manage to overcome it. Arnie Hessel meet Jessica Lanning, Jessica is from England." The young woman winced appealingly, "From Scotland actually, that's a bit like my calling you chaps Austrians Mister Hessel." She replied, "Please call me Arnie, and as the great leader would insist, we are all part of a greater Germany now." Jessica seemed a little flustered by my invitation, "Oh, I thought."

Now it was my turn to wince slightly, "I won't be too upset if you were to hold me extra tight to compensate for my lack in that department." She smiled as she led me to the dance floor. When we got there she stood on her toes and pulled my two arms around her neck locking them around her ingeniously. I smiled at her thoughtfulness; no one had ever done this simple act of kindness for me before. The music was American big band swing and we started to dance. "Where in Scotland do you come from?" I asked, "Edinburgh," she replied, "And why does an Edinburgh girl come to Germany?" She looked at me curiously, "You're very inquisitive for a stranger." I looked at her for a long moment before responding, "I don't intend to stay a stranger."

Jessica laughed again, I liked that laugh a great deal, "I was warned wasn't I, a very determined chap. I'm reading politics at London University. This is the place to be, this or the Soviet Union, if you're interested in such things, the two great social experiments, it's all happening here isn't it." Her spirit was determinedly jolly, but there was more to this young lady if I could find out what it was.

"Do you approve of what's happening here?" I asked, "I came to learn, it's far too early to make a value judgment, but I can understand it all though." Although we continued to dance I think she felt my body stiffen as I reacted to her words. "Then you might well be unique in this room, explain it to me if you would."

She wasn't in the least perturbed, "It all flows from the iniquitous Versailles Treaty forced on your leaders at the end of the Great War. It was too humiliating by far and for Germany what's now happening is a natural reaction to that indignity. It was totally unfair." I was beginning to not like this girl so much, "So you approve, of all this?" I looked at the posturing uniformed Nazis, the flags and the bunting.

She stopped dancing and looked up into my face, now quite serious, then like a cloud it passed and she smiled her most dazzling smile, "I came to have fun tonight, don't you want to have fun?" I couldn't help smiling in response, "Of course, the New Year is approaching and we must celebrate, out with the old and in with the new.

In another part of the hall my parents were standing in a small group of dignitaries that included Joseph Papp, the evening's main speaker.

"A very worthy speech Herr Papp." Said Bertie, "Joseph, please, mind you the name is the only Jewish thing about me I can assure you!" Papp led the group's laughter. Bertie, keen to be part of the inner circle moved closer to the man, "Many thanks Joseph," he paused, "A word to the wise, we are all wondering when the Fatherland might re-introduce general conscription, so far all we get are hints?"

Papp leaned in conspiratorially, "Well if I had a son, and who knows if I don't eh?" he led the group in more laughter, "I would tell him not to make plans beyond March, although, of course, this is entirely off the record you understand, non attributable." The men in the small group nodded whilst the women looked at each other as women will do, "That's good news," said Bertie, " Very good news, that will keep the young men out of trouble, teach the hooligan element some discipline and respect for authority..." Papp interrupted him with an imperious wave of his arm, "Enough of business, tonight is a celebration and you haven't allowed me to socialize with your charming wife at all, and she's clearly so shy as well as being so pretty."

He bowed to Bertha who kept her eyes downcast which Papp had misinterpreted for her being shy and demure, whereas in fact, it was to conceal her fear and loathing, "Forgive me," replied Bertie, "this is Bertha." She nodded her head in the direction of Papp, her distaste almost palpable.

Papp turned back to Bertie after looking over her fine figure as if she were his to take as he wanted, "Do you mind if I take her for a spin on the dance floor old fellow?" Before Bertie could reply Bertha spoke, "I'm terribly sorry Herr Papp but just for tonight I have to beg your indulgence, I'm not feeling particularly well."

Papp bowed from the waist in what he took to be a most gallant gesture and kissed her hand, "Of course, I hope we have other opportunities to dance together soon, I wish you the most speedy recovery." He smiled at her and then turned on his heels and moved to another group. As he left Bertie grabbed his wife by her shoulders and quietly hissed in her ear, "You idiot, don't you realize the opportunity we have just missed!" She recoiled from the severity of his grip, "But it's true, I do feel ill, people like him and you make me feel sick to the pit of my stomach!"

Bertie sneered at his wife menacingly, "I don't have to tolerate such behavior any more, you do know that don't you?" he asked, "I know the divorce laws, go on do it then, why don't you, make us both happy." He shook his head, "All I have to do is renounce the marriage because of the taint of your Jew blood and you'll be out of my life for good, with nothing, no money, no alimony, property, nothing!"

Bertha looked out at the dance floor, and quietly uttered three words, "Nothing except Arnie." This deflated her husband completely; it was as if all his energy and self-importance simply vanished, "Except our son." He intoned quietly.

I was unaware of this drama in any detail as I felt their stares in my direction and turned to smile at my parents, as ever they had clearly been arguing, and I just hoped it wasn't about me. Despite everything I did love them both, if not equally, or in the same way. I was still dancing with Jessica and I found her refreshing and fascinating. "Marlene tells me you're quite the famous painter?" she said, "she's exaggerating, I am a much better decorator." Jessica smiled at the small joke and then continued, "She showed me your special painting of her, the private painting."

I felt my face go bright red; Marlene had promised me that she would never show that painting to anyone. "That was totally painted from my imagination, apart from Marlene's face of course." Jessica just carried on smiling, "You must have a truly remarkable imagination, to have imagined that mole on her inner thigh."

I had nowhere to go in this conversation, so I tried to deflect the determined young Scottish lass, "Hey, didn't we come here to have fun, let's talk about something else, like any moles I might discover on you were I to paint you for instance."

Jessica's smile broadened, "You forget I was warned about you, all about you." Now it was my turn to smile knowingly, "As these military types would tell you it can be much more rewarding to outflank a well prepared defense." The music came to an end and Jessica unclasped my hands from around her neck and stepped back one-step. "You're a very unusual man, but I'm not the kind of woman who disguises her womanhood with feminine fripperies, I'm no man's coquette."

I liked her abrupt declamation, but I wondered what had happened in her life to make it necessary, "I consider myself duly warned, so you lust after woman's emancipation, not men's bodies, and on this we are as one."

She smiled again, and she was much more desirable when she smiled, almost irresistible, "First their minds, then their bodies." She responded quickly.

"I must return the compliment, you're a most unusual woman, can I be equally direct?" she paused for just a moment before nodding, "Of course you can."

"Would you like to go to bed with me?" I asked, and this time it was her turn to blush, but I was relieved to note that she hadn't run away, "If I said yes you'd think me the most awful tart wouldn't you?"

"No," I answered honestly, feeling the familiar thrill of excitement at the possibility at intimacy with a new and exciting woman. "I think it would be wonderful for both of us." She laughed throatily and as she did so tossed her head back, "You must have some Irish blood in you, you're so full of the blarney," she leaned in close, so only he could hear, "and I am the most awful tart, the answer is yes, but on one condition..."

Arnie nodded, "I haven't told you what it is yet," she said, "Almost anything." I said.

Later that night I found myself in Jessica's bedroom, she was semi nude on a bed, but instead of making love I was painting her. I was still fully clothed. My paintbrush was clamped between my teeth as my study of Jessica took shape on the canvas. The more I studied her the more I wanted her. I was making love to her with everything but my body and she luxuriated in this sensual knowledge, fully aware of her power over me.

"This is without doubt the next best thing to being touched by genius." She teased me. I bent down to my easel and dropped the brush from my mouth, "I promise you the real thing is better, and you'll shortly know that is no idle boast." She smiled again and stretched like a big cat displaying her magnificent body fully; the woman was torturing me. "Get about your painting you naughty boy!" she said, "I've heard of singing for your supper but never before painting for a ..."

She hushed me with a finger to her lips and with her other hand she stuck the brush back into my mouth silencing me, "A deal's a deal. I'm yours for one night when you finish the painting, which I get to keep forever and ever, remember?"

I recommenced the painting, and somehow my passion for this special woman grew with every brushstroke.

Eventually we both got what we wanted but I remain convinced that I got the better end of the deal. Although they say anticipation is nine tenths of the joy of making love on this occasion I don't think they were right. Jessica was every man's dream, a lady in the drawing room and a whore in the bedroom. She was clearly more experienced than me, and although that caused me to wonder where such wisdom might have been gained I soon lost that reservation when I felt the benefits of her carnal knowledge.

She was so giving and tactile, I experienced every inch of her and she me, I felt all her body, every undulating and pulsing part, she caressed me with her tongue, her mouth and her soft small hands. I used myself as well as I can, and her small noises grew in volume as our first kisses turned to open mouthed passion, our tongues exchanging more than words. I felt her tongue explore me and how I wished I could use my hands as cleverly as her hands tugged and stroked me.

Jessica felt comfortable with her own rhythms and soon she was dictating the pace for both of us to achieve ever more intense gratification. Without thought we became one being, sliding into one another, her breasts above my lips, swinging ever more temptingly to my lips, her openness pierced by me. Now she rode me like an accelerating horse, harder, faster, the pace increasing until we were totally lost in the rush to fulfillment and then, we were there, pumping everything into her, and her juices coating me, our perspiration mingling from this most wonderful coming together.

I slowly realized that I felt as if we had been in some extreme sporting event. Neither of us could quite catch our breath, the intensity, the passion between us just beginning to dissipate. "Better than a painting?" I asked, "You are the perfect lover." She answered, "Really?" I said, genuinely surprised by this unexpected compliment. "Yes, do you know how sexy it is for a woman to control making love with a hunk like you?"

I thought about this for a moment or two, "Is that what its about, control?" I asked, "Yes, to a degree, control, speed." she felt me under the sheet which we were both now under, "and endurance, you're a bull of a man, a bloody lion, and every woman wants that in her bed whatever they might say to the contrary."

She rolled on top of me and kissed me again, with growing passion. I couldn't rid my face from its silly grin, " and you're a woman without shame or remorse." And then we made love again. This time we were even slower and our build up more measured but no less exciting. I felt my heart beat to an accelerated pace as the woman played me as if I were her plaything. She was strong enough despite her willowy frame to move me as she wanted and she had no inhibitions in the bedroom. Afterwards I lay with my head on her bosom, her arms around me. "You use your mouth like other men use their hands, its wonderful." I smiled, "Do you give written references?" I asked. She traced the features of my face with her hands, "No, you're my secret and I'm keeping you all to myself. She must have felt my sudden discomfort as I turned my head away from her touch. I started to laugh and this broke the mood, at first she thought I was crying and she was concerned, "what is it, what's wrong?" but soon realized it was laughter not tears. She was fairly outraged at the way I had broken the spell cast by our lovemaking, she whacked me on the shoulder, and "You're mocking me!" I couldn't stop myself laughing, "Tell me what's so funny or I shall bash you with this." She held the pillow above me.

"Who would have ever thought, Arnie Hessel, sex object, plaything of the world, Casanova, gigolo!" she bashed me on the face with the pillow, I began to laugh again, "You're getting a bit above yourself young man. You love women and it shows, that's nothing to get too excited about."

But we were now both laughing, "Now show me my painting." She jumped from the bed and rushed to the easel before I could say a word. She stopped as she looked at it, "You bastard, it's wonderful and, its depraved." I studied her as she regarded my painting of her, "If it's wonderfully depraved then I have captured my subject, perfectly."

She strode back toward me on the bed, her wonderful body reflecting the light coming in through the big picture windows, unaware and uncaring of anyone who might be peeking in. She stood by the bed looking down at me, "How did you know I wouldn't just smash your depraved picture on your head, am I such an obvious tart?" Jessica was genuinely angry with me, her chest heaved as she crossed her arms and appraised me.

"Why do you say that?" I asked her, "Because I can never show that painting to anyone, let alone sell it." It was my turn to smile again, "I never thought of that, and of course it was a present, and you being a lady would never think of selling a present. I never sell paintings to friends. I give friends my paintings. What even makes you believe you could sell it, what market is there for the works of Arnie Hessel, my only value on the market is as a freak, a curiosity, people don't think I realize why they buy my paintings but I do, its just an update of going to the freak show at the circus and seeing the bearded lady or the midget for a little bit of money." She got back into the bed and lay beside me above the sheets, "You're being ridiculous, self pity really isn't attractive." I shook my head in reply, "My realism isn't self pity. At college I used to think that I was as good or better than the rest, but since then some of my fellow graduates have already had exhibitions, made sales, been seriously reviewed while nothing has happened for me except the odd critic who deigns to say that my work is most unusual before passing on to some other, more mainstream artist."

Her eyes narrowed as she studied me as if I were a particularly loathsome zoo exhibit. "You're nowhere near so appealing when you're like this." She commented, "Like what?" I asked, not knowing enough to keep quiet, "Do you really want to know?" she asked, "Yes," I replied, "Self pitying, winging, moaning and pathetic."

I inwardly winced at her evaluation, "That's unfair!" she was silent, "You sound like my mother." She smiled and kissed me briefly, full on my mouth, "She must be a wise woman, but surely you're not confusing the two of us I hope." I kissed her back, "Never, she's nowhere near as bossy as you!"

She tickled me on my belly, "that's so cruel" I laughed, "We Scots have to take every advantage we can, being only a small but bonny country, perhaps you need some authority in your life." I found myself very pleasantly pinned by her chest resting on mine, "And you're a bully, but I certainly don't want anyone telling me what to do, and it doesn't matter whether they're right or wrong, I can make my own mistakes thank you."

"Mister independent are we?" she inquired, "No, not really, without the support of my parents I would have starved on the streets long ago. I have no idea how I shall ever make a living." Suddenly she sat bolt upright, "I could sell your paintings for you, I could be your international agent."

"I don't want to dampen your enthusiasm, but have you ever sold anything, do you know about selling?" But she was already getting up and moving purposefully into the bathroom where I soon heard running water. "Come on!" she called, "It's time to get going, all we have to do is find someone with money who is as greedy for your depraved paintings as I am for your body and their money!"

My memory of events is that almost instantly Jessica had appointed herself my official international agent. Cards were printed and a sales campaign, more like her personal crusade commenced. As I watched her prepare I thought it would take a brave or foolhardy soul to deny her anything.

Jessica arrived at the first gallery with her hopes sky high. She checked her appearance in the glass front of the building and adjusted herself minutely, although there wasn't a hair out of place, she looked wonderful, fresh and although trying to conceal it, nervous. But it was as if she had some contagious disease, within less than a minute she exited the gallery, less happy but still determined.

Despite my wishing for success I was still certain that this would turn out to be just another disappointment. If I had known the crushing rejections Jessica suffered my worst fears would have been confirmed and I would have insisted she stopped. I spent the day pacing around my Spartan room as she was ejected from all the galleries of our town.

After a day of universal rejection Jessica was pleased to finally meet one gallery proprietor who was more sympathetic. He nodded a great deal as he examined my canvases. "How many complete canvases did you say are initially available?" he inquired, Jessica was suddenly excited by this turn in our fortune.

"Fifteen presently, and given a little time perhaps nineteen or twenty, why, are you interested in an exhibition of Arnie's works?" He looked very closely at one of the paintings before responding, "This artiste, Arnulf Hessel, has he never exhibited previously? His name strikes a chord, but I can't quite place the name." Jessica shook her head; "This would be his professional debut sir, anything to now have purely been steps on the path leading to your door, if you were to launch him you would forever be remembered as the father of a great career."

The Proprietor now studied Jessica with the same intensity as he had previously shown with the paintings, "Are you involved personally with Herr Hessel?" Jessica found the new direction this conversation was taking a little uncomfortable, "Why do you ask?" he smiled but his meaning was clear to the young woman especially as he moved closer and rubbed her hands with his own, "Oh I think you're a big girl, you understand, we scratch each other's backs, no one needs know, except the two of us. It wouldn't be so bad and your friend would be launched. We could rub each other up the right way"

Jessica looked up at the big man as he leaned forward to nuzzle her ear and as he attempts to do so she kicked him hard in the nether regions. He howled in pain and hopped from foot to foot whilst holding himself. Jessica gathered up the canvases and the rest of her stuff and made for the door where she stopped and turned; "Now you could say you can rub that the wrong way, bye." She called as she left the gallery.

I laughed with Jessica when she told me the stories and adventures from these first, totally unsuccessful days but it didn't make us any less disappointed at the totally barren outcome. We sat at my kitchen table surveying our bare existence and lack of future promise. I must have shaken my head for the thousandth time, and Jessica exploded, "Will you stop shaking that head of yours, its not the end of the world, we haven't begun to fight yet." She swigged from the bottle of red wine we were sharing, "I told you exactly what would happen didn't I." "You give in too easily." She responded with her usual defiance and speed, "I'm a realist." `I said, "You're a bloody pessimist." Jessica insisted, and just then, to save the day the door burst open. In strode our great friend Helmut. I jumped up to greet him and he grabbed me in one of his usual huge bear hugs.

"Why didn't you tell me you were coming you old fool?" he grinned, and turning to Jessica continued her sentence, "he is worse than that, he is a bloody minded, obstinate pessimistic fool!"

He kissed both Jessica and me despite not knowing her previously. He gazed at her appreciatively, "Well introduce me you cad!" "Of course, this is Jessica, a beloved flower of the finest English womanhood Jessica this is Attila the Hun, keep your legs crossed at all times in his presence."

Helmut and Jessica both laughed before she jumped into the conversation, "By the way Helmut I am most definitely not English, I am Scottish." Helmut laughed again, "Of course you are dear lady, of course you are. So, why are you two looking so glum? You didn't see me arriving through the window by any chance?"

"Jessica is learning the hard way how difficult it is to live by art alone. She has had a very difficult time I'm afraid." Before Helmut could respond to my description Jessica spoke, "I can speak for myself you know." "Of course" I said, "so how would you describe your experiences?"

"Bloody awful which is why Helmut needs to pour us all another drink, and make mine a double." Helmut did as he was asked, he was always keen to have a drink himself and it didn't matter the circumstances, venue or time. "Fancy your allowing this fragile flower of Caledonia out on to those cold Teutonic streets whilst you sat here on your fat ass in this warm studio, shame on Arnulf Hessel."

Helmut snorted in disapproval, I smiled at Jessica and shook my head, "You're to take no notice of this very silly man, he loves me really." "Not when you're stupid I don't. I have told you what to do many times and you just don't listen. You prefer to suffer you idiot!"

I was so fed up with this speech that I found myself shaking my head yet again, "Not your mad scheme again, Lord preserve us all." Jessica cut in, "I'm interested, what mad scheme is this?" Helmut smiled again, and turning from me was about to address himself directly to Jessica but I interrupted him, "It's not an idea as much as it's a trick, almost a con trick."

Helmut spoke to Jessica, "Shame on you Arnie, it is strictly legal and proper, now shall I put the lady out of her misery or will you?" I sat down again, knowing that no power on earth would shut my friend up, but at least I could make my feelings known, "You explain your strange idea, you're so much more suited to explaining criminal concepts larceny being so close to the heart of all aristocrats."

Helmut was not particularly amused as he resumed his explanation, "Well, as is well known, unless an artiste is safely dead in today's Germany his art has no sales value whatsoever, in other words you have to be dead to have a future."

"My word," said Jessica, "we kill Arnie and then we market him, wonderful!" she giggled, "Very droll." I said, "Droll or not, it happens to be nearer the truth than we would all like to admit, no one in Germany has spare cash to buy art unless it's a certain investment with good returns, most folk need every penny just to make sure they eat, but what if there was a way to make excellent art available to everyone for a few coppers and at the same time make the buyer feel good, what would you say then?"

It all sounded so plausible when Helmut outlined his dubious plans, "This sounds very interesting," said Jessica, "Carry on."

It was less than a week later that my garret had been converted into a small print works, complete with a press, inks and every variety of the finest card available. The machine was antiquated but, with the combined efforts of Jessica, who turned out to be a hidden engineer via her father's wise upbringing, and Helmut for the muscle, it worked. The team was turning out reasonable facsimiles of my best paintings in postcard size.

Helmut held up several to the light pouring in via the window, and rifled through them, grunting in satisfaction. "Not so stupid now eh. Postcards of the works of our pet genius, on the other side our little message explaining who and what Arnie Hessel is, and we never ever claim this is a charity, but neither do we say we are not a charity. We send these cards out in packets to every house in every street at Christmas or other holidays.

If the people receiving our cards as a gift decide they wish to reciprocate by sending us a little something, perhaps some money, it would be churlish to refuse. If they wish to throw them away or use them for free then I shall lose the money I am willing to invest to launch this concept. I have every faith that the average German family will do the right and honorable thing and make us all immeasurably rich!"

"And I say again, for the umpteenth time, that is a shabby and shameful way to get rich, that is if it were to ever work."

Helmut became serious, which was happily quite rare, "You once told me that I would have to learn the new order's rules in order to have a chance of survival and their first rule is that the strong shall devour the weak. You will be very weak indeed my friend, a half Jewish penniless artistic cripple. Don't you see this could be your ticket for survival? Rich men make their own rules, they are much harder to push around, whatever the rules are supposed to be, even the Nazis will know that."

"Listen to him Arnie," said Jessica, "he knows what he's talking about."

Helmut focused his winning smile in my direction, "I don't know if I would go that far Arnie, but how about giving the idea a try and we'll see how it goes, you've got nothing to lose." "Except my self respect!" I replied.

Jessica stood and with the most unladylike of gestures turned her back toward me and lifted her skirt so I could see her perfect camisole covered bottom. "And here is what I think of self respect!"

We couldn't remain serious and all of us roared with unrestrained laughter. I walked over to the printing press and examined the first batch of postcards neatly placed on the table next to it in small piles. I noticed that my partners in crime were watching me to see my reaction but I tried to give nothing away. "I have one question for you Hynie. If you answer satisfactorily I might, just might, possibly, consider your ridiculous proposition."

Helmut leaned towards me in anticipation, "Yes?"

"How much do you think we can charge for a pack of cards?" I asked. Both my friend and lover laughed again. Helmut grabbed me in one of his huge, all enveloping bear hugs and Jessica threw a bunch of cards into the air to celebrate.

It was very soon after that happy moment that she was out pounding through the streets, now softly carpeted by the first snows of winter, knocking on doors. At one particularly fine house a maid answered her knock, "Yes?" the maid asked, "May I speak to the lady of the house?" Jessica asked, "Who shall I say is calling?" Jessica smiled, "Oh she doesn't know me." The maid's attitude suddenly hardened, "If you're peddling something then you can get yourself to the back of the house, to the tradesman's entrance, a bit bloody nervy aren't you girl?"

Jessica stood her ground in face of this onslaught, as ever when faced with confrontation she seemed to swell with imperious self importance, "But I have a gift for madam and I will thank you to mind your manners or feel the back of my hand." The maid immediately became contrite, "I'll fetch madam straight away," but before she turned to go she hesitated, "it was a silly mistake, just a stupid mistake you understand?" Jessica smiled to herself as the woman retreated into the house, "Bloody Germans," she muttered, "either at your throat or at your feet." An overweight lady, dressed in frumpy blouse and long black skirt arrived at the door, she eyed her pretty visitor suspiciously, "My maid said something about a gift?" she asked. "Yes that's correct." Jessica beamed at her, "Forgive me, but we don't know each other do we?"

Unperturbed Jessica handed the lady a small attractive beribboned box, which the woman immediately began to unwrap. "I am here to help the crippled artists of Germany, by demonstrating to you, a lady clearly able to discern honest effort and true German artistic expression of talent." The lady is impressed by both the contents of the box and what she's hearing, but still unclear as to its meaning.

"The paintings are charming, but it would be embarrassing to accept such a gift from you. Why should a disabled artiste give me any such gift?"

"It's Christmas even for the disabled madam, and they also want to spread some joy and happiness."

The lady of the house clutched the cards to her ample bosom and fought hard to suppress the tears, "Then, in the same spirit let me give your invalid friends some token of our love and appreciation; would they perhaps like some nice cakes, I've just finished baking?"

Jessica smiled an almost saintly smile, "Well a cake would be lovely and very kind, but perhaps even more appreciated would be a small cash donation, that way we can facilitate their every need."

I well remember Jessica looking a lot less happy by the time she got back to our little apartment and stood by our small coal fire as it fought a losing battle against the biting cold. "I stood talking to that fat frau for a lousy few coppers, the cards are worth much more than that!" Jessica protested. I was glum with these poor initial results but I wasn't very surprised. The local folk of Darmstadt had never been over generous in any matters concerning me. Helmut didn't seem much concerned. "I knew all along it wouldn't work, don't say I didn't warn you, perhaps if we were in Berlin or somewhere else that they appreciate some art, but here, never."

Helmut didn't answer straight away; instead he simply started extracting money, paper money, from every pocket in his coat, jacket, shirt pockets and trousers, making a huge pile of cash in front of us.

"What's all this?" I asked, "Money you dumb ox, what do you think it is?" he answered, "I don't believe it" I said, and meant, "This is just our first day's profits, you'd better believe it."

Jessica ran her hands through the cash and was silent for a moment, then asked, "How much is it?" "A lot, you little mercenary woman." Helmut responded. He turned to me, "Now you must believe me, we've made it. You'll have more money in a month than most men earn in a whole year." I was spellbound, "this means that hundreds, maybe thousands of people will see my paintings."

Helmut leaned closer to me and put his arm protectively around my shoulder, "Thousands, maybe, one day, millions of people will see your paintings." I turned and kissed him on the mouth, he laughed and Jessica joined us in a group hug after throwing the money in the air.

Chapter Thirteen

Darmstadt
1935

It had been a long while since I faced my father across the living room of our family house. I had long avoided his disdain and constant, harping criticism. He sipped tea and barely controlled his anger under an icy veneer.

"I have heard what you and your friends are up to, and needless to say I don't like it one little bit. What's more I absolutely forbid you to continue. Do you understand me clearly, I will not allow it!" I waited a moment, not bothering to waste my breath in arguing a hopeless case. My father became even angrier at what he would consider my insolent silence. "Do you not realize the harm your shabby little business enterprise can do to my standing in the Party, it could ruin me, it could pull us all down like a pack of cards?"

"Why do you always ask me questions and then answer them yourself?" I replied, "Don't get clever with your father." He said more quietly, now he was trying to be more conciliatory, "Why are you always so argumentative, what's good for me is good for you also, why can't you understand that, do you want them to measure you and your mother racially, do you not understand what that could mean?"

"All I see are those bloody black uniforms and hate filled faces. What would be good for this family is if we were on the same side, the right side against those very people that you consider to be your friends." My father stood up and started to pace the room unable to suppress his fury over what he considered my stupidity. He leaned closer to me. "It has long been clear to me that you have too much of the Jew in you. You're the product of my biggest single mistake, you're mistake number two."

Now it was my turn to be infuriated, "Marrying my mother was the best thing you ever did, she's far too good for you." I stood and faced him; neither of backed away, how I wished I could smash my fist into his face. "I could divorce her just like that!" Bertie clicked his fingers, "What's stopping you?" I asked, he was suddenly not so sure of himself, "I don't know." He sat down again, as if the air had been let out of him.

"You still love my mother don't you, that's why. Perhaps you've still got a spark of humanity left in you." He raised his hand as if to strike me in the face but stopped his impulse. "Go on big man, or haven't you got the guts to hit the cripple?" My father subsided, moved back slightly and lowered his head. "You don't understand how it is, you simply don't understand."

"Oh I understand all too well, you make me sick, you've chosen the new religion rather than your family." Bertie looked momentarily disconcerted by this, but it was only a passing shadow in his eyes, nothing too definite, or obvious. "I still care for your mother, I like and respect her very much, but I'm just not in love with her any more. But none of us want to see her utterly defenseless." He almost made it sound plausible, but I was no longer an immature boy, I could see through him, and respond.

"You sound like some stupid child. This is your wife, the same woman you married, and she has been your wife for a quarter of a century. You can't explain this away with some wooly platitudes."

There was a moment of cold calculation between us, as the fury abated but the anger remained, my father continued, "Don't you understand, under the law, the consequences? If I divorce her because she's Jewish then you might be automatically disowned as a non-Aryan. That's the only thing that has held me back. Whatever our disagreements you are still my son, I still love you."

"Do what you want, and so will I!" I wasn't quite sure what I meant, but I wanted him to understand that there would be a reaction from me and he didn't have my blessing.

"Perhaps we could reach an accommodation, you quit your ridiculous business and I arrange a chance for your mother to get out. Otherwise I shall do my duty for the Party and the Fatherland."

"Do you know how ridiculous this whole conversation is, my business or my mother, while you weigh up a choice between your wife and the Fatherland. This is all some sick joke."

"Put it whichever way you like, but if it's a joke no one is laughing." He replied." I decided that I couldn't win this argument with my father, but I didn't want to lose it just yet either. "Would you give me some time to make the necessary arrangements, I couldn't do everything necessary immediately?" Father was clearly relieved, he even smiled and the tension in his shoulders relaxed, "I'm glad to see that you're finally seeing sense. Of course I'll give you some time, I'm a reasonable man, a pragmatist, is a week sufficient?"

"Ample." I replied, hoping he didn't notice the insincerity in my smile as he forced me into his wooden embrace to seal the deal.

It was at the end of that week that I was driven to the town's Gestapo headquarters by Helmut in his swanky new Mercedes. I looked at the tension in his face and looked at my own reflection in the car mirror, willing myself to appear calm. Nothing must reveal my inner thoughts. "Are you sure you can do this alone?" He asked me, breaking my focus. "This is between my father and me." He clapped me on the shoulder, "I shall wait for you." I nodded to him as one of the guards at the building who recognized me opened my door smartly and I jumped out.

Whatever I thought about these Nazi thugs you couldn't help be awed by the sheer sweeping swagger of their flags and bunting, their never mind the quality feel the size of our reach, the colors of our revolution, the cut of our uniforms, the symbolism of our new order. For their growing number of fanatics it was as if they were supporting the best-dressed football team in the world.

I marched in the imposing building past the billowing Nazi flags and armed sentries. Inside all was ordered, antiseptically clean and almost mechanistic; not a natural habitat for an artiste. I had my father's carefully written instructions to take me through the corridors, up the central sweeping stairs, down more, seemingly endless echoing corridors. I felt myself accelerate all the way until I reached an imposing set of wooden double doors, again guarded by two armed sentries, the one on the right recognized me, smiled and tapped quietly on the door. He opened it and I walked inside. There, in the large, room with its high ceiling I found Kurt, my father's young bespectacled aide and secretary, he looked up and pasted on his formal forced greeting, uncomfortable as ever in my presence. I never knew if his discomfort was due to my never discussed disability, or whether he was aware of my being only half Aryan, and the other, half, possibly the disabled half, being Jewish!

"Hello Arnulf, your father is expecting you, he said you should go straight into the office. What do you think of your father's new surroundings, we're moving up in the world, pretty impressive eh?" I mumbled something in response, knowing I shouldn't trust myself to talk to this little bastard whatever his origin or position. He knocked on my father's door and without waiting for a response opened it for me and stepped aside as I entered the inner sanctum. It was palatial, dark, with wood paneling on every wall. The only relief from the gloom of so much dark wood was the six floor to ceiling picture windows.

My father's desk is, as ever, fastidiously neat, he turned to his aide, "Kurt, why don't you take a coffee break, my son and I have some family matters to discuss." Kurt almost wagged his tail, "Of course Herr Hessel, straight away," he turned to me, "is there anything I can get you, a tea or coffee, perhaps a glass of water?" I declined and as he left the room he continued smiling, "It was a pleasure to meet you again Arnulf, I look forward to our getting to know one another." He nodded to the two of us and finally left the room. "What an ass!" I said to father, "He comes with the job," he agreed, "but yes, he is a bit pompous isn't he. Why don't we go and sit down more comfortably over by the windows." He directed us to two big armchairs next to the huge fireplace, which was dominated by a life size, stylized portrait of Adolf Hitler. He followed my eye line to the painting, "I've already told my colleagues you could paint a much more flattering but realistic painting of the Fuhrer that would more realistically capture his magnetism. You should consider that a priority."

He paced up and down opposite me, the fire crackling loudly in the background as I sat in my chair. "I like that you have come to visit me here, its important that a son sees where his father does his work. Well, what do you think, impressive isn't it?" He indicated the huge room, its drapes, its rugs, everything reflecting my father in all his Nazi glory. He had arrived, found his destiny and was immersed in its gory embrace. "Very impressive indeed." I agreed, thinking what was to be gained by further argument. I looked out of the window from my chair, which was overlooking the front of the building down to the ground far below, I looked back to my father when he continued to talk. "I presume as you're here that you've reached a decision for sure. I'm confident that it will be the right decision." He smiled expectantly.

"So do I father, I hope so to." "What's it to be then, I want to hear the words, there must be no misunderstanding between us, what is it to be, your card art business or your mother?"

I stood up to face him, "the answer is obvious, isn't it father?" My father smiled, "I'm so glad you've seen sense my son." I walked to the other side of the room, but still facing him from some distance. "Yes," I said, "How else could I decide when faced with the choice of my mother being divorced and thrown to the tender mercies of your Nazi party colleagues? How else could I possibly decide?"

My father looked out of the open window, unable to meet my stare he appeared to be studying the comings and goings in the town below, "You always personalize issues too much. You take after your mother like that. It's the emotional Jew in you. But National Socialism is not personal. It is a movement for the greater good of the country. The individual is simply less important than the group. You just have to look how things are already improving in Germany..."

He never even sensed me running towards him until it was too late for him to do anything about it. His reaction as he turned in my direction as I barreled into him was shock and a look of almost comical astonishment. That's why I laughed as he flew out of the window as if shot from the cannon, unable to resist my huge momentum. I watched him drop, almost as if it was in slow motion and then normal speed as he crashed into the cold unforgiving concrete far below. The fall was clearly fatal, I had murdered my father, and I felt relief.

I saw people move toward his still body and quickly moved back from the window. I heard myself pant, and didn't know why. I remembered our plan. I flicked off my right shoe with my left foot and pulled the handle to the door open with my stockinged foot. I sneaked a look and there was no one in this smaller office. I put my shoe back on and quickly left the room as fast as my feet would carry me.

Meanwhile Helmut ran over to Bertie's body, turned it onto its front and was seemingly seeking to revive it by the time the men and women from the building had encircled them. Kurt, who had been discreetly smoking a cigarette around the corner, and hearing the commotion, had run to see what was happening. Kurt he saw it was his boss and mentor who was the victim. "What happened?" Helmut turned to him, "He just jumped!" I had, by now, just managed to exit the building from the side entrance and joined the back of the crowd. "You're trying to revive a bloody corpse you fool, let him be." Kurt ordered Helmut, who seemingly distressed tenderly laid his own jacket under my father's shattered head. "Who are you exactly?" Kurt asked Helmut, "I am a long term friend of the Hessel family." The soldiers and Gestapo officers sought to restore order immediately, moving the crowd back from Bertie's body.

Helmut took this as his cue to return to his car and get in. He started the engine and gunned it into action. He was out of the square before he half turned to see me hidden between the front and back seats, and uncomfortable squeeze for someone so bulky as me. Everything had worked as planned, even to the extent that he had left the door of the car slightly open and the front seat pulled forward so that all I had to do was wedge myself in place. Everything had worked, and then the realization had dawned on me, I had just killed my own father. Whatever he was, whatever he planned, I had to live with this terrible fact, for the rest of my life I was to know I had killed a man, and that man was my own father. What kind of man did that make me?

I became aware that Helmut was talking to me, "Arnie are you all right?" All I could think of to say was, "Drive Hynie, just drive!" The car sped from the square, and we were both unaware that a particularly vigilant local police officer noted our haste and wrote the details of our car carefully into his notebook.

Later that night Helmut and I sat at the kitchen table drinking tea. There was a polite knock at our door and we both feared for the worst. Helmut went to the door and opened it. He returned to the kitchen before our new guest, and looked shocked, stunned even. The Rat, who had tortured us both, so recently, followed Helmut into the room. Ratwerller smiled as he looked from one of us to the other.

"Good evening gentlemen, you remember me don't you, Ratweller is the name. Our paths seem to cross so often perhaps I should move in here with the two of you, yes?" Helmut looked at him, the hate quite obvious, whilst I did my best to restrain my natural inclination, which was to spit in the bastard's face. "I remember you very well Herr Ratwerller," said Helmut. I fought to control my fear, hating myself for this weakness, but terrified of falling into this terrible man's control once again. Ratwerller pulled out a chair for himself and sat down. "I'm sure you won't mind my joining you like this but I have some very sad news..." He looked at us, particularly me, waiting for a give away reaction. I don't believe I gave anything away as the clock seemed to stop ticking, "What is it?" I asked.

He appeared not to notice my question, removing his hat and smoothing his jet black, greased hair. "I thought, you know, as we all know each other so well I should be the one to personally deliver this news." He was savoring the moment; the bastard was enjoying the irony of his delivering the news to me. "Is it something I should also know about?" asked Helmut. Herr Ratwerller smiled toward Helmut, "Oh yes, I think you should know all about it, what do you think Herr Hessel, do you agree with me?"

I feigned indifference, but don't think I pulled it off, this man Ratwerller made you react as if he was pulling your fingernails down a blackboard, he set my teeth on edge without effort. "I don't know what he's talking about Helmut, but no doubt Herr Ratwerller will tell us all about it in his own good time."

"Oh come on, play the game Arnie, you know I know and I know that you both know, it's a fun game, we can all play." He toyed with both of us, as dangerous as a viper. Both Helmut and I kept quiet and still, aware of the Gestapo goons stationed just outside the door waiting for the slightest excuse to cause us yet more pain. "You always enjoyed talking in riddles." I said to Ratwerller. "Go on." He said, "I do so enjoy to reminisce, remember, for example, the name you and your little friends used to call me at school?" I didn't answer, "You used to call me a rat, remember, you called me a rat. In fact so many people heard that name that in the end the new children in the school thought that my real name was rat!" he finished the sentence with crashing his fist down on the table. "I didn't think that was very funny, did you think it was funny, Helmut, or you Arnie?"

We both shook our heads; it wasn't worth picking a fight when you didn't have any weapons available. "This is a familiar situation for you isn't it Arnie..."

"What do you mean?" I asked as he stood up and walked around the room until he was standing behind me, I turned to face him, "I'm getting tired of your games Herr Ratwerller, so tell me this news or get out!"

Ratwerller smiled and stopped his pacing, "Games, words such as games, one realizes in my trade that the first casualty of the criminal fraternity is the sanctity of the German language. For example, murder suddenly becomes an accident or suicide."

Helmut looked at me to see how I might react but I wasn't stupid enough to give the game away at the first hint of trouble. Rat had seen the look and it was enough for his animal instincts to prompt one of his rictus smiles. "I think Arnie and I understand one another perfectly, don't we?"

I let the silence build for a moment, "I think we always did." I replied, "Arnie!" cautioned Helmut, "Perhaps you should wait for us in the other room Helmut." He looked between me and my old adversary, "Are you sure that's wise?" he asked, imploring me with every fiber of my being to back away from this confrontation. Rat turned to Helmut, "Be a good lad, and run along." Helmut reluctantly left the room to the protagonists,

"What do you want?" I asked him when the door had closed, "Who said I want anything, I could take anything I want anyhow."

It was my turn to smile, "If you didn't want something from me I would already be in your special little room being questioned with your special methods." He nodded his head, "that is, I admit, always fun, but I do require something from you in return for my co-operation."

"First," I said, "I want to know what you know, exactly." He sighed, as if the weight of the world was on his shoulders alone, "Too much as ever, I know enough to put two and two together, and in this Germany this is more than sufficient. Or to put it another way, possibly there are reasons I could make it all disappear as if in a puff of magical smoke. Wouldn't that be nice and you'd never need to know how."

"So its blackmail, name your price." I said, "Blackmail is such an emotive word, such unpleasant connotations, like patricide or murder, don't you think?" he replied, "What sort of pleasure does it give you Ratwerller, playing with people like this?"

"I just like precision in all things, speed without accuracy is useless, much better with complex issues such as these, to be clear as crystal." I looked into his ice blue eyes for some clue, but there was, as ever, nothing there to read, he gave none of the usual signals, he seemed devoid of any emotion. Not for the first time I wondered if he had ever felt anything other than hate. The tap in the old sink dripped as I waited for his next step, he noticed my glance at the sink and walked over to the faucet and turned the tap vigorously, the drip ceased. "What do you want?"

"I prefer a long term relationship." He responded, "and you know I am not a greedy man, for my protection, my mentoring, I want you to have every incentive to succeed."

"What does that mean, precisely?"

He paused thoughtfully, then smiled, "I truly believe in your talents, Arnie, you have a future in whatever society takes shape, selling those cards of yours, a wonderful business scheme, there's every likelihood of success, an outstanding return on your friend Helmut's investment. For my sponsorship I would be gratified to receive twenty five per cent of your gross return, without deductions of course."

I didn't need to think about it, I didn't want any kind of relationship with this man, "How about instead of that I give you one thousand English pounds, now, wherever you like?"

Ratwerller laughed as if I had said something very amusing, "No, that simply doesn't satisfy my long term plans. I want us to be partners."

I tried something else; "We've established you're a whore even more than you're a Nazi, so all we're really discussing is your price."

Ratwerller giggled in that high pitched whine of his, it was an almost obscene and unnerving sound, "You cannot upset me with such obviously contrived abuse, after all those are my techniques, you cannot have forgotten the lessons I gave to you so recently. No, above all I am a businessman with pragmatic objectives, more than anything I have to receive profit for the future to be rosy. I shall have a little document drawn up and you shall all sign it, and it will donate twenty five per cent of your entire income into a charitable trust in Switzerland. It is this or those big nasty chaps with their nasty ways will be driving you and your friends back to a very uncertain future. Which is it?"

"Five per cent." I answered, he smiled, "I'm not too unreasonable a man, but I am getting rather bored with this, I shall be reasonable and I am prepared to reduce it to twenty per cent, but that's it, I will also have your books checked every week."

"Fifteen." I tried, he cleared his throat as if to call out to the guards outside, "All right, twenty it is, but I don't want us to have any contact."

The Rat stood before me and bowed incongruously, his smile a token of his happy agreement, "Fair enough, we have an arrangement, now, details, bloody details, do you wish to inform your fair mother of your father's tragic accident or would you prefer me to fulfill this function?"

I tried to keep my voice from shaking, I wanted him to understand that I was no pushover, "I shall do what I have to do, I always have, and I always shall."

Ratwerller walked toward the door where he paused and turned, "Why do I always get the impression that every one of our conversations ends with one of us always threatening the other. If you had the use of your arms you might be a formidable foe, but as things stand; well, I shall never turn my back like your daddy that would be a big error when standing next to an open window. Anyway, I look forward to a long and mutually rewarding relationship, goodbye."

After he left Helmut returned. I told him about our new partner, and, as ever, he shrugged and was supportive, the whole world was still his plaything and I wished I shared his optimism.

He drove me to my family home and offered me his support, but I told him I would prefer to handle this alone. I found mother alone in the garden, allowing the last rays of the day's sunlight to warm her. She looked very much as she had always looked, her age betrayed by some grey in her hair, and the slightly still way she carried herself so erect. It must have been a trick of the light, but just for a moment, before she heard my approach, she looked so young and carefree in that wonderful garden, like the young woman she had been. My approach to her momentarily blocked the sun from her, and she felt the shadow and turned. She smiled that wonderful smile of hers in greeting, and then there was concern.

"Arnie, how lovely to see you, I wasn't expecting you, its such an honor for you to call these days. Come inside and I can make you a little something to eat." Then she noticed my grim expression, "What is it, you're not in trouble again are you; something is wrong tell me."

I wasn't used to bringing such news and didn't know what to do except for what I had seen in films or read in books, "Come inside mother, you had better sit down." She allowed herself to be ushered toward the house but before she got there she stopped and turned to face me again, "It's your father isn't it, he's dead!" she said this with unintentional loudness, startling herself and me in equal measure. I wish, oh how I wish I could have reached out to enfold her in my arms at that moment, she simply slumped to the floor, as if all the air had suddenly been sucked from her body. "He's dead, he's dead, tell me he's dead!"

I nodded my head, but I was unable to hold my mother's disbelieving stare, I looked away, "He fell out of his office window." She laughed at this news, "He fell out of the window, don't be so ridiculous, he was careful in everything he did, such men don't fall out of windows, he is not a clown making a pratfall, he is not some Charlie Chaplin, such men as your father do not fall from windows!" she was shouting now, she stood up and looked directly into my face, "You're saying that he fell out of a window, he just fell from a window, this simply isn't possible for him, he was not the type to fall from a window. This is ridiculous, he is the most careful man in the world." She stopped talking and sensing something in my manner, she held my face between her hands, intensely staring into my eyes, seeking the truth, "You know something more Arnie, I can always tell when you're holding something back, tell me what you know, you always do in the end, tell me what it is, you'll feel better for sharing."

"What does it matter, he's gone, at last he's gone. Now we still have each other, and we can get on with our lives, isn't that better?"

"But he was my husband, I must mourn for my husband. You don't simply close of a bit of yourself like you would turn off a light. I need to know what you're hiding from me." She let my face go, and we stood facing each other as she again stood. "Nothing mother. Honestly, nothing at all. I just can't forget how wicked he was to you recently and to me for so many years. I could never forgive and forget, even if you could."

Her voice tore into me, "Whatever he did, however he behaved, he was my husband and your father, and we are a family and in our own ways we all loved each other once, and you will respect his memory, for me, even if for no other reason, and I don't care even if you have to put on an act you shall, do you understand me?"

The next thing I remember about that time was our standing inside the cemetery. Six uniformed officers of the Gestapo transported my father's remains, housed in an ornate, heavy casket draped in a Nazi flag to his grave. There was a large crowd, perhaps four or five hundred, peppered by local dignitaries attending the burial service. I wondered if they were there to make sure he was dead, or whether any of them cared anything for him. I hope he would rot in hell.

Ratwerller was in attendance, he always had enjoyed a funeral, and so was Helmut, to lend me moral support. My mother stood proud and erect, refusing to show her emotions, as father would have required of her. The clergyman read the service as the coffin was lowered into the waiting earth. I looked from the coffin to my mother and Ratwerller leaned near to me as I did so. "I can help get the Jewess out of Germany, for the right price." I tried to ignore him, but his proximity made that impossible, "That Jewess is my mother, and now is not the right time, this is her husband's funeral. Don't you ever let your greed rest?"

He shook his head, "Don't your people say business is business. We all have to look to the future and there is no future for Jews in this country, no future at all. Anyway Arnie, aren't you being a touch sanctimonious about all this given the circumstances. Wasn't it you, the loving son, who put your dear daddy in the ground. We're both whores and murderers, so name the deal. She'll be safer, and I shall be richer. What's wrong with you Arnie, not catching a conscience at this late stage? I do hope it's not contagious!"

I looked at mother as she looked at the coffin's final descent and the first shovels full of earth were emptied onto it and I knew what I had to do.

Chapter Fourteen

The Wolf's Lair - Berchtesgarten, Germany
Summer 1939

The large airy room overlooked a breathtaking panorama of snow-capped mountains. There were about twenty guests standing in the room, chatting convivially, if somewhat stiff and formal. Among the group were Germany's new order, the elite of the party and the state. I was standing next to an attractive blond woman, her name was Eva.

"Have you been here before Eva?" I asked, she nodded, sipped from her drink and replied, "Oh yes Herr Hessel, many times, but I have never seen you before. Of course like everyone else in Germany I have heard of you, seen your cards and of course purchased many. They're charming and you must be very rich!" She giggled again, and held her hand in front of her mouth as if horrified by her words, but I decided to humour the obvious gold digger, after all she was very attractive, I bowed to her. "Thank you kind lady, let us say I have enough money that I no longer need to count it any more." She giggled again, "Perhaps I could help?" she asked. "This is my first time here," I said, "And perhaps my last, so tell me, what happens next, more drinks then we say our goodbyes without ever meeting the Fuhrer?"

She stopped playing the coquette at this moment and leant closer to me, then whispered, "You are about to find out." I turned to follow her look as Adolf Hitler entered the room. He was smaller than I had imagined, and quite thin. His silly moustache and strange hair seemed right on his head. He was dressed in typical German country gentleman's clothes. Smiling broadly and holding the hands of two very pretty little blond girls he walked through the throng who greeted him like a god. "Come along my girls, it is a nice party and you can play anywhere and with anyone, just keep back from the edge. Hello everybody, lovely day, yes?"

We all chorused back greetings to him. Almost everyone present shouts "Heil Hitler" and raises their arms in salute, everyone but me. I had the excuse that I couldn't do so, but I was secretly glad at that moment, because I would hate to salute Hitler. He had been properly briefed and realized that the only person not making the standard salutation must be me and he walked directly to me. I bowed so that he should know I wasn't being offensive. "Hessel, we like your work." He said by way of greeting, "Thank you sir," was the only thing I could think of.

"You are an example others must follow. Made a success of yourself despite a disability. To be admired. We will put you to good use for your country." I swallowed nervously as he stood looking up into my eyes, "thank you my Fuhrer." He smiled, and his smile was very winning, for a moment I found myself forgetting all the horrors, the stories, the rumors and just saw a kindly man, "You mustn't be worried. Germany would never persecute workers, only shirkers parasites and this will do with the utmost vigor and severity. Your working with us will finally put pay to the false propaganda that we deal unfairly with the handicapped and mentally deficient. If we did that I would have to eliminate half of my entire general staff and almost every one of my ministers!"

He laughed at his own joke and I had little alternative but to join in, as did others, who hadn't even heard the joke, but were too nervous not to. "We shall speak later, in private. We have great plans for you, historic plans. After dinner then."

He patted me on the shoulder and turned away, leaving me alone with Eva who was clearly captivated, "You certainly made a good impression with the Fuhrer." I smiled at her, "You think so?" She snuggled up to me suggestively, "Is it true that one God takes away one sense he compensates with the other senses even more?" she asked, "We could find out later, together in my room." I suggested, "Later it is." She agreed.

Dinner was agreeable if overlong and too formal for my taste. I noticed that Hitler ate hardly anything but nibbled and sipped as if he was to be sociable. I wasn't near enough to hear his discussion with the obese man to his left, but time passed quite swiftly. After we were finished I was ushered into Hitler's private quarters and sat opposite him in his study. The fat man who was next to him at dinner was taking the leader's blood pressure as we talked. "I should introduce you to my physician, his name is Doctor Theodor Morell," the corpulent man barely looked in my direction as he ministered to Hitler. "He keeps me in tip top condition. Mind you if he didn't then he would probably get a permanent ailment himself, like dead ha ha?"

Morell barely raised a smile; he had heard the joke before. The thing I noticed about the doctor was that he was always sweating, and he stunk like a pig, his personal hygiene was lamentable.

Hitler and I sat in two winged armchairs facing one another; a fierce blaze flamed in the elegant open hearth. I had declined the offer of an after dinner brandy, and so had the Fuhrer. Morell whispered something in Hitler's ear, "You don't mind if the doctor here gives me my little herbal injection do you, it makes me feel very excellent, not squeamish are you?"

I didn't get the chance to respond as the doctor gave Hitler the hypodermic. "Have you calculated the reason why I can trust you and the doctor here totally, one hundred per cent?" I was too nervous to respond as the doctor mutely stared at me, his injection kit packed away, "Because you're my nearly Jews." Both the doctor and I froze, we knew that Germany's leader had total control of our destiny in his hands, but all he did was laugh, "Not to worry, we're not monsters, the half of you both that looks after my needs is more important to the Fatherland than the Jew half. You'll be perfectly all right as long as you keep me happy, understood?" I just nodded as the doctor, who was wearing full uniform clicked his heels, "Good night my Fuhrer."

Hitler waved his doctor away and turned his full attention back to me.

"You know a major war is inevitable I imagine?" He asked, "Yes sir."

"Good, we will win of course. It is our country's destiny to control Europe, possibly more. Mussolini and the Emperor of Japan will join us in common cause, but it is Germany who will truly lead. Of course I have tried to avoid this war, you do realize this yes?" I nodded my head, "Yes sir, everyone in Germany knows that for a fact."

Hitler nodded his head, "That drunkard, that buffoon Churchill, he has stirred up the old bulldog, but it has been asleep for so long it has forgotten how to bark let alone be the lion it once was. Even that vacillating fool of a Prime Minister." now his face contorted into a very fair impression of the British Prime Minister, Neville Chamberlain is being forced, against his best judgment, to resist the tide of history. It's a pity you know, we could work with the English. They're basically German you know, what a combination we could have made, but they have become weak just as we regained our pride and our strength, and the weak must always be swept aside." Even though I disagreed with everything the man said I could understand his almost hypnotic hold on the people of my country. He was so compelling, so certain, saying the words we all craved to hear. But I knew that I could never let my guard down for an instant in his presence, it could be fatal, so I asked, "How could I help, in my humble way my Fuhrer?"

He smiled again, and it was as if the sun had broken through the clouds of war stirring all around us, ""You will record our victories on your canvases for the nation. Your work will immortalize our conquests. You will be my personal war artiste; I have personally selected you for this heroic task. You shall be answerable to me alone. You will be free to go wherever your work takes you, with total license to see anything go anywhere at any time. And if you should die in the cause of our beloved Fatherland I give you my pledge of a state funeral. How does that sound?"

The man was offering me a state funeral if everything went wrong, how could I possibly refuse? I feigned delight, but this was liberally mixed with genuine astonishment, "This is an incredible honor sir, I am certain I am not worthy of such a thing, my father would have been so proud."

He shook his head, "No false modesty young man, I shall be the judge of who is worthy. I hear your late father was a good Party man, it's a pity he wasn't here to share your glory. Of course I shall want to see everything you do, naturally you will leave your partners to run your business, no room or time for commerce when we're making history eh. This work will require your total dedication. We would give you the rank of Colonel in the army for this service, and of course, all the benefits. Do you find this agreeable?"

I recognized this request to be an order in all but name, "Naturally, it will be an honor, when could I begin this task?" He clapped me on the back, "We can begin in one week; and when we, the German people put down our weapons you can lower your weapon, your paint brush."

He stood and so did I, and I clicked my heels like a good soldier in salute before I left the room. I don't even remember if I took advantage of Eva's kind offer. The next few days passed by in a blur of activity. I had a great deal to arrange. Firstly I had to make my business arrangements. My main office was in Berlin and Helmut was shocked when I told him the news. "And you agreed to paint pictures for the swine?" he asked, "don't you see the opportunities this gives us Hynie? Besides which what choice did I have with our esteemed leader you either do what he says or you are broken, you still have to learn to bend with the wind. Under that business suit you're still the proud Junker." He laughed at my jibe, as ever Helmut was at ease with the truth. "How will I run the business without you Arnie?"

It didn't take me a second to know the answer, "Like always, profitably, anyway, perhaps the Fuhrer will be wrong and we won't actually go to war after all." Helmut shook his head, "No, he's right about that, there will be war, but who knows how big and with whom and exactly when, once you open Pandora's box anything can happen."

"Do you think we'll win?" I asked, "It depends on who is we doesn't it, do you mean Germany?" he answered with his own question, "No, in this instance any country who is against Germany, how could we side with these Nazi monsters?" Helmut stood as he heard me rant, he was clearly disturbed by these thoughts, "You know what I think of these Nazis and their jumped up leader, but I am a German to the core of my being. If asked I would still fight for my country."

We looked at each other, I was astonished and angered by Helmut's statement, "Are you mad? These thugs stand for everything that we are against. How could you even think of fighting for them under any circumstances when the patriotic thing to do is to fight against them?" Helmut was now becoming as angry as me, he stood at the head of our boardroom table and thumped his fist down on its mahogany surface, "Right or wrong this is my country!"

I looked at him, and wished I didn't feel it necessary to respond, but I had to, our friendship might depend on it, "So suddenly it is not my country? And in this new country no one is allowed to disagree or question?" Helmut hesitated as he heard the quiet seriousness of my tone, "We are not discussing semantics at college any more, and this is talking treason!"

"It seems to me that it is your Nazi friends who do that with every new amoral act." Helmut tried to placate me in response, "Perhaps we should simply agree to disagree. Whatever it is you plan to do, just keep it to yourself. We will always be friends, won't we?" he asked, and at that moment I knew we could not be but I would try once more to make him understand.

"You've been my arms Hynie for such a long time, let me be your heart." He smiled but I could see that such an emotional plea was not getting through to him, his reply was simple, "Perhaps the time has come for one of us to use his brain old friend." At that moment, with nothing resolved between us the telephone intercom interrupted, "There is a telephone call for you mister Hessel" came the voice of my secretary, "Who is it?" I asked impatiently, "I've told you a million times not to put anyone through when we're in conference." She paused, but then nervously continued, "I don't know who it is, but he said it was urgent, he told me to tell you precisely these words, that he represented the football team management, and that when I told you this you would let me put him through." I knew what is was about instantly, "Put him through." I ordered, "Herr Hessel?" the man's voice asked, "Yes," I said, "this is Arnie Hessel, to who am I speaking?"

"Never mind my name, there is a football match this Saturday at three o'clock, can you attend?" Helmut looked very suspicious, "Yes," I said, "Saturday at three, usual pitch?" The man said yes, and the connection was cut.

"You're playing a very dangerous game Arnie." Said Helmut, "You know I always enjoyed my football."

At the appointed time I was outside the university lecture hall trying my best to blend into my surroundings. The lecturer stayed at the podium after he had finished. He was middle aged, unconventionally dressed but an otherwise unremarkable looking man. I entered the hall when I thought everyone had left. "Good afternoon Professor." He smiled, and beckoned me closer, "Ah my prize student, do I find you well, I understand congratulations are in order, is it all confirmed?" Now it was my turn to smile, "How many no armed Jewish artists have been enlisted to be Hitler's war artist do you know?"

"You are honored, Hitler's personal war artiste, an honor indeed," he said before continuing, "It could not be more perfect, you will be of extreme use to the movement." I couldn't resist a question, "Where exactly do I fit into the movement?" He paused and regarded me seriously, as if I was some obtuse academic question, he shrugged, "Naturally I would like to respond directly to that question, but these are strange times, strange times indeed, in these peculiar circumstances I am none too sure where I fit let alone you, I only know the person who recruited me and you, because I recruited you, and that's it. We have security questions that transcend any of our personal issues, you understand?" It was my turn to shrug my shoulders, "I worry that we might be used to little or no effect, I want to be useful."

The Professor lit his pipe and fussed for a moment with it, and then took a long satisfying pull on it, expelling a puff of aromatic smoke that smelt rich and middle aged, "I came to my conclusions through my belief in Christ. You came to the same conclusions through your Socialist conviction. All I know for certain that I feel a sight better doing something to combat this evil rather than doing nothing. We might still smell that Nazi shit, but we are two Germans among many other like minded Germans proving by our actions that we won't swallow that shit!"

We both laughed quietly, and then I asked, "What are my orders?" as I did so a young woman entered the hall, she clattered over in high heels. I had a chance to look her over as she walked across the room. Early twenties, she was now voluptuous, wearing a tight black skirt and a figure-hugging sweater. Her long blond hair, framed her oval shaped face with her large widely spaced spice blue eyes. The first thing I remember noticing were her cherry red lips smiling as the Professor introduced us as she approached, "I think you will remember your friend Arnie?"

"Marlene!" I said, totally surprised by this turn of events, "Hasn't it been a long time Arnie?" she said and came over to hug me to her, I inhaled her wonderful smell, and enjoyed the moment. I turned to the Professor, "the Movement is playing cupid now?" he shook his head and smiled kindly, "It's not quite like it seems Arnie, you should learn not to jump to conclusions, I'll leave you two to make up for some lost time, I'm not authorized to hear the details of your brief, all that remains is for me to wish you both good luck."

With that he left, Marlene and I sat facing each other. "What's this all about, and how did the Professor know we'd been friends?" Marlene was as playful as ever, and now, as if no time had passed she teased me with that wonderful smile and her natural flirting totally captured me in an instant, "Lovers you mean, you do remember don't you?" "What, you told perfect strangers our most intimate secrets?" I teased, "No," she said, "but you were always so old fashioned. We were lovers and it was never such a secret."

"Why have they brought you in on this?" She smiled again, very much in command of the situation. "You always were such an inquisitive boy, and that's why I told the Professor to recruit you." She let that rest with me for a moment, "So you're the Professor's boss?" She touched my cheek with her hand, remembering some intimacy; "something like that, more like a chief guide than a boss, but yes, the instructions you've been acting on have originated with me."

"Why did you expose yourself to me now, isn't that breaking security, in the cell system we're never supposed to know more than one person up and one down so that if we're caught we can't give any more names and the chain has time to disperse."

"Yes, but I was always prone to exposing myself to you, remember?" she couldn't help but tease me, "We had the need to change the rules for this situation. You will need an assistant for such an important client, and that is going to be me. I qualify for several reasons, we have a long history together, since we were children, and that can be checked from Darmstadt, where everyone knew we were an item. I went on an art appreciation course; remember, at the university, that was my first degree. It's perfect."

"Yes, and perhaps we can make love at all of the Fuhrer's best battlefields." She didn't smile at this weak little joke, "Don't you get it, and this is the most wonderful opportunity for the Movement to create a structure together with all of our friends in the military."

"Of course," I said, "but can't we have a bit of fun on the side. This is all going to take a very long time, and everything sounds so worthy and meaningful and serious, can't we have some fun meanwhile, you and me, like old times?" She looked at me as if I was a naughty and petulant child, and perhaps I fitted that description, all I knew was that I wanted her as much as ever as soon as I saw her again. Now that she had added power and authority to her undoubted sexual attractiveness made her almost irresistible to me. I wanted to tell her about how I had missed her but it was all coming out of my mouth as if I was an uncouth idiot.

"Why do you always bring the focus of every situation to you Arnie, you always did that, and it's very tiresome, there are more important things in this world than you." I was chastised but not defeated, "That's not what you once said to me, you said you would love me forever, after university we were going to get back together, forever. You went away and you never came back." She looked at me for a long moment and then smoothed my hair back from my brow, "You always did have lovely hair, so thick and strong;" she took her hand away and broke the spell, "this is childish, love has nothing to do with now, understand?" she paused for me to respond, but I remained silent, "This is just too dangerous for love, I don't mind going to bed with you occasionally, we both have needs, but just as friends. We don't have time to play. Can you keep your mind on our mission, the Movement needs us to do this."

There was no sense in my begging for more, she had her mind made up, and Marlene was the most determined woman I knew except for one other, "I have to get my mother out of Germany, can you help me do this?" she looked at me with increasing skepticism, "Is that your condition for your continued co-operation?" I was angered by her manner, "You know me better than that, but it is a condition for my mother to go on living. Or is the Movement so important that details like my mother don't matter?"

As ever Marlene had the capacity to throw me off balance, "Professional curiosity, is it true that you killed your father?" I wasn't sure it was wise to reply, but did so anyway, "No, he killed himself, I just helped him out of the window. What about my mother?" Marlene looked me directly in the eye and paused just for a moment, "Of course the Movement will help their own, there was never a question that we wouldn't, whatever you do. By the way, there's another detail for our cover story. "

"What is it?" I asked, and for the last time that day she shook me rigid, "We have to get married."

It seemed like only a few minutes after this that Helmut was plonking a top hat on my head. I recall standing in front of a full-length mirror in my family home in Darmstadt. I thought we both looked very silly in our morning suits but the consensus between the great powers, mother and Marlene, was that this was as much a necessity as the white dress my bride was to wear, the flowers and all the other paraphernalia attendant at any "decent" wedding.

Helmut looked at me in the mirror's reflection, "It's not too late to back out old friend." He said, his tone only half joking, "I don't want to back out you fool." I replied with almost undue haste. "Keep your top hat old fellow, it was awfully sudden you have to admit. If she's in trouble I know a nice old fellow in Frankfurt could make it all go away, you know, sort her out, and he's a fine medic, no trouble, just a little money and the problem is gone."

I acted outraged, "She is not in any trouble, but you will be if you don't go downstairs right now." "Fair enough old chap, keep that ridiculous hat on." We grinned at each other, realizing quite how silly we both looked.

Down in the garden there was a crowd of our relatives and friends assembled in the grounds, which mother had organized into a magical al fresco-wedding arena. Mother looked particularly radiant and happy as she stood chatting to the parents of Marlene. I spotted several men in dress uniform amongst our guests. The preacher looked pointedly at his watch as I hurried to my position next to Helmut down the red carpet. As I approached several of the young men I had gone to the academy with shouted out ribald comments to me, which I did my best to ignore. Just before I got to my position Ratwerller stepped out in front of me. He clapped me on the shoulder, and quietly, so no one else could hear, leaned towards me and spoke, "I always seem to want what you've got." I couldn't walk past him without causing a fuss in public, and I didn't want that on such a day, so instead I stood facing him, with a stupid smile fixed on my face, "What do you mean?" "One day I would like to have your bride, but I can wait." He smiled and stepped aside and I decided to ignore him. As Ratwerller moved to resume his seat Helmut surreptitiously stuck out a large foot and sent the Gestapo man sprawling helplessly onto the floor in front of the entire assembly, many of who laughed at his undignified sprawl.

Ratwerller was clearly furious as he meticulously began to brush and smooth his uniform down as he struggled to his feet. Before he could vent his anger the small group of musicians struck up the wedding march and all eyes turned down the aisle where Marlene appeared. She was a vision.

I vividly remember thinking that she was more angel than woman at that moment, the wedding guests spontaneously sighed and murmured their approval. She had seen Ratwerller on the floor but not the cause, she moved to help him regain his footing. He smiled at her, "Are you all right Herr Ratwerller?" she asked, he was clearly delighted by this turn of events, "Just a clumsy trip, I'm fine, but thank you for asking, but might I be the first to kiss the bride?" before she could respond he firmly kissed Marlene on the mouth for a little longer than he should, or she should have allowed, had she not been taken by surprise. Marlene pulled away from Rat and turned to face me, her face flushed and angry, but I smiled to reassure her as if it didn't matter, but when she drew up next to me I whispered, "What did you let that creep kiss you like that for?" She looked at me as if I were stupid and her smile concealed the strength and emotion of her next words, "I do what I have to for what I believe in, that's more important, after all I'm marrying you aren't I."

The preacher coughed to get our attention and we dutifully both turned our smiling faces toward him. The marriage ceremony then continued in time honored German tradition. We accepted his blessing and Helmut, as the best man placed the rings on our fingers after we exchanged our vows.

Thus we were married, to all appearances as a happy couple full of all the normal joys of newlyweds. We kissed deeply, still in full lust with one another. My mother was the first to congratulate us, "Marlene, my daughter, now you promise to always look after my boy, yes?" Marlene hugged my mother, "Of course I promise mother-in-law" "No," my mother said, "It's mother or Bertha now." "I shall call you mother number two!" My mother leaned very close to my new bride's ear and whispered so only the two of them knew what was being said, "I know about the so called arrangement, but I also know the truth. You really love my boy don't you?"

Marlene whispered to mother whilst looking at me, "Of course I love him, I always have. But how else could I capture him other than to make it impossible for him to refuse my proposal?"

Both the women laughed conspiratorially and hugged one another. Helmut clapped his hands for attention, and when everyone had fallen silent, "Ladies and gentlemen, it falls to me as the best man, in every respect, to propose the toast to my very good friend Arnie Hessel, who you see before you looking as good as he's ever likely to look and the astonishingly beautiful and wonderful Marlene, how did he ever get so fortunate. He did nothing to earn such luck. Seriously they are such a fine couple, and Arnie is an example to us all. I can today announce wonderful news, that Arnie Hessel has been selected personally by the Fuhrer himself, Adolf Hitler, from amongst all the artistes in the Fatherland, including poor unfortunates like myself, to be the country's official artiste and to record the historic times we are about to pass through!"

The crowd turned and applauded me wildly, and despite myself I found their cheering wonderfully exciting. Helmut continued, "Marlene is better known to some of you than she is to me, those of you from this town have watched her flower into a symbol of perfect Germanic womanhood. From my all too brief friendship with her I have learned that she is indeed a woman worthy of Arnie. United they represent all that is good and decent in the Fatherland." the guests applauded enthusiastically, "therefore, without further ado, the toast is Arlene and Marlene, Mr. and Mrs. Hessel!"

People in the crowd called out, "Speech Arnie, speech!" and I, shy as ever, stepped forward, "Thank you Hynie, for those few kind words, and the rest of them, that were not true at all. As far as the wonderful words are concerned I have been telling Helmut for years how terrific I am, and it is very rewarding that he finally recognizes this." The crowd laughed, and I continued, "Ladies and gentlemen, relatives and friends, thank you so much for coming, thank you for your wonderful gifts. Now it only remains for me to ask." but before I could finish Ratwerller rushed up to me and spoke urgently into my ear. I must have paled as Marlene asked me if I was ill. I hushed her and stilled the chatter of our guests, "Ladies and gentlemen, I have an important announcement," the guests fell silent, "It has just been announced from Berlin that Britain has declared war on the Fatherland. We are at war, long live Germany!"

Marlene stepped forward so that she was by my side and led the singing of the national anthem. As everyone joined the rousing chorus we all heard the sounds of the air raid sirens.

Chapter Fifteen

Warsaw, Poland
October 1939

Marlene and I walked down the long series of stone steps leading from the imposing structure that housed the Polish State Art Museum. Now huge swastika flags fluttered proudly from the recently conquered city buildings, including this historic structure, evidence of the country's crushing and rapid defeat.

"I can't believe this is all happening so fast. How could the Soviet Union make a treaty to carve up Poland? What did the Polish people do to deserve this fate?" Marlene looked around the handsome city, "they existed between two hungry, greedy giants, that's what they did wrong. Is the meeting set with Hecht?" "Yes," I replied, "but our friend the General doesn't sound too sure anymore. How do we know we can trust him?"

She nodded, "It works both ways I suppose."

That night, it was with a great sense of unease that Marlene, now dressed as my chauffeur was later driving the staff car with which I had been supplied by the local German army people. We pulled up outside a large darkened building that had, until recently been a hotel, but now all the signs were out. There were no guests that night. A tall army officer, in greatcoat opens the back door of the car as we stopped outside the main entrance. "Herr Hessel?" he asked, "Yes." "The General sends his compliments. He has asked me to apologize, but he is confident you will understand. He has a staff meeting and will not be able to attend this evening. However he did ask me to deputize for him, and to buy you a meal."

I looked from the officer to Marlene and she almost imperceptibly shook her head. "No that will not be necessary, but please thank the General for his kind offer. Did he say anything about any future arrangements?" I asked, "Not to me sir, I'm sorry, is there anything else I can do, a message perhaps?" I smiled, but told him, "Yes, please tell him we will always remember him." The officer was clearly not thrilled to be the bearer of such a menial message, but promised me he would pass it to his commander. "I shall pass that message to him sir, have a good stay in Warsaw." He stepped away from our car, "Let's go," said Marlene quietly, "the smell of cowardice sickens me." She drove the car away from the curb, "But that was stupid, do you think you will scare a general with veiled threats from a disabled artiste? We need friends not more enemies you fool. "

"Don't call me a fool, it might have been a foolish thing to say, but I'm no fool." She raced the car through the half empty streets. "I'm not a bloody machine, I have feelings. The man should realize that one day, when this is all over, everyone will have to account for his actions."

She nodded her head, and I saw her eyes assessing me in her driving mirror, "And that makes you the judge and jury? Don't forget who is the boss between you and me and remember, you obey my orders!"

"Yes sir!" I said, she didn't smile, "Perhaps he felt he was under suspicion for some reason, you mustn't jump to conclusions in this game, learn some patience." I was fed up with the way she was always seemingly lecturing me, "That's rubbish and you and I both know it, he got nervous and he didn't want to risk his fat ass. I got it, you're in charge, what now?"

As we turned the corner to drive towards the hotel Polski in which we had been billeted we came to a juddering halt as we taken a wrong turn and nearly collided with a floodlit security barrier manned by some Waffen SS guards. The first of the men had one hand on his machine gun and waved us down with the other. Beyond him we could see hundreds of bedraggled men building a large brick wall blocking the main street. "Papers, let me see your papers!" he demanded, and Marlene showed the guard both sets of our documents. His hard features softened when he saw my Colonel's rank and Marlene's pretty face. He saluted us. "Sorry about this, but you'll have to turn around and go via Adolf Hitler Strasse, used to be called Avenue Leopolski or some such Polish name. Just about a half kilometer further up on your left, and it'll take you all round this rabble."

"Who are these people?" I asked him looking towards the men building the huge wall. "Jewish labor battalions, being put to good use for a change, are building a wall for their ghetto. All the vermin of Warsaw will be living behind these walls. Keep the rest of the place free from their Jewish stink which can't be a bad thing eh?"

Marlene was watching me closely, I could feel her intense stare and knew she was silently instructing me to keep silent. "Thank you for the directions." She said to the guard as she turned the car away from the construction. He waved us cheerily as I saw endless truckloads of Jewish people being driven into the ghetto past us in the other direction. They looked dazed and confused, and of every age and type imaginable. Old men and women, boys and girls, men and women, rich, poor, the Nazis made no distinction, all Jews were being rounded up and forced into the ghetto. The trucks were off loaded and their pathetic passengers were unceremoniously dumped to walk through the gate one at a time, with their one bag each. The names of the new ghetto dwellers were checked off on a list. I wanted to stay and see what would happen to them but Marlene rushed to drive us away.

As my head was turned watching the slave workers laboring with their bricks and mortar one of them, a younger man who had been carrying something on his broad back was casually struck by a guard with the butt of his rifle, instinctively the laborer turned and swung his fist into the guards face, knocking him to the floor, the Jewish man realizing what he had done shouted something but it was lost in the sounds of gunfire as several of the guards shot him, riddling his body with bullets. As we pulled out of sight the last thing I saw of him was the growing pool of his blood forming around his head as the guards circled his body.

"Shouldn't we do something about that?" I shouted at her. "What do you suggest?" she asked by way of reply.

Later she held me as I shivered in her warm embrace in our bed. For once I had Marlene naked with me and I didn't want anything more than to take comfort from her. "Tell me you love me." I said, "Never," she responded, "Why not?" She kissed me on my neck, which she knew I couldn't resist, "This is pure animal lust." she licked the end of my ear, I shivered with pleasure. "You disgust me, you lecherous beast, go on admit it, you love me desperately. I know you do, just admit it." We became a bit more passionate, I couldn't help it, our legs were entangled and I loved the feel of her wrapped around me, I was becoming harder and we both kissed with more urgency. Now we were both becoming aroused, "You say it you bastard." She insisted, "Easy," I said, kissing that spot between her ample breasts, such a sweet lovely valley, now becoming hot, "I. love. You." I said, between each kiss of her cherry red nipples, left and right, now prominent and aching to be touched. With my knee I moved her so that we were sideways on to each other, me slightly behind her, her lovely posterior half perched on one of my legs, this left a very attractive opening which I thrust myself into. She smiled as we coupled languidly, slowly, we made a rhythmic loving dance of growing passion, she held her own breasts and touched her own nipples for the pleasure of us both was increasing, "Where did you learn to make love like this?" she asked, "It was very hard for me." I joked as I momentarily paused, "Don't stop now!" she insisted, slamming hard back onto me, "why won't you say you love me?" I whispered to her, with each word she moved her hips until our breath was becoming hurried and united, "Because you are big headed enough already, now shut up and make love to me!"

We were even more passionate that night than ever before. I don't know what it was, perhaps what we'd seen, or the danger we were in, or maybe we were just falling ever deeper in love with one another. Later I sat up in the four-poster bed with its red canopy and looked down at my beautiful sexy wife who was still sleeping prettily with her arms and hair framing her perfect face. "I know you really love me," I whispered as she lay there, still asleep and the phone rang, breaking the spell. Marlene opened her eyes but closed it as soon as she caught sight of the bright sunlight streaming in through the half closed drapes. "Go away world." She sighed, but the phone continued its insistent ringing, not to be ignored. "Come on," I insisted, "You can hold it for me." I told her, she came awake with that minx like smile playing on her full lips, as she reached across my body for the phone she said, "that's what you said last night." We both laughed as she picked up the receiver from the night table and held it to my ear.

"Yes, this is Colonel Hessel, yes, I will accept the charges." I heard the operator attempting to put the long distance call through, "It must be mother, who else even knows where I am and cannot tolerate long distance telephone charges." Suddenly the whistling and crackling stopped and the operator spoke again, "Putting you through sir." And then the line was clear, and it was mother. She was very animated and at first I couldn't understand what she was trying to tell me. "Mother, yes I am fine and so is Marlene, but what is it you're saying?"

Her voice paused, then realizing that her call to me might be overheard by a nosy operator or others she resumed; "I need to receive a call from our friends, about a football match, I believe I have to be invited if I wanted to go see a match, you understand, and I don't want to miss the entire season, and I will if I wait for an invitation, its getting close and then there'll be no games left for me to see."

It was my turn to pause and gather my thoughts, Marlene, who was also listening as she held the phone to my ear smiled eagerly and nodded her head, excited for my mother and me. "If my friends can arrange a ticket for you it would be essential for you to go. Let them make the arrangements and don't let anyone else know you're going so it will be a surprise for all our friends. And don't worry, they know how to arrange a match I promise you, just trust them and don't ask any more questions. It will all be fine. You'll enjoy it. You understand?"

My mother had regained her composure, "I'm looking forward to it, and I shall wait for the call." The line went dead, and the operator was immediately speaking, "I am sorry but we got disconnected, do you want me to try to reconnect you?" I was disconcerted by her having clearly listened in to our call, but I was learning to be more careful with my outbursts of temper, "No, thank you that was fine." Marlene put down the telephone, was the disconnection a coincidence or not I wondered. "What happened?" she asked, "We have to get her out of Germany before its too late." I insisted, Marlene got up and pulled on her silk robe, she sat on the chair by the dressing table, looking at me in the mirror as she combed the knots out of her long hair. "The Movement is not your family's private escape route. Everyone involved with us is in terrible danger."

I stared at her hard for a moment before I continued, "they have rounded up my mother's entire family and sent them to a place called Theresienstadt, have you heard of this place?" I asked, she puffed out her cheeks, "This is good news, this is not one of the worst outcomes, we have information that it is planned as an ideal community for the Jews of Germany, it could be a lot worse for your family than this place. We have heard it might also be used as a transit camp, perhaps for people to be released to America or Britain." I was not too reassured by this, "I have heard no one ever comes back from these places, no one ever comes home." I insisted, "and that is never going to happen to my mother, you know the rumors as well as me, they are killing people, and I don't like it when you use the word Jews, its Jewish people, I like us to be called Jewish people." She appraised me coolly, "so now you're a Jewish person?" she asked, "and before you never gave a damn about religion."

I shrugged, "I won't let these Nazi bastards define me." She lit a cigarette, and paced, which she always did when she was angry, "You would expect me to expose our entire Movement for the sake of one person?"

It was my turn to hold her stare, "For this person I have already killed my father, so yes, whatever it takes is what I will do.

It was very soon after my return to Germany that I visited the large antiseptic office of my nemesis, Ratwerller. We faced each other across his large metallic desk. He peered at me over the neat folders he was working on. "What can I do for you Herr Hessel?"

"You know the reason I'm here." I said, "Yes, of course I do, but I do so enjoy it when you're forced off your silly little artistic pedestal where people like me can't touch you because of your special friends, and now you're down in my gutter, where we're all in the mess together. How is our Fuhrer by the way?" He smiled in his feral way, as usual with utter insincerity, "Very amusing Ratwerller, let's get to business. What's it going to cost?"

He sighed and made a triangle of his fingers, "This is so delicate a business. Such arrangements are risky, costly, extremely costly." he enjoyed elongating the moment to extract the maximum aggravation from me, but I was older now, and not so easy to excite with his usual nonsense. "The price?" I asked, "But what's money when it's set against the value of one's dear mother, eh?"

"You were always so perceptive." I answered, and this is the moment when my life was to change direction, "but what if the price wasn't just money?" he asked me, I wasn't sure which way this conversation was going, but I was becoming progressively more nervous, "What else do you want, a special painting?"

He smiled again, "No, I do appreciate your work, very good it is too, and especially its financial attractiveness, but art and money are not everything. After all we do not live by bread alone. I have developed a taste for other things. Like all men, the flesh is weak unfortunately."

"What else do I have that you want?"

"I do so admire your choice of lady"

"What do you mean?" now I was very anxious, which is when Ratweller became hard edged again, "Don't play the fool with me, you know exactly what I mean. I want your wife." We stared at each other; I didn't know how to reply. I was genuinely outraged and incredulous, "You want Marlene, my wife Marlene?" I laughed, "but you're a queer aren't you, what would your boyfriend say?"

"I really think she's cured me of that nonsense, but in any event if she hasn't my boyfriend and I can share her bum whenever the mood takes us. She would probably learn to love getting it in the ass, like I do. Two whole men instead of one half of one man, what's not to like, a little penis here or there, it isn't an end of the world decision is it?"

"You're obscene, this is madness and in any event Marlene won't go near either of you scum." I snarled this into his face but he remained as calm as ever, "Well your mother and I shall be relying on you to convince her." He concluded, "There are millions of women out there who I could buy for you, and many of them are as attractive as Marlene, why does it have to be her?"

Ratweller clearly savored this moment, "Because she is yours."

I started to stand up but realized there was nothing I could do to him, "It's men like you who will pay the price for such crimes when the Nazis are wiped from the face of the earth." But instead of being concerned by this his grin became wider.

"It is men like me who shall be long gone when and if there is such an outcome. Or haven't you noticed that your silly little Christian resistance movement has shrunk now that we have taken control over most of Europe. Sensible folk back winners, and we are winning!"

"I have more faith in human nature than that." I said, but he dismissed me with a wave of his hand, "Let's discuss politics some other time. At present all I want is one wife, on her back or front, to be decided, with her legs wide open, willing me on, or your mother will visit the camps. Deal?"

"Maybe I don't need you for this." I mused, "Maybe I can get my mother out without you." The Rat laughed out loud, "Perhaps, why not try it and see?"

"I will pay any other price, but not this." I insisted, "It is, as ever, entirely your choice Arnie, you came here and asked for my help, not the other way about."

"We are going around in circles, it was you and your people who rounded up all the Jewish people in this town." Ratwerller agreed, "Yes, I was obeying my orders, but I missed out your mother, and of course, you." I let a long pause develop, "If such a thing was acceptable to Marlene, what guarantees will you give me that you will really arrange for my mother to escape?"

"Oh, you don't accept my word as an officer and gentleman?" He mocked me, "OK, I shall accompany your mother safely to Switzerland myself and our deal only comes into effect when she is proven to be there?"

"I would have to travel with you."

"All right." He concurred, "But why Switzerland?" I asked, "I can count all my money while I'm there. Such a comforting race the Swiss, their bankers, so wonderful." I didn't have to think about this for long, "I still can't trust you. How do I know you won't arrange little accidents for my mother and me?"

"You're so plebian aren't you Arnie. Why would I, a practical fellow cut off my principal source of income and fun? There simply would be no joy in fucking your wife if you were not present to know about it in every detail." He responded, and in his twisted mind I knew that this answer was honest. He wouldn't kill me while he could make me suffer and make

157

money from me. "I will make you pay a hundred times over for this you bastard." Incongruously he reached over and stroked my face before I could back away in disgust, "such a pretty face, it's a pity I can't get it up for you or I'd have you instead of the pretty little Marlene, but you're wrong again, its me that makes you pay, not the other way about. Now you run along and all you have to do is let me know when you've arranged to deliver Mrs. Hessel to me on a plate, with her legs spread and as soon as that's all in place, as it were, we shall make arrangements to smuggle your mummy out, agreed?"

I turned to leave, I just couldn't trust myself to speak with the disgusting man any longer, nor did I know what I would have said.

I went to meet my mother and wife at the family's old home and when I got there they were seated having tea in the drawing room, facing each other, chatting amiably, seated on two of the four brocade armchairs. As I walked in they both looked up at me expectantly.

"What did the little monster say?" asked my mother. Before I could reply Marlene looked at my crestfallen face and tried to deflect the question to give me some time. "Perhaps its something you need to think about, a business demand?" But I knew there was no way around these moments and questions, "Ratwerller was his usual self. But the one thing we're all agreed on, even him, is that mother has to get out of Germany before it's too late to do anything. Later will be too late."

Mother bridled, hating to be directed by anyone now that her tormentor in chief, my father, was no longer alive to bully her into submission. "Arnie, you forget that I am as German as anyone else in this country. Where else would I live, what could I do? I don't know any other way of life." I couldn't believe she was that naïve, "There is no choice for you between a German way of life and another style of life, your choice is between staying and dying or going and living!"

The harshness of my words made my mother start to weep, a sight I could never deal with, Marlene neither. She moved over to comfort my mother, putting an arm around her shoulders. My wife then spoke to me, "You don't have to be so rough with your mother, and she deserves respect." I felt as if I had wounded my mother unnecessarily but it was for her own eventual salvation, "I don't mean to bully you mother, you know that don't you? But you must realize that we have to get you out of Germany while its still possible for us. Remember when I was a boy and you told me when and how to pick my fights, never to give in? Now its your turn to fight, but not here, where they will kill your voice, but from outside, where you can do them the most damage."

Bertha looked up at me, dabbing at her eyes with the lace handkerchief, which she kept perpetually up her cardigan's right sleeve, "You understand, I am not crying for myself or this house, it is only bricks, and they can be replaced by another house somewhere else. But they have removed my family. I simply do not know the fate of my brother, sister, mother, cousins; all of them gone. I fooled myself that somehow they will be all right, but now I know they will all be murdered and any chance I had of ever seeing them again, embracing them one more time, has vanished forever."

"That's not true, they have been taken to the new Jewish labor camp, I already told you." Said Marlene, but Bertha shook her head slowly, "Rivers of blood and death will result from these Nazi madmen, mark my words."

I didn't have the heart to lie to her, when it was obvious that we agreed, "These are terrible times, I didn't think you still thought so much about your family, you never speak about them, see them or anything, and they treated you so badly when you married father." She looked at me mournfully, and spoke through her tears, "I think of them every morning, when I wake up and before I go to sleep at night."

Marlene sought to find something positive to say, "I'm sure they will be fine, you know how it is with rumors, they usually turn out to be silly stories." Mother smiled bravely at her daughter-in-law, "No, we all know, no one come back, once they're taken away, that's it."

There was a moment when none of us knew quite what to say, but then I tried to reassert control over the way the conversation was going, "That's why we can't let the same fate overcome you. We are going to take you to safety in Switzerland, then the world will be your oyster, and you will be in charge of your own destiny again." Marlene joined me in the attempt to bring some enthusiasm and optimism back to my mother, "Where would you go, if you had the choice, England, America or maybe even Australia?"

Mother replied instantly, "Palestine. I would go to Palestine."

This surprised me totally, I had never heard my mother express any opinion on the Jewish people's ancient homeland, I was incredulous, "Why Palestine, its hot and dusty, full of people in conflict, don't you want some peace?"

"Because I have finally realized that is where all Jews should live, and if necessary fight. If others say that I'm nothing but a Jew I shall not disappoint them, and once I get there I shall never run again."

Later, after Marlene and I had said goodnight to my mother we strolled through the garden, each lost in our memories of the place. We were both reluctant to talk more, but knew there was no escape, "How are you actually going to get mother out?" she asked, "I'm not certain yet." Marlene stopped and we faced each other, she looked into my eyes, her habit when she was determined to force the truth out of me, "Everything you do Arnie, is calculated, you already have a plan, what is it, can I help?"

I still tried to prevaricate, "Rat says he will help with this, and you know how resourceful he is."

She nodded, but wasn't satisfied with my response, "and the Rat is very greedy, so what has he asked for this time?"

Something about the manner of my hesitation before I replied set the mental alarm bells ringing in my wife's head, "What is it, what does he want, what aren't you telling me?" I couldn't answer, "Is it something to do with me?" she asked, as ever intuitive, "It is you, he wants you."

Marlene was very calm, and this made me more nervous than if she were ranting and raving at me as I had expected, "And what did you answer, when he made this proposal?"

"I said no of course, I said no." Marlene shook her head, "No you didn't," I was trapped, "OK, maybe I didn't say a total no exactly, I wasn't strong enough, its my mother, can you forgive me?" She caressed my cheek and smiled, "You still don't know how much I love you do you, for you I would let the entire Gestapo have me if its what you needed."

"I cannot allow it." I answered, "You silly man, you'd risk your own mother's life because of your ridiculous masculine pride, you know he can take my body, but he can never take my heart and mind."

"I just cannot stand the thought of that man touching you, seeing you, knowing you."

She shook her head again, "He could have my body a thousand times but he will never know me, whatever happens, I shall always be your woman." She kissed me and I responded.

Chapter Sixteen

The German/Swiss Border
1940

There were four trucks and a car in our convoy through the mountain roads and their hairpin bends leading to the German and Swiss border. Our car was a Mercedes and was driven by Helmut, our ever-faithful friend, with us for every major adventure, wanted or otherwise. I sat next to him; Marlene was in the back of the car. The trucks each had two heavily armed Gestapo men guarding them. The vehicles had tarpaulins covering their contents.

We were within a few minutes of the border when Helmut took another swig from his whisky flask, which he had been taking large nips from throughout the long drive. He offered it to me, and again I declined. "Why so glum?" he asked me, "The very finest Scotch whisky, nothing ersatz about it, I can assure you. How about it Marlene, would you like a nip, to keep the cold off?"

She took the proffered flask and drunk from it and passed it back to our friend. "Better?" he asked her, "Much thank you."

Helmut looked between the two of us, and then he smiled one of his knowing smiles, which usually indicated he was about to get something wrong, "What is it, you two lovebirds had your first big married row?"

"We're that obvious?" I said, seeking to keep the conversation bland, "Why else would you be this miserable. We're going to a perfectly nice neutral Swiss and German friendship gathering to exhibit the very finest German art, the majority of which is yours. We shall have a lovely few days of pretentious chitchat, Edelweiss and cuckoo clocks and both of you look like the entire world has caved in on your pretty heads. Now cheer up or I shall have to bang your heads together."

I smiled, despite not feeling like it. "Have you got all our permits?" I asked him. "For the hundredth time, I have got all the bloody stupid permits, in triplicate, including your letter of accreditation from Herr bloody Hitler. What else can they want, a counter signature from God?"

"I'm just being an old woman aren't I. You're right let's have a sing song." I started to sing my favorite song, Lili Marlene. The others soon joined in, and the soldiers in the trucks, hearing this, joined in loudly.

It was a fun moment, and it served to break the tension that existed in our car. It was only a little while longer that we pulled to a halt by the German border crossing. There we encountered two bored sentries who snapped to attention when they saw the impressive credentials that Helmut proffered on our behalf. One of the sentries suggested we all wait in the car as he rushed busily into the small green wooden hut that apparently served as the border guards' office and mini barracks for this out of the way crossing point.

I exchanged an anxious look with Marlene, and hoped the worried look on her face wasn't as obvious to the border guards as it was to me. We saw the guard on the telephone and he occasionally looked up from his conversation to our car. I could just hear snatched of what he said through the open window, "Yes sir, I shall keep them here until you arrive. Yes sir, understood." He replaced the receiver and walked from the hat to join his colleague. They spoke with one another, and both men turned to face our car.

As this was happening our convoy guards alighted from the trucks to stretch their legs, pleased at this pause in the long journey. A couple of our soldiers joined the border guards in some unheard banter, no doubt at our expense, and they all looked at us and laughed. Helmut turned to me, "Wait here, I'll go and find out what this hold up is about."

Helmut got out and approached the soldiers, meanwhile Marlene leaned toward me, and "Do they suspect something?" she asked.

"Only if some particularly repellant rodent has been captured and turned, and that couldn't have happened so fast." I said it, but I wasn't sure that I was right. Rat would sell his soul for the price of a cup of coffee.

Helmut's imposing presence had the effect of making the soldiers straighten up as he joined them. "We have a busy schedule, what appears to be the hold up?" he asked, in his best officer class, patrician voice. The senior of the border guards fell back on the most heard words of the Nazi era, "Orders sir." He paused, "We're following orders." Helmut looked at his quizzically, "But we have signed authorization from Adolf Hitler, who dares question such orders, someone who wants to spend the winter in Russia?"

The guards wished they were anywhere else at that moment, but orders were orders, "A superior officer will be along very shortly sir, and I'm sure he will have answers."

But Helmut was not to be easily deterred, "Don't you think the Fuhrer's own orders to." he looked at the paper and read it out loud, "To let the bearer pass without let or hindrance, and I quote, to assist in any way deemed fit by the bearer, far outweigh any orders by any petty bureaucrat in an out of the way crossing, don't you?"

"Yes sir." The guard responded, "Good," said Helmut, "then raise the bloody barrier and let us through right now." "I can't do that sir." He insisted, "You are now disobeying a direct order from the Chancellor of Germany, the Fuhrer, Adolf Hitler himself. No one does that, you will be shot you fool!"

The guard swallowed hard, but didn't budge. Helmut turned his attention to the other guard, "What about you, do you also want to get shot because of this clown?" The second guard clearly didn't know what to do, "No sir, but it'll be just a few minutes and we can sort this lot out."

Helmut was towering over them both, and I thought he might hit one of them, but at this point, with him clearly attempting to intimidate the guards, that the senior one of the two calmly pointed his rifle at my friend. "Please sir, can you wait in the car?" he said it very inoffensively, but Helmut wasn't easily deterred, "I am giving you both one last chance!"

The soldier prodded his rifle in the direction of Helmut, no longer cowed, but determined to follow his orders. "Now sir, be a good gentleman, walk back to your nice comfy car please sir, we'll have this sorted out shortly. There's a good gentleman."

Helmut had no alternative but to do as he was instructed much to the amusement of our own military escort who clearly relished the puffed up aristocrat ordered around. Helmut returned to the car and slammed the door shut. "No luck?" I asked, fighting hard to suppress my own nervous giggles. "You would think we had no papers, this is outrageous!" His shouts drowned out a noise from somewhere in the rear of the car. Arnie turns toward the back of the car by reflex, "What was that?" asked Helmut, "Face the front, don't look around!" commanded Marlene urgently. Helmut, suddenly paler did as he was instructed, "We owe you an explanation." I said to my friend.

"I don't think I want to know whatever it is you're about to tell me," was his response. "We shouldn't have involved you without your agreement, but the less people that knew the safer it would be for everyone. You understand?"

Helmut tried to force a smile, but it was not easy for him, he was as scared as the rest of us. "Just tell me its someone that is terribly important, someone you can't do without. I'd hate to be risking my skin for a smell bloody sewage worker, or even worse, a Communist!"

"It's my mother." Helmut nodded his understanding, "Of course, we have no choice. God help her." He concluded, "God help us all." Said Marlene, realizing better than any of us the terrible danger we were facing.

At that moment a military staff car pulled up alongside us. In it were four SS men and our old friend Ratwerller. The SS men looked calm and assured, and they were soon chatting with the border guards as the Rat walked slowly over to our car, his smile doing nothing to conceal his deadly menace. "Oh shit!" said Helmut, but not loud enough for anyone outside the car to hear.

Marlene turned to me, "I thought we had a deal with him?" "And we do, let me do the talking." I answered. "And if you can answer his questions you'll have more from me later!" interjected Helmut.

Ratwerller leaned in through the open window of the car. He smiled as pleasantly as his feral, narrow face would allow. "Good day my old friends!" None of us replied. " Very moody, but we can soon change people's moods. We have ways to cheer people up. I am told I can be very amusing. What do you say we do a little old fashioned search of your nice shiny vehicle."?

Ratwerller called over to his men. "You know what we're looking for, come on, get on with it."

Two of the soldiers previously guarding the convoy were ordered by the SS men to unload the contents of their truck. I watched the search with Rat standing right next to me. "What's this all about?" I whispered urgently to him, "Who knows what we might find?"

I looked at him, "You never ask a question to which you don't already know the answer."

As I was talking to him I could sense Marlene doing something in the back of our car. I couldn't hear, but I knew she was hushing my mother. From my position I could see the contents of the first truck on the road and the SS men were now inside poking around. Ratwerller opened the door for me and ushered me outside, where Helmut joined us.

"You people issued us with these bloody papers so even you must know they're genuine. We have an official German art exhibition to mount inside our neutral neighboring country and you are about to ruin all those arrangements. You're behaving as normal, like the school bully you always were. You are an idiot and I am going to report you to a superior." Helmut finished, but he hadn't succeeded in wiping the smirk from Ratwerller's face.

"Oh come on, don't you want to see what we're going to find, aren't you just the tiniest bit curious?" Rat mocked us, "Humor him," I said to Helmut, "He's a very sick man."

"Yes, humor me, I am very sick." The Rat confirmed. Two of the SS men pulled the contents out of a long thick cardboard tube. Very carefully and deliberately they unwound a canvas, exchanging loud sarcastic comments about the abstract art. They held it up for Ratwerller to look at, but he shook his head.

Another soldier poked around the seemingly empty shell of the truck with his bayonet whilst a Gestapo officer crawled like an inverted crab under another one of the trucks, examining it minutely with a torch.

We all watched the search progress. Ratwerller moved closer to me, "Where is the merchandise?" I knew what he meant but I didn't want to look at him, the effort at appearing cool and unflustered was proving too much for my self-control. "What so you can cancel the deal? No you find the merchandise yourself, if there is anything to find"

He looked at me with disgust etched on his face, "Idiot, I am not trying to find the merchandise!" He hissed in my ear, "this isn't my doing, I have superiors and they don't trust a half Jew whatever the Fuhrer says, and they won't you nailed on a cross, just like the Jew doctor who looks after him."

"So what happens now?" We watched the various soldiers continue their search. "I can't rely on anything other than your greed, that's always been reliable. How do we fix this problem?" I probed him, but he was clearly agitated and not in control of this situation. He dragged on his cigarette; smoking was a habit that he had adopted more and more over the last few years.

"I can't rely on you or your word, only your greed." I observed, "Just this once, we don't have to love one another, but, we do have to trust each other, we both have much to lose."

I said, "Yes, if she's caught, we're questioned, we talk, you're implicated and..." "We're all dead." He finished my thought, "Now tell me where she is so I can misdirect my friends away from the scent." Helmut, who was standing nearby, shook his head, as if to say don't tell him anything. I raised my eyes to heaven in mute reply, meaning what choice do I have? "Under the back seat." I said, trusting my instinct rather than my brain, which was shouting at me not to tell him anything. Rat sneaked a quick look at the SS and Gestapo men crawling all over the trucks and then turned back to me. "I thought that's where she would be." Having said this he marched towards the trucks without looking back.

The area around the stationary convoy was littered with hundreds of pieces of artwork, most of which had been already thoroughly searched. Ratwerller arrived at the nearest group of searching men. "What have you found, anything interesting?" A Gestapo man in the back of the truck facing Ratwerller shook his head, "You've searched every truck, every exhibit?" asked Ratwerller.

The leading SS man, now perspiring heavily from his efforts removed his cap and wiped his brow, "Every single thing has been looked at twice, at least twice, sir, every bloody centimeter sir." Ratwerller snarled, " Then search for a third time until we find something!"

The Rat stood overseeing his men as they redoubled their efforts. Eventually the men had clearly exhausted every possible hiding place and had discovered nothing not already written on our customs declaration forms.

Helmut and Marlene now lounged on our car's back seat having opened the picnic hamper and spread its fare across the rug now covering the leather. If you listened carefully, and I did, you could hear the sound of a woman quietly whimpering and crying. "Not too much longer, keep strong for a little bit longer, we'll be there soon." Marlene said quietly and soothingly, inelegantly wedged into the tiny crawl space we had created beneath the seat.

Below the seat it was very dark and hot, too claustrophobic for one person, we had stuffed two women into this tiny space, and neither was my mother. These were two younger women.

My smile of relief faded when Ratwerller and his men walked towards our car. "Are you satisfied, can we continue on our journey now?" I asked, "We haven't quite finished yet sir, we would like you and your companions to all step from the car so that we can search you."

Helmut and Marlene scurried from the car to join us next to the car. We stood in a loose semi circle around Ratwerller and his men. He eyed Marlene like a man assessing some horse he was thinking of purchasing. She averted her gaze, aware of his intention. "Please, madam, remove your coat." Marlene removed her coat as asked, which she handed to Helmut. Her fine body was emphasized by the static electricity making her dress cling to her every curve. Rat looked at her from head to foot. She looked vulnerable and undeniably desirable. Ratwerller looked at her with a mixture of desire and contempt. The SS men almost drooled with appreciation but were restrained by the presence of their strange but dangerous boss. "You," Ratwerller said to the first SS man, "Search her, very carefully." The SS man was surprised, "Sir, regulations, shouldn't a female officer undertake such a body search?"

Ratwerller looked away from Marlene for a moment and snapped at the man, "Scared of what's there, just do it man!" Helmut stepped between the SS man and Marlene, blocking his path. I looked on knowing there was nothing I could do at this moment, the other men under Rat's orders all raised their rifles and aimed them at Helmut who spoke urgently to Ratwerller, "What could she possibly be hiding under that dress?"

Ratwerller looked at Helmut but spoke directly to the first SS man, "Find out everything she has got under that dress, NOW!" he shouted, but Helmut determinedly stood his ground but before the situation could deteriorate any more Marlene stepped in front of her friend and protector, she raised her hands. "Go on, if you must, search me. But all I have under my dress is the same as any woman." The soldiers almost schoolboy lust turned to ash when confronted with Marlene's overpowering female assertiveness. Almost apologetically the SS man starts to touch her as he searches, but being cautious not to offend her or exacerbate the already volatile situation.

Ratwerller's anger turned to fury, his imagined sexual degradation and humiliation over his enemies was publicly backfiring. "You call that a search you oaf?" He shouted and pushed the SS man aside. Now he and Marlene faced each other. "You will remove all your clothes, including your under garments, at once." He instructed her, "Here, out in the cold sir?" she teased him.

Ratwerller thought for a moment and then smiled. "No, of course not, where are my manners, we shall continue this in the nice warm hut, if that would be more convenient?" The question was, of course, an order. She nodded and followed Ratwerller into the hut, the guards aiming their guns at Helmut and me. There was nothing I could do as Marlene turned at the door of the hut as she followed the Rat inside, she smiled bravely and then vanished. "Your woman likes to play a bit doesn't she mate, what can we do?" said the SS man, "Follow orders!" I spat at him.

Inside the hut Marlene and Ratwerller stood facing each other. "Now madam, disrobe, please." She tugged at the zip in the side of her dress, "The blinds?" she asked, and he released the blinds, the room went dark as the sexual electricity mounted as she let her dress fall to the floor in a silky sheath. She faced him in her black satin knickers; a brief brassiere held her generous breasts and her black seamed stockings were held up on her shapely legs by her matching suspender belt. Ratwerller was fascinated and repelled by her. "And the rest." He said huskily, for the first time facing a mature and sexually attractive woman. "You want to see everything you've bought? OK, I will show you everything." She undid her bra and let it fall to the floor. After a moment when she hid her rose tipped breasts from his view she decided it was hopeless so she let him see her and she placed an elegant foot on the desk in front of her, and unclasped one suspender and pulled down a stocking, then repeated this with the other leg. "Am I the first woman you've seen?" she asked him, he didn't ask, he just wanted to see her, every inch. She removed her knickers slowly, letting him see her full womanhood.

Ratwerller grunted something unintelligible, and came over to be close to her, to breathe in her aroma. "Bend over the table." He instructed, "You'll find me better than any of your little boys." She teased him. Ratwerller was now inches behind her, looking at her very closely, "This is a search, what are you talking about?"

He used his hand to search her intimately, and then as he wiped his hand on his handkerchief she spoke again, "You're stopping now?" she thought she had mastered him, but she had misjudged his sexuality. Without warning he unzipped his trousers and holding her hips in place he forcefully penetrated her. There was nothing she could do, he was using her for his pleasure and he was merciless as he used her in every way until she was unable to bear the pounding, her legs turning to jelly and her breasts sore from the vicious mauling he gave them, twisting and pinching her nipples until she screamed for her to stop. He stuffed his handkerchief into her mouth to quieten her. "How do you like to be ridden like the bitch you are?"

Marlene hated him, but her body reacted involuntarily to the stimulation and this encouraged Ratwerller even further. She cried with the pain, humiliation and powerlessness of her situation and this excited his perversity further.

Outside the hut we could hear her muffled screams and crying and occasionally his grunts, shouts and exultation. Even the SS men were embarrassed by this situation. Helmut tried to lead me away from the hut but I had to be as close as I was allowed. The tears streamed down my face unbidden. My humiliation was abject and total, and at this moment I swore quietly that I would wreak my revenge on Ratwerller, not just for me, but also for Marlene.

It was about thirty of the longest minutes of my life before they came out of the hut and walked towards us. Marlene managed to keep a neutral expression on her face but the Rat was beaming with pleasure. I couldn't face Marlene when she tried to kiss me. "Remember what we said, whatever he did, I am yours forever?" I tried to smile at her, but I wasn't as brave or strong as she was.

"You slut." Said Helmut, he slapped her face hard; "I do that for my friend because he cannot." One of the SS men moved menacingly towards Helmut but Ratwerller held up his hand, "Surely that was just an observation rather than a criticism?" He turned to me. "I must say the good lady was co-operative, most open and co-operative." He smiled at me, encouraging me to ask questions, but I wouldn't give him that satisfaction. "Can we leave now?"

"Yes, of course you can, but remember we want to see precisely the same goods returned to the Fatherland when this exhibition is over. Understood, precisely the same goods." Ratwerller emphasized. We got back into the car as the trucks, now re-loaded with their contents, all started their engines. Ratwerller waved his arm towards the crossing point and the barrier was raised. We passed into Switzerland leaving behind the hell that was our country.

We pulled to a halt after crossing no mans land at the Swiss Customs Post. The German drivers and guards left and filed back toward Germany, still gossiping about the extraordinary events they'd just been ordered never to discuss with anyone.

Swiss guards and drivers replaced the departing Germans. A Swiss customs officer examined the documents Helmut handed to him. "What was the hold up sir, we heard you arrived at their end a long while back?" the customs man asked him, "Just some formalities, you know how we Germans like our papers to be perfect." Replied Helmut, "We have that in common sir, well this all appears to be in good order, have a nice stay in Switzerland."

We were trying to regain an air of normalcy in the car as we pulled into the countryside of Switzerland, but it was impossible, the tension crackled between us all.

About half an hour later we pulled into a dark forest clearing. Several of the guards rushed back to the edge of the road and blocked off the entrance to the clearing with trees that had been prepared for the task, but it would look to the untrained eye as if some trees and rocks had fallen onto the road, blocking it, from the mountainside.

This was the one moment when I could assume command, and it was a relief for me to do so. Marlene had been quiet and withdrawn and Helmut was also seemingly delighted to be active. "Open the back up." I commanded him, and he rushed to comply. "There's a catch underneath the centre of the seat." I told him. He pressed the catch and the bottom of the seat sprang open. He looked down and was astonished by what he saw. He found, instead of my mother, two teenage girls who breathed deeply and smiled at him as he helped them out of their hiding place. Helmut was unable to understand who these girls were, and he looked at me for guidance. For the first time that day I smiled with genuine happiness.

Marlene supervised the guards who were scrambling beneath each of the trucks. They quickly unscrewed the panels holding the big petrol tanks in place that revealed more hiding places next to the real and smaller petrol tanks. They reveal Bertha Hessel suspended upside down by webbing belts to the chassis of the truck, her position having been cushioned by a great deal of rubber and sponge. "Get me out of here for pity's sake!" she spluttered, "I feel like a bloody old bat!" Although her face was lined with fatigue I was thrilled to see she was otherwise well.

The guards very carefully released her from her confinement and lifted her to shaky feet. I rushed over to her and she embraced me as I kissed her face. It was nearly all worth the price. Helmut was totally perplexed as another eight escaping refugees were freed from their ingenious and virtually undetectable hiding places. Marlene had, by now, assumed total control over this operation. One of the guards, a dark swarthy man wearing a black beret, walked over to my mother and me. I was never to learn his or the other names of the men who had risked everything that day. "Come on, we have to go now, there's no time to stand here." He insisted. "Just one minute young man." She insisted, "Marlene come here a minute," Marlene smiled at my mother and hurried over. Helmut and the man with the black beret backed away a few paces, aware that they were intruding on family business.

Bertha spoke to my wife and me, "You know my son, that the work Marlene does is more important than you or your vanity, and a woman is physically weaker than a man so she has to use every weapon at her disposal. Arnie you understand you will have to grow a great deal to be as big as your wife, because she's a giant." Marlene burst into tears, but tried to hide them in front of the people relying on her, and I felt totally inadequate and small minded. Marlene and my mother hugged, each comforting the other. Bertha continued, "If you learned anything from me my son its that what counts is the person from the inside out. Remember what I tell you now, it's still the same."

"I'm not a little boy mother, don't talk to me like this." "I'm your mother, so I have to." She admonished me, "But I'm not the little boy I once was." She smiled and playfully smacked me on my ass, "For me you will always be my little boy." Before we could continue the man wearing the black beret interrupted, tapping his finger on his watch. "No more time," he said in his heavily accented German. Mother hugged Marlene, and then me and then forced us into a three-way embrace. While we were huddled she added, "Remember, we only have each other to love without question." She released us and then joined the rest of her group, where she turned and waved, "Look after yourselves and love each other."

She turned and followed the others in her group, the man turned to us one last time, "I shall get your mother to her destination I promise, and maybe we can all meet again, shalom, next year in Jerusalem." With that he led the group into the forest and out of sight.

"What did he mean?" asked Helmut, "Shalom means peace, and Jews have been saying next year in Jerusalem for the thousands of years since we were dispersed around the world by the Romans. Adolf Hitler has made it possible for my mother."

"So now your mother goes to Palestine and you're a Jew?"

"Yes, it seems in today's world we don't have any choices, so some of my people are going home."

And I wondered if I would ever see my lovely mother again.

Chapter Seventeen

Berlin
Spring 1942

It was one of those balmy wonderful nights that Berlin does so well. Crowds swirled outside the theatre after the premiere for the new play. The women were in their best evening dress, the men mostly in uniform. I was standing next to Helmut, he was in his usual louche dinner suit and cape, I was in my very smart Colonel's uniform given to me courtesy of the Fuhrer's command. We both saw Marlene being escorted out of the building by Ratwerller; it still hurt me almost too much to bear to see them arm in arm. As usual Helmut tried his best to distract me, to block my line of sight, anything to stop yet another confrontation.

"Get out of my way." I told him. "Why do you punish yourself like this?" I shrugged my shoulders, "I don't know old friend, I really don't know." Marlene smiled at the people being introduced to her by Ratwerller, unaware that I was staring at her.

A portly man, wearing the dress uniform of a general greeted me enthusiastically, "Herr Hessel, what a pleasure to run into you again like this. It's been what, a couple of years at least." I recognized him at once, General Kleist, not a bad old stick, and he liked my work, which recommended him to me immensely. I smiled, "Good evening general, how pleasant to see you again, forgive me if I didn't see you straight away, I was a million miles away. Refresh my memory, where was it we last met?" He laughed, full of merriment, "You've forgotten me already, just how many fat old generals do you meet?"

We both laughed but then he noticed my eyes were still drawn to Marlene and Ratwerller, "Beauty and the beast eh. I can understand looking at her, but he's no treat for the eyes." I nodded, and then turned to face the general directly, "She is beautiful, and she was once my wife."

"Oh, I am sorry if I have said something to offend you." "No," I shook my head, "Forgive me, its me that is rude, now I remember, we were introduced by the Fuhrer himself, how could I possibly forget that."

The general was delighted we had moved the brief conversation to an easier topic, "Yes, that's right, at the Wolf's Lair." He looked at Helmut, "I'm sorry," I said, "This is my colleague Helmut Von Thysen." They shook hands, "I think I know your family." Kleist said to Helmut, "Most people appear to do so." Replied Helmut. "I have heard very good things about the two of you, your fame and business acumen precede you. You're legendary, its almost as if you had a bit of the Jew in you to be this good at squeezing people for the maximum money, just like the chosen people." He laughed, but Arnie and Helmut forced themselves to join him.

"How about the two of you join me for dinner, there's a wonderful place near here, does the best food, and a tasty dessert if you know what I mean, they import the steak from the north and the women from Paris, a good combination yes?"

"That would be very nice." I started, trying to find an excuse not to join him, "No buts, let's get out of the madding crowd eh, I insist, it will be my treat?" he ignored our protests and barged his way happily through the throngs of revelers.

We arrived at the restaurant in the company of Kleist who seemed totally unconcerned that we quickly became the centre of attention as we took our table. The general sat opposite us and we now had the opportunity to look more closely at our surroundings, the place was like a giant womb, hot and red. The other occupants were mostly discreetly hidden behind drawn curtains, each in their private booths. Ours had the curtain open as Kleist soon had the drinks and food flowing. Soon three beautiful French girls wearing very little but skimpy maids outfits and saucy smiles joined us. Kleist ignored them except when one of them put her hand on him under the table and he swatted it away, "Not while we're eating dear heart, you can spoil a man's digestion. These French women, so eager to co-operate with their conquerors eh?"

I was fascinated and repelled by the man's Rabelaisian gusto; he was just such a happy pig as he gorged himself on his vast greasy sausage and sauerkraut. Bits of his food dribbled and squeezed from the side of his thick-lipped mouth as he attempted to combine talking and eating simultaneously, "Your business spreads faster than the Reich itself. You boys must be making a bloody fortune, not that I have anything against making a fortune you understand, it would be un-Germanic to be against making money so we can pay more tax eh?" He laughed and wiped his mouth on his sleeve. "What plans do you have for the future of the business?" he asked me.

"I'm just a painter, its Helmut who runs the business." I responded, "He's just being modest, most of the original ideas are his, and all the good paintings." Helmut said, the beer rapidly going to his head, "You know how it is general, what with the war and the business I don't have time just to sit and do my painting anymore, we're more of a business than anything else." The general laughed and raised his glass to us, "You are more of an industry than a business, I haven't seen your figures, but they must be most impressive. Let us drink to the business!" Everyone at the table took a drink to toast our business, the young lady next to me held my glass to my lips with one hand and surreptitiously felt me under the table with her free hand, "I've never had one of our disabled boys before, I'll do you for free." She whispered in my ear, but before I could explain that I was disabled long before the war and she didn't have to service me out of misplaced patriotism the general continued. "To have a business such as yours in the middle of this war is a great comfort. A comfort I don't presently enjoy myself. I have been stuck away on the freezing bloody Russian front where your balls have to be wrapped up warm or they freeze up and fall off. My business is nearly kaput. I don't know what I am going to come home to."

He was near to tears of self-pity. "I thought you were a professional army man?" I inquired, "What me, no, ha, my wife should hear you say that. No I have a print works in Munich. I am a printer, not a soldier, that's what I am, Kleist the printer. The Kleist Printing Company, that's me." "Oh," said Helmut, "I've heard of you, that's the biggest printer in Southern Germany!"

Kleist beamed proudly, "It is the biggest print works in the whole of Germany!" his good humor evaporated as he continued, "But now the its government work at government controlled prices and this isn't so good, but perhaps providence smiled on us all tonight."

"Go on," suggested Helmut, the general was now apparently stone cold sober, "I can print your cards better, cheaper and in bigger numbers for less than you pay anywhere else, I guarantee that for special friends, and I can even guarantee that they will be distributed throughout the war and all over Europe, come on tell me that you're not interested."

It was a tempting pitch, it could solve all the problems with costs, printing and distribution that we'd been encountering as our enterprise had grown too fast and become unwieldy. "How did we become your special friends to get such a special deal general?" I asked, "I'm not an unreasonable man, for a factory owning general, I want you to flourish and at the same time we should also make a profit, it isn't unreasonable eh, if we are to be long time in a working relationship with each other eh?"

I was to find out the answer to that question a few days later when we visited the general's house in Munich. It was a huge and garish mansion that only the newly rich, with more money than taste or experience could relish. Set in a couple of hectares of neatly trimmed gardens the home seemed to reflect everything unappealing about the man and his money. Helmut and I were ushered into the hall with its immensely high ceiling and overly ostentatious and grotesquely overlarge crystal chandelier by a frock coated butler. Both Helmut and I followed the man as he led us to the drawing room.

The general entered with a very amply proportioned young woman, "This is my little princess, my daughter, Kathrin." The one word that didn't do her justice was his inappropriate use of the word little; she was very large, very pretty but ovoid. However she had a winning smile and despite her potentially slow metabolism a lovely personality. She saw Helmut and I at the same moment the maid brought in tea and cakes. Clearly she was under strict instructions not to eat as she forced herself to look at us rather than the food but I felt her attention stray toward the cakes occasionally.

I realized this was a set up almost immediately, the fat girl and the cripple, a partnership made in heaven. To give her some credit I could see from the way Kathrin looked at me that she recognized the situation for what it was, but was resigned to her fate. "Hello Kathrin. Any cakes for a hungry man?"

She beamed at me, "You like cake Herr Hessel?" "I love cakes," I stipulated, "But only if you can help me with it?" she moved over to me and looked me straight in the eye, "You can call me Kat, all my special friends call me Kat." "OK Kat, I think we can be special friends." Helmut read the signals and smiled, as did the general, deal done!

I think Kathrin saw me as a challenge to fatten up and she wasn't worried about me not having the use of my arms. In fact she saw this as a potential advantage, it meant she could always take the initiative and I could never hit her as the general had often done as she'd being growing up. I exchanged a happy glance with the general, some things, it was understood, such as business, being far more important than any others. I sat next to Kat and opened my mouth; she started to feed me and never stopped again for many years.

The wedding ceremony took place at the registry office; it was brief and awkward. Only a few richly dressed people attended. I stood next to Kathrin and we were both happy enough and the General was more relieved than thrilled. I was so busy thinking about the business I almost didn't hear the registrar tell me, "You may now kiss the bride." I did so without any great enthusiasm but Kathrin saw this as her first opportunity to take ownership of the romantic situation, as she grabbed the back of my head in both her large hands and returned the kiss with enormous gusto and stuck her tongue into my mouth.

This was to be my first experience of Kat's other hunger. She was a very earthy woman, and this was immediately revealed in our seaside hotel bedroom. Kathrin went after me like a tigress, with no subtlety or style but enormous energy and power. I felt like I had been ravished. No intimacy was a problem for this woman; she would wipe me in the toilet as if I was her baby, and then make love with me as if I was the only man in the world. I was to find more to recommend this girl as time passed, but above all I was pleased to be with a person who woke up happy and always seemed pleased to see another day. It was to take me out of my more introspective moments as I shared her simple joys.

Our first morning together, as man and wife, I was standing by the window of our large honeymoon suite, looking out of at the sea below. I was dressed in my pajama trousers and Kathrin was sitting in our bed, consuming a deluxe box of chocolates imported from Belgium. "Are you happy?" I asked her, "Happy?" she said, playing with the word, "Yes," I said, "You know, with me?" She smiled and popped another chocolate in her mouth, "Look what an appetite you gave me, you wore me out, you're very good in bed, very imaginative, much better than I thought you'd be, very, acrobatic; are you happy with me?" Now it was my turn to smile, "Of course I am."

She stopped eating for a second, "I know some people think I'm fat, but I hope you see me as voluptuous. Daddy was especially generous with my dowry. A half-share in his factory, and a large amount of money, you must be very happy with that."

"I think you're voluptuous, and you know, a dowry is normal. And I was comfortably off already, you know that, I think you're very special, voluptuous in fact." I kissed her on the cheek. She shook her head and ate another chocolate, "Look I'm a practical girl, you just have to keep me well fed and looked after in the bed department, that's all I ask, I'm old fashioned, you can do what you like as long as its not in my face or on my doorstep, understood?"

I laughed, "If everyone in the world was more like you there would be no wars!" I was very happy at that moment, we had an understanding, and we could, I thought, both live with that quite happily. "I see it like this eh, you like to paint and fornicate, I like to eat and fornicate, what's the problem eh, you go and paint a nice picture, make us some money, and I shall find a nice patisserie. We shall meet for lunch at one and maybe have a quickie and a siesta, sounds nice doesn't it, now hurry along my little apple strudel, all this talking is making me hungry."

I smiled at her, sharing her humor, "you said making love makes you hungry." I scolded her, "Everything makes me hungry, even breathing. You don't want to reform me do you, I like eating, I don't even mind being voluptuous." I looked at her Rubenesque body and shook my head, "Never, of course not, eating, for you, is an art form!"

The rest of our honeymoon was, on the surface, a light-hearted pleasure for the two of us. Perhaps this was not love's first dream, but it was a very serviceable arrangement that made Kat, the general and myself very happy.

We returned to the rather large house Kathrin's father had purchased for us his wedding gift. "He might not have table manners," said Helmut who was waiting for us by the stairs to the front porch, "But my god, he is a generous fellow!" "It's good to see you to Hynie!" I called to him, trying to hush him from embarrassing Kat, "OH, I don't mind, daddy is a bit below stairs sometimes, but he's a lovely fellow." She hugged Helmut; the two of them had become firm friends very quickly. "Did my friend look after you appropriately?" He asked her, "If you know what I mean?" wiggling his eyebrows theatrically. "I know what you mean you naughty boy," she giggled, "....and Arnie did very well in that department, in fact I don't think I can walk without being bandy!"

"That's enough of the detail Kat. I invited my friend here so he could carry you across the threshold on my behalf." I said this mischievously, never one to lose an opportunity to challenge my friend, who was plainly annoyed by my idea of a joke. Kathrin looked at me and wagged her finger in my direction in admonishment, "You're a very naughty boy sometimes."

"That's exactly my thought," said Helmut, "...so I had better be running along to leave you two lovebirds to your cooing." He was about to turn but Kathrin caught his sleeve in her not inconsiderable hand, "But I do like the idea of being carried across our threshold. It is supposed to be lucky you know."

Before Helmut could react she put her arms around his neck and daintily for someone of her size, jumped into his arms. Helmut staggered but kept himself upright. Kathrin smiled appealingly, "Let's go Hynie." She insisted. Helmut nearly buckled under the weight, but one step at a time; he managed to carry my wife into the house with my laughter and that of Kathrin ringing in his ears. It was at this moment that Helmut realized the two of us had set him up and this only served to increase our laughter until he was no longer able to hold my wife aloft. They collapsed in a heap onto the floor. "Very funny you two!" he called with Kathrin sitting on him, "I can see you have perfectly matching warped humor."

Kathrin pulled Helmut up easily, "I thought you were going to burst!" she said, and I added, "You went redder than a tomato!" We all laughed but something about the look on Helmut's face made both Kathrin and I pause, "What is it?" I asked, "You've got your marching orders again old friend."

I was annoyed by this but not half as much as Kathrin, "I shall put a stop to this, I shall phone my father, this just isn't fair, we only were married a few days ago, it isn't right eh?" "Yes," I agreed, "We just got married and it's the first time I've laughed like this in years!"

Helmut brought the mood down to a more sober level, "It isn't a party that you've been invited to, and it's a war Arnie, our war." What is it Hynie, what's really wrong?" I knew him well enough to know that his sudden change of mood signaled that something was seriously troubling him. "I also have to tell you that I am going to the front."

"Of course, if you want to come with me, that's fine, I can make arrangements I am sure. We can fix it up." But something about the stiffness of the set of his shoulders, the stillness of his eyes, the way he clenched his jaw meant that there was something more serious for him to consider, and then I realized what it was, "You bloody fool, you've done it haven't you, you've bloody volunteered to become more cannon fodder just like all the rest of the idiots. I'm right aren't I, that's it?"

Helmut squared up to face me, "Yes it is, and I'm proud to volunteer to defend the fatherland. I know you would do the same if you were able."

"Bravo!" said Kathrin, "Shut up both of you, don't you understand, my friend here is a lousy painter but he's an even worse fighter, he is going to get killed and to achieve what?

Helmut stood his ground, and Kathrin started to eat some nougat from the bag of snacks she carried with her in case of emergencies, she always ate in the face of conflict. "It would be better to live for your country rather than die for it, enough fools are doing that already."

Helmut smiled as if he was invulnerable, " I will come back, I promise." He squeezed my shoulder, "How will I run the business without you?" He was already walking away, down the path and out of our lives, he stopped at his car, before he got in, and "The business runs itself these days. Get one of your three hundred staff to be the butt of your bloody stupid jokes until I get back!"

He stood by the door of his car and I could see that there was no point in arguing with him; his mind was made up, "Promise me you'll come back you big idiot." I said, as if he could really keep that oath. "I can't shake your hand so." he hugged me in a masculine but spontaneous gesture. "Our lives are more like a melodrama every day." I said, "The world is falling apart, and there are no neat patterns or happy endings any more."

With that he got into the car and started the engine. "Don't get yourself shot." I called to him as he put the car in gear, "I will try not to, and look after that new wife of yours, she's all right." I returned his smile, "Better than that, she's also rich and happy!" He drove down the driveway, waving to me out of his window. I spoke to myself now; he was too far away to hear, "Promise me you'll come back old friend." I turned back to my home and Kathrin.

Chapter Eighteen

Tremendous bursts of gunfire sent showers of earth into the air around me as the Soviet fired their shells screaming at us. Our soldiers from the once proud 6th army were no longer recognizable as human beings. They ran from hole to hole in the wreck of the city. They had now been fighting for nearly four months to try and take this place, and it had become the great set piece battle of the war. It was rumored that there had already been more than two million casualties in this one battle, and there was still no winner or loser. Perhaps that was the message of this war; there are no winners. I looked around the wreckage, the buildings were truncated husks and the men darting between them shadow glove puppets dancing for their lives between the bullets of the snipers. I had come to the conclusion that I was both invisible and invulnerable. No bullet yet made had my name on it. I could run through the charnel house without a scratch, my job being to record these momentous and stupid events for posterity on my canvases.

I was convinced that I could safely rest my easel on the small hill constituted by fallen masonry and the bodies of soldiers from both sides. There I sat painting, puffing on my cigarette whilst the world was coming to an end in the apocalypse enveloping me.

I was blissfully unaware that a Russian sniper was observing me in minute detail through his rifle site, and had decided that he liked my work and the crazy way I did it. He must have been watching me as I tried to paint with my mouth, recording the carnage all around me. Quietly and slowly he put down his gun and picked up his crossbow. He aimed it very carefully and smiled just before he pulled the trigger. Moments later the arrow lodged itself in the corner of my picture, inches from my face. Attached to it was a note, "Keep your head down," it instructed me. I looked around for its source, but the shooter was too well camouflaged. I decided to keep my head well down. At least I had one fan on the other side!

I saw incredible and terrible things in those days in Stalingrad. No other battle could prepare you for what I saw. The number of bodies torn asunder, the dead unable to be buried in the hard unforgiving frozen ground, the snow, the cold, the unbearable cold that froze through your bones, it didn't matter how you dressed, you could never get warm. The spent, twisted metal everywhere, as if a giant toddler had thrown a tank here, a tank there, discarded torn buildings and cars, bits of flesh that were once living, breathing people lay unclaimed, seemingly uncared for. It was hell, and still it went on, unrelenting. I painted in a frenzy, somehow if I painted these scenes they might never be repeated, surely if people saw this ultimate destruction amongst the acts of heroism, stupidity and bravery they would realize the futility of it all.

I didn't notice the young soldier running in my direction across the scarred earthen landscape and then I spotted him only because the Russians opened up their small weapons in his direction as if he was a moving target at a fairground. I found myself cheering him on, along with other German soldiers who were witnessing his progress amongst the bullets whipping up the ground around his running feet. He ran, paused, sprinted, twisted and turned to thrown off the aim of those targeting him. Somehow he made it to my position unscathed; he saluted smartly, then stood, panting heavily as he looked at my painting with approval.

"Colonel Hessel?" he inquired with studied courtesy, "Yes," I replied, whilst thinking there couldn't be too many other colonels who were painting this scene at the front who were without the use of their arms. I couldn't hear the next words of the young soldier because just then there was a juddering series of artillery shells exploding all around our position, one of which blew both of us onto the ground. He carefully replaced my now dirtied painting back onto the somewhat broken easel and then, satisfied, he pulled me back onto my feet. "What is it you want, you can see I'm busy," I said, somewhat ungraciously. "General Paulus' compliments Colonel, he wishes to invite you to return with me for dinner." He said this with no trace of a smile of incongruity.

"I'm still too busy, can't you just send him my apologies?" I only needed a little while longer and I would have finished my painting. "I'm sorry sir, but I am instructed to bring you back with me, I think we might shortly be withdrawing to a new position." I looked from the boy soldier around the general mayhem, "But the Fuhrer says we are winning!"

His eyes followed mine as we both witnessed the white faces of the dead strewn all over the ground like discarded confetti from this wedding of death. The smoldering rubble clamors for the eye's attention against the burnt out, once deadly machines of war which stand here and there as monuments to death in battle. "So, General Manstein is going to save us all?" I asked him. "Those are General Manstein's men sir;" he said this whilst pointing to the dead bodies on the ground, "Come along sire, we must get going or we'll be cut off."

"No, you go, I want the world to see this through my eyes." I told him. The soldier took a last lingering look at me, considered me mad and bade me farewell, "Good luck sir, I'll tell the general you were unable to dine with him tonight." He smiled and so did I, and then he ran off, the same way he came. I don't know if he made it, but I hope he did, he had a wonderful smile.

The darkness closed in but I hardly noticed as my painting took an almost demented intensity. I didn't even feel the terrible cold creeping into every pore of my body. To anyone who glimpsed me they must have thought I was a frozen statue.

Eventually the inevitable happened and the Russians surrounded me, approaching ever closer until I was ringed by them, their guns inches from my face. I didn't move even when one of them prodded me with his bayonet. He barked a command that I thought must have meant, put your hands up. The one command I could do nothing about. Then a sergeant moved to the front of the crowd of bemused Soviet troops and said, in poor German, one syllable at a time, "Put, your, hands, up!" I told him in German, "I can't move my arms." But the phrase book he held didn't contain that answer so he hit me around the head with his heavily gloved hand instead. I didn't move. Another soldier cocked his rifle, "I'll shoot the stupid bastard."

He placed his rifle muzzle in my mouth and prepared to fire. Before he could do so, another voice shouted, "Halt!" The soldier removed the gun from me and joined his colleagues as they turned to the Russian officer. He wore no insignia, but we could tell from the way he carried himself that he is accustomed to instant obedience. "We need information, we already have enough bodies!" He walked up to me, and studied my painting, "You paint well enough for a German with no arms." He said in heavily accented German. I wasn't sure whether his words were meant as a compliment to me, but leaving me alive was certainly to be encouraged, "Thank you, sir?" He understood that I was asking after his rank, "I am a political officer Colonel, I don't carry rank. Bring him along." He instructed the two guards who were perpetually at his side.

The soldiers roughly grabbed me from both sides and forced me to march behind their boss who first took my canvas before leading our little group away into the gathering darkness.

We arrived at a Russian bunker, which, from the mess everywhere was apparently a rapidly deserted German position. The place was concrete grey, damp and cold. The light flickered as if the thud of the heavy artillery affected its supply. More likely the intermittent effectiveness of the small generator I had seen on the way down had more to do with the dimness.

We sat on hard wooden chairs facing each other, the Russian officer and me. He smiled pleasantly, "We are not the same technically as your Gestapo. Apart from the politics I mean, that bit is obvious I think. No, we don't bother with a good guy bad guy kind of routine. I do both, so for now you get the good guy, and then without warning I shall be the bad guy." With that he casually walked over to me and hit me on the nose. I felt the blood trickle down my chin.

"I appreciate that so far you have been most co-operative, or that would have been much worse, maybe a kick in the balls, always good for an opener, or for the very annoying, some fingernails out with the pliers, well you get the idea don't you?" "Yes, thank you, I get the idea." I didn't want to be hit again. "So the facts, you are Arnulf Hessel. Otherwise known as Arnie. We have established that you come from the town of Darmstadt in Germany. You are a painter and businessman by profession. You are a good painter, maybe even an outstanding painter. Did I tell you that already?"

"Are you going to release me?" I asked, "Do you mean ever?" he asked, seemingly quite reasonably. "I think we might, one day, but I suppose that would depend on your condition of release, there's release alive, like you are, or there's slightly damaged, or very much so, or there is dead. One way or another all things come to an end as you know. Tell me why I should let you go in your present condition?"

I looked around to see that there was no one else looking or listening, there was not, "I'm on your side, I am against the Nazis." His face twisted as if tormented by this question, and he shook his head sadly, "I do have difficulty with that point. I hear what you're saying I really do. But you would be surprised how many truly committed Nazis become Communists in this room just before they face the firing squad. Tell me why I should believe you, you are, as you have admitted, Hitler's special pet artiste; and I can see why, you are very talented, and the crippled thing, only adds to the appeal. But how do I know you're on our side, you're going to have to prove it I'm afraid. Go on, convince me."

"How could I convince you?" I pleaded, I knew how dangerous my position was, this man could shoot me and no one would ever know anything about my fate. "Well you should try very hard or you could be leaving here dead." He laughed at his joke, I found myself doing the same, and this mystified him, "Why do you laugh when your life hangs in the balance?"

"Every side must have one of you." I said, "What do you mean?" He asked more insistently, "I know your Nazi twin, his name is Ratwerller, we call him Rat, he did the same things to me, no he was worse, he also stole my wife!" I laughed again, "don't you want to live?"

"What difference would it make?" he paused before answering, "None really, but I live to collect knowledge, that's my reason for being, I exist to gather information for the collective. Tell me the story of this man Rat, and your supposed resistance activities."

So we spoke, it must have been for hours, because even in the gloom of that dunk bunker streaks of light eventually seeped in and I realized that another dawn had come. "Your stories are simply ridiculous." He concluded, after having told me many times that I had simply fabricated them to stay alive as long as I could. I was too tired to answer him. He looked at the notepad he had been meticulously writing my story on. "You will have to do much better. How can anyone verify any of these names, dates, times, places? You understand that I personally would love to see a man of your talent be released."

"Oh, is this the good guy talking?" I asked him, he smiled. "Yes, but its true nonetheless, I would like to believe you comrade, but how can I know, really know that you're not just another Nazi liar?

As he finished his question a huge brute of a man entered the bunker, he looked me over, as if measuring me for something. He looked over to the officer who nodded. The brute approached me as if he was running up to the start of an athletic event. Then, with all his might he started punching me, face stomach, face stomach, face stomach. I threw up what little food I had consumed, but still he didn't stop. The officer shook his head, as if shocked by the violence, "Help me to stop this." He pleaded to me, "What do you want from me?" I shouted, "The truth, tell me the truth!" he shouted back to me.

"For God's sake, how many Nazi spies do you think they sent to bloody Stalingrad without the use of their arms?" he nodded, but didn't display any humor, "You would be the first."

I lost my temper, "Shoot me you bloody fool, I can't stand to listen to your shit anymore!"

The Russian laughed and looked at his watch, "Perhaps some breakfast and a nice cup of tea, but first a little test of the electrics eh?" With that the brute whipped of my clothes as if I were a little boy. He dragged over what looked like a car battery from the side of the room where it had been covered by a piece of material. It had leads coming out of the device and I understood that this was going to be worse than the beating I had already taken.

"I thought you were the good guy." I tried to say through my broken teeth, "And the bad guy," he said, "But I told you the truth." I insisted, " We don't trust many Germans around here, I can't think why." As he talked the other man attached the leads to my balls with little care for my comfort. "Is there anything I can say to stop this?" I asked, "I'm no hero, I have nothing to tell you." With that he flicked the switch and I felt searing my pain tear through my groin and permeate every pore of my being. Just when I thought I would die, with my body in convulsive shock he broke the connection, "How was that, comfortable?" he asked, "Perhaps a little more juice?" He turned up the power and left it on a little longer, I was sure I would die, my heart must have nearly burst. "Tell me everything." He said, "I have told you everything!" I said, forcing the words out of my mouth one at a time. He turned the current off again. I exhaled, the sweat pouring from me despite the freezing temperature.

"Perhaps its time for breakfast, but before we go." He threw the switch again, and left the room while I writhed in agony, passing out from the agony. I don't know how long I was unconscious but when I came to my tormentor was back in his chair eating his breakfast. He looked happy and refreshed. "Tuck in," he said as his colleague solicitously fed me the promised breakfast. Between mouthfuls the Russian officer spoke as if we were old friends, "The battle goes well comrade. We are decimating the invincible German 6th army, chopping it into little pieces. What do you think of that; You Aryan super beings, beaten by us sub humans?"

"I don't like killing, but I would make an exception of you." He laughed, "You have big balls friend, big cooked balls!" he observed, "But we know you kill your enemies when you have to."

"But I don't like killing." I insisted, "Even your daddy?" "What do you mean?" I asked, "Your mother sends her love." "I don't understand." I said, "We can find out anything, we're everywhere, you know that don't you?"

"No I didn't" He beamed at me, "Killing that bastard of a man was a patriotic act, why not admit it to me, this is not a Nazi court."

"If you know so much then you must know that everything I've been telling you is true. What else do you want?"

He gathered up all his papers and fastidiously straightens them. Satisfied, he folds them twice and inserts the package into his greatcoat pocket.

"You must be tired Arnie, we've been talking almost non stop for two days. Have some rest. We shall talk again later. Now I have to go."

The Russian walked out of the bunker before telling me if I was free, but the hulking guard with the gun told me that I wasn't. I signaled to the man that I wanted to stand up and he nodded that this would be all right. As I did so waves of dizziness and nausea overcame me temporarily. I staggered over to the dirty mattress on the floor in the corner. I collapsed onto it and was almost instantly asleep.

I don't know how long I slept. The next thing I remember was being the sound of gunfire. I opened my eyes and saw my sadistic brute of an interrogator being riddled by bullets fired by the machine guns of a ring of grinning German soldiers who were surrounding me. The leader was the young messenger I had met earlier, immediately prior to my capture. "I could kiss you." I said to him as he smiled and pulled me to my feet, "I thought you boys would be half way back to Germany by now." The young man dressed me hurriedly with the help of his fellow soldiers, "The General's compliments sir, he said to tell you that if you don't come for dinner this time he shall have to presume you're snubbing him deliberately."

I laughed along with the soldiers. "I am a bit hungry now I think about it."

The contrast between the dank, cold bunker and the long disused ballroom of the seconded palace could not have been more pronounced. Now I found myself in ancestral glory brought low and mean by the terrible conflict. But the glory of what once had been was still visible to the discerning eye. How I wish I had been here to see what it once was. Now it was bedlam as the Russian's final big barrage of heavy guns opened up. Four senior German staff officers were gathered around a large map discussing strategy. It felt unreal to me, so recently being tortured during my interrogation to be present amongst such opulence and chaos. I had been ushered into the room by my young guardian angel. He had cleaned himself off since my rescue and had taken the opportunity to render me the same service.

He was ramrod straight as he led me into the swarming activity of the huge room, so inappropriate for its present purpose. Men and women of every rank were hurriedly gathering up everything transportable and packing the resultant bundles into crates that other soldiers wheeled away on metal trolleys in a never ending parade. The Adjutant led me through the chaos, "Forgive the mess Colonel." He informed me with the gravity of the situation readily apparent, "Such mess seems to be following me everywhere I go these days."

He left me standing at the end of the room as he approached the general staff at the map table. They whispered to and fro. They all had their backs to me and I was beginning to get impatient when they all turned to face me, in fact everyone in the room turned, and all were holding a drink in their hands and beaming at me, full of good humor, General Manstein raised his glass in my direction, "The Fuhrer himself directs me to lead a toast to our honored guest, Colonel Arnulf Hessel, now Iron Cross Second Class, and the father of twin sons, the toast is Arnie Hessel!" everyone raised their glasses and toasted me and I was, for once, unable to utter a sound. I must have been smiling stupidly, having no idea that Kathrin was pregnant with twins, or that the due date had been so imminent. The Adjutant kindly held a whisky glass for me to drink from, and the hot liquid pouring into my empty stomach soon hit home hard with a lovely glow.

The wonders of the German army and air force High Command was soon evident when they managed to extract me in one piece from the hell that was Stalingrad, returning me to the warmth and security of my own home within a day. Soon I was kneeling and cooing like a big soft teddy bear for my two lovely baby sons who were laying in their beautiful blue double pram, a personal present from Hitler.

I realize I was prejudiced but the boys were clearly the most handsome and brilliant babies ever born. Kathrin was sitting on a stool next to the pram, rocking it with one hand and eating a ham sandwich with the other. She looked every inch the earth mother as she smiled at her babies and triumphantly to me. I kissed her cheek tenderly. I was busy making silly faces, which the boys were studiously ignoring. "Did you have a nice time when you were in Russia?" she asked me. I could happily have killed her right then, but perhaps her happy lack of knowledge was a blessing in disguise. "I've always wanted to visit Russia. Do you think we might go there one day, when all this unpleasantness is over? I thought this over, "I think we might be getting a visit from our Russian friends first." I said, "That would be nice, new friends." Kathrin said, unbuttoning her chemise and placing one of our boys at each breast where they began to suckle hungrily. These are two boys who will never suffer malnourishment I thought. "You don't mean that the Russians are winning do you. Don't be so silly; Herr Hitler says we're winning so we must be winning. Where has he ever been wrong before?"

"Oh, and the long lines outside the shops, the rationing, the shortages, the bombing of our cities, they are all part of his master plan yes?"

"You're such a silly boy. Open up all our cupboards and you will see they are as full as ever. It's just a matter of knowing how to shop." She smiled again, "and being connected, but that was always the case wasn't it?"

"You do realize there is a war on don't you, and we really are losing?" She shook her head and looked down at the boys hungrily suckling from her, "Don't you go upsetting our boys you naughty man, wars a man business, if the world was run by us women there wouldn't be any wars. We're not so silly."

I sighed in exasperation, "What shall we call our sons?" This brought a smile back to her face, "I thought the older one should be called Bertie, after your father, but what do you think of calling him Adolf?" I could barely control myself at either choice; "Adolf, no I don't think Adolf is entirely appropriate here, can you imagine the little fellow with a silly moustache?"

196

she chortled, "Oh you're so silly." She chided me, "I was thinking Eric, Eric is a good strong name."

Kathrin nodded her agreement, "Yes, I like Eric, you can't abbreviate it, and I do so dislike it when people shorten a name, so Eric and Bertie it is." I smiled because she hadn't realized that she had already abbreviated the name Bertie. "Will you wheel the boys into the garden for us so that they can see their lovely garden." "I'll get the maid to do that, I could do with a little sleep for an hour or so, I've been so tired since I had the little darlings. Don't let them catch a chill out there, keep them wrapped up nice and warm."

I nodded and added, "We can just sit in the sun and have a chat, my boys and me." The maid, Gert, wheeled the pram out through the French windows. Kathrin left the room for her nap and I followed the pram outside to the garden.

We ambled toward the rose garden, my favorite part of the estate. Gert, the nursemaid, put on the brake of the pram and made sure the boys were well covered up and then left us alone to get to know each other. I couldn't help but smile as the two boys lay happily in the sunlit pram. It was then that I heard a low buzzing sound. At first it sounded like a very large bee but it was hard to place. I looked for a source but seeing none I almost dozed off even though the almost frosty. But that noise was getting louder and more insistent. Again I heard that sound, now closer and somehow it was becoming alarming. I studied the sky and there it was, one lone aircraft. Initially I wasn't worried but then I understood it was coming directly for my house, the biggest in the district, perhaps a natural target of chance. I could now see it was a lone RAF Lancaster bomber, what was it doing here, in this sleepy place, coming to visit me in my garden.

I looked from the airplane down to my two lovely baby boys, Eric and Bertie as they gurgled happily up at their new daddy. The plane was so close now, coming right for us, I looked at it, willing it to go away, but now it was blotting out the sky. "NO!" I screamed forlornly as I saw the bomb door was open and from

it a deadly cargo was being unleashed on us. I don't remember
if any other sound came from me as the bomb fell towards us. I
found myself racing the bomb toward the house but the bomb
won that race as it fell through the roof disintegrating it as if it
were some plaything made out of cardboard. The noise and the
shattering impact threw me back as my home simply evaporated
in a huge ball of fire, crashing and flaming in an incandescent
explosion as the world changed for us in that instant, and would
never be the same again.

The next period of time was a blur for me. I was once again
in mourning, and this time I didn't know if I could ever truly
recover. How many times does a man have to be struck down by
fate before it is acceptable for him to simply give up? I had no
one to ask but I tried to keep myself in one piece emotionally
because I still had my boys, and they needed me. But every time
I looked at their innocent faces I felt tears well up in me, and I
wondered how I was going to manage.

The shock stayed with me for a very long while. Burying
what remained of Kathrin was so traumatic I couldn't remember
more than the sketchiest details.

The next main event I had to force myself to organize was the
baptism of my boys. Despite his many drawbacks General Kleist
was a rock during this difficult time. He stood at my shoulder
and served as my stand in to hold the boys for the priest to
dip their heads in the baptismal font. I almost burst into tears
again as first Bertie and then Eric had their heads wetted, "Keep
it together son." He insisted to me, "I don't understand, why
would anyone want to hurt Kathrin, she never hurt anyone in
her life." He held himself straight as he stifled his own anguish
in order to help me through, "The Americans just had a spare
bomb left after their raid on Frankfurt, it was simply a target of
opportunity, nothing personal. Just war, that's all, just war."

I cried, oh how I cried that day and then the general's words
came to mind, and I cried no more, "Be strong Arnie, your sons
need you now." I looked at my boys, and I felt some of Kathrin's

sweet strength fill me, and then the general whispered to me again, "And the Movement needs you strong." I was so shocked that for a moment I didn't exhale, my breath trapped in my body. Kleist nodded his head and smiled, my tension evaporated as I saw in his eyes that he was telling the truth. But now that I had come out of my initial shock I was angry, "So, even my family is using me, haven't I given enough, more than enough?"

I looked away from the general and saw Marlene standing next to Ratwerller, "Do you want his world for your sons to grow up in?" Kleist asked, and I noticed that Ratwerller was smirking whilst Marlene was unmistakably sympathetic. "We haven't lost yet," I pledged to my family, living and dead, "We can still fight."

Chapter Nineteen

Frankfurt
March 22, 1945

In Frankfurt the Nazi flag still flew defiantly outside the sandbagged building, which housed the city's Gestapo headquarters. This street, like most of the others in the ancient city centre had been recently and relentlessly bombed by the allied onslaught. I found myself alternately cursing and cheering the waves of American and British bombers. They took it in turns; the Americans were over us in the daylight hours and the British at night. Seemingly never ending waves of heavy aircraft droned over our country dropping their immense loads of destruction down on us.

I had heard about what happened to my hometown in September of '44, they had literally wiped Darmstadt off of the face of the map. My town, once inhabited by over one hundred thousand people had been decimated. I had seen pictures of the almost unbelievable catastrophe but it was hard to reconcile those images with the beautiful ancient place in which I had grown up. But now such overwhelming, almost apocalyptic carnage was commonplace in Germany. We were being systematically brought to our knees.

The stench and mess of the bombs and the resulting horrific bloodbath was everywhere. Rubble was being cleared this morning like every other recent day. This revealed the gristly crop of the freshly dead and maimed. It was hard to believe that the mounds of smashed bricks were once proud buildings that had stood for so long.

There was an air of lethargy and defeat permeating every fiber of the worn out rescue parties as they sought to find life amongst death.

A very young blond boy drove me to the headquarters. He didn't look more than sixteen and he was wearing an ill-fitting brown suit. The once mighty Nazi machine was really reaching down far in the barrel if they were enlisting babies like this one. As we pulled up outside the once grand building the boy opened the door for me politely enough.

I had become middle aged without noticing I realized as I saw my reflection in the car window when I got out. Perhaps stress had accelerated my ageing. I straightened up, glad that my suit was still the finest cut and style. At least I would maintain those things I could control. I was ushered past the guards into the building and up a huge sweeping staircase to the familiar and magnificent set of double doors.

We entered and I was whisked past the busy office staff straight to Ratwerller's office. He stood and personally pulled a chair back for me opposite his own across his vast desk. He sent the boy out and asked how I was. "What do you want?" I asked, he made a tutting sound and shook his head. "No one is all bad," he admonished me, "the way you seem to think I am. I could be so insulted. But of course you're right about one thing. I did ask you to visit me for more than social purposes." "Get on with it Ratwerller." I growled.

"Perhaps the problem is that we're just too familiar with one another, you know the saying, familiarity breeds contempt. All these years we've been friends, sharing so much, in every regard, we should be the very best of friends, almost like brothers yes?" I waited, knowing that he would soon get tired of his baiting. "For example here I am seeking your advice, your guidance, your succor."

"Nervous that the Russians might get here before the British or the Americans? In that case I would recommend you follow the cyanide option for yourself, save everyone the trouble of a trial." "Do you think they'll be particularly bothered by me, a petty bureaucrat, I haven't be so bad, not when compared to some of my colleagues? My position was often misconstrued and misunderstood. I was just following orders. Like all soldiers must. My heart was always with the Movement. You'll recall how you and your associates were repeatedly allowed to carry on your noble resistance thanks to my personal intercession." I smiled, "And the fact that you were creaming off so much money from me. I'm sure that the Russians will be most understanding and sympathetic to all this rubbish. Are you rehearsing this for me? How charming."

"No, I think perhaps its time I went on a nice long vacation. I've not been allowed the luxury of a holiday in so long. Everyone needs a break, don't you think?"

"You didn't get me here to recommend a hotel did you, if the rat's are going to scurry away just go into the nearest sewer where you belong."

"Arnie, you really don't like me very much do you? Despite the fact that with my protection you've become one of the wealthiest men in this city."

"What is it, have you spent all the money you stole from me? I will gladly give you a bit more if it guaranteed you would vanish forever."

"Such hate," he hissed, "Can't we be friends, now it's nearly all over?"

"I prefer being your enemy." I looked into his eyes and as usual the dark pools gave nothing away. "We need each other, even now Arnie, we need each other. I made it possible for your genius to flourish, to leave questions unasked, questions that would have led, could still do, to a firing squad. You don't get it do you. I knew that with you I was always at a big disadvantage. You might not have the use of your arms, but you do have talent, look at how you can paint and draw. Me, all I can do is destroy and pull things down. I knew from when we were boys that my only real talent was to recognize the gifts of others, and to capitalize on them. We are inseparable; I think the correct word is conjoined. Two bodies feeding on one heart, and that heart would be yours."

"Are you really going to wait here to test your theories in front of a Soviet firing squad, I don't think so." Ratwerller smiled mirthlessly, "We still need each other. I have to get out of Germany and you will assist me."

"Why should I, our pasts have cancelled each other out." His smile grew wider, "I'm like a magician, remember that, I always have something up my sleeve."

"For this trick, to get me to help you when I am enjoying watching you squirm, I don't think you have anything left."

"OK, let's try this one on for size. I know where your friend Helmut is, do you?"

"He's at our headquarters." But I could see that my information was out of date, "Not any more." He told me, "Now he's at one of those awful camps. You know what they're like, not very nice, not too many people use the exit door."

"You've put Helmut into an extermination camp, is he all right. I will go straight to the Fuhrer himself about this. You forget I have the ultimate ace up my sleeve."

Ratwerller pulled open the central drawer of his desk and held up a piece of paper and examined it, "No you won't, and you'll read this note." He placed the paper in front of me on the desk. "So you forced a confession out of him. Hitler knows what such confessions are worth, do you think he'll believe this shit?"

"Well it was the best I could do at short notice, and you must admit it's very plausible. You sound like a very naughty boy, taking advantage of the Fuhrer's kindnesses. And it doesn't mention me once, did you notice that?"

"What will happen to Helmut?"

"If we co-operate, then nothing will happen to Hynie, nothing at all."

"And if I don't?"

"Well you won't have long to find out, I think he'll be having one of the camps special showers in;" he looked at his watch, "one hour, give or take a few minutes. And for sure I can arrange some nasty little car accident for you just to make it a perfect day. Who knows what would happen to those charming little fellows of yours in that situation. I suppose they would be taken into care. It's as I told you, we really do need each other."

"Is it for pleasure that you do this to me? You don't need me any more. You've got more money than you could spend. I'm sure you must have prepared your escape route long ago organized with your pals in the SS."

"I'm a businessman remember." He sighed, "haven't I proved that in our partnership? You will go on earning for me long after this nasty war is finished. Besides which you're a much better ally for me than the SS. You have credibility with both Hitler and the Movement. That's a win win." I tried not to allow a flicker of emotion show on my face now that Ratwerller had revealed that he knew I was with the resistance, but I had to know what he know, even at the cost of my own security.

"How did you know?" "Does it matter, I know." He replied, not bothering to conceal the triumphant look that surfaced on his face. "OK, we still need each other, what now?"

"It's time to leave Germany." He answered, "OK," I said, "But now, at the risk of everything, I have some conditions of my own, if we do this that's it, no more money, no contact, we're finished with each other, forever, agreed?"

"Yes," he said, "We have a deal."

As he said these words there was the sound of rolling thunder above us, and the bird songs seemed to stop as the shrill sirens sounded, the world held its breath and hell visited Frankfurt.

The building exploded around us and as the room blew apart Ratwerller jumped over the desk to protect me from the mayhem. The next moments were chaos compounded by terror, screams and deafness. I didn't realize that I was one of those screaming as we plummeted downwards with the building as it evaporated around us.

When I regained consciousness I found myself trapped under Ratwerller and a mountain of rubble. I tried shifting my body away from us, but he was wedged on top of me. I suddenly remembered that Helmut's existence would depend on my waking Ratwerller, if he was still alive, and getting him to find a telephone that was working, or Helmut would be murdered like so many others.

"Help, help, we're trapped!" I screamed at the top of my lungs, before I understood that I couldn't hear myself, my eardrums were ringing but useless. No one came, but I felt Ratwerller stir groggily, "Wake up you bastard!" I shouted into his ear, but I didn't know if he could hear me, or whether there was any sound coming from my mouth. "Ratwerller you little bastard, wake up!" I shouted, and at last he began to respond. He opened his eyes and we were staring at each other, inches apart. Now we were really conjoined I thought, unable to separate by even one centimeter. "What happened?" he croaked, and I could hear him a little, "we were hit by a bomb." I replied, "Don't shout, I'm right here on top of you." I hadn't realized that I was shouting. He tried to move off me, but something was trapping him on top of me. "I often thought what it would be like to be intimate with you Arnie, but this is not what I imagined." We both grimaced at each other.

"Can't you at least slide off me, your weight is crushing me." I said, "What do you think, I'm enjoying this, I have half a building on my back and I am protecting you from it and you are complaining." We lay there, with acrid smells and dust choking us for what seemed like an age, but in truth wasn't very long. However we tried to shift ourselves we were pinned helplessly to the ground. Ratwerller began to breathe erratically, "Do you think anyone knows we're here?" He sounded panicky, "Of course they do, and the one thing about you Nazis, the record keeping is meticulous."

"When we get out what are you going to do with Marlene," I asked, "So you do care?"

"Of course." What do I care? You can have her back, I'm finished with her now."

Not long after this we both heard the scrambling noise of the search and rescue teams, "Hello we're here!" I shouted, and within another few moments we were being dug out of our tomb. "If you don't get Helmut out of that camp in time all bets are off." I hissed in his ear just before we were pulled out, "Don't worry," he said, "he's been downstairs in a cell all along."

As always with Ratwerller I wasn't quite quick enough to find out the truth before he was gone, vanishing in the confusion and mayhem that surrounded the days bombing. Over one thousand people had died in those few minutes, but I didn't know where to begin to look for my friends.

The only person I knew who might help me was still living in one of the finest addresses in town. The roads were all but impassable, cratered by the huge bombs. But nothing was going to stop me finding that house. Eventually I found my way to the house I remembered from my childhood, once it had belonged to my grandparents, but now it belonged to Ratwerller. It was untouched by all the devastation around it, as I staggered up the stairs to the front door it was opened and there stood Marlene. She saw the disheveled state I was in and brought me inside.

As she cleansed my wounds with the easy familiarity of past intimacies she let me come to my senses in my own time. Initially I didn't know what to say, but it felt wonderful and cathartic for her gentle hands to wash my wounds. "How are the boys?" she asked eventually, incongruously I answered with extreme formality, "My sons are well, thank you." She finished her ministrations, and stood back from me. Our shared intimacy was over.

"Why did you come here?" she asked me, "I don't know." And that was the first honest words from me to Marlene for as long as I could remember. "We were married, we loved each other, there was too much left unsaid, we never finished properly, we need to tie up everything. It was no way to end our marriage."

She looked into my eyes, "You're right, but you knew what it was about. We did what was necessary."

"Will you help me this time, the movement has had enough of us don't you think?"

Without a moment's hesitation she nodded her head, "Of course, what do you want?" "Just like that, no conditions?" I asked, "I'm not Mister Ratwerller. You want my help, now or ever in the future, you have it."

"Let me tell you what it is first, you might not be so quick to be so generous."

"I gave myself, body and soul for our country, you deserve whatever is left." At that moment I wished I could wind back time, to what might have been had our lives not been contaminated by this poisonous war. Now we were two sad people looking to each other for comfort and memories.

"Do you remember when our lives were simple, eating, breathing and making love?" I asked, "Yes," she whispered wistfully, "Maybe one day it can be like that again." On saying this she reached across the distance between us with her hand caressing my cheek. I'm not ashamed to admit that I wept for us. "I'm sorry Marlene, but I don't think I'm mature enough to deal with the thought of you with him. Whatever the motive, I can't deal with it."

She looked at me as if I was a silly boy, and she was a woman, full grown, mature and pitying my inadequacy despite her love and warmth. "What do you want me to do?" she asked, anxious to change the subject.

"Get my sons to my mother." Marlene was surprised by this, "To Palestine, why?"

"There they can grow up as Jews, they can be themselves."

"But their mother wasn't Jewish, or their grandfathers."

"Hitler made them Jewish. Will you do this for me Marlene?"

"You know the answer Arnie, your boys will be safe with me." I smiled, knowing that this was the truth.

Hours later and I was with Ratwerller who was driving us in his open topped car fast down deserted country roads. He was dressed in full uniform. I watched the world as we sped past, it was as if the war had forgotten this corner of Germany, it was totally untouched. I looked at the Rat and wondered what twisted logic motivated him.

He was singing a Wagnerian aria from the Ring cycle, apparently happy with the glorious winter day. "How do you sleep at night?" I asked him. He briefly looked away from the road, "Like a baby, I sleep the sleep of the just. Your problem Arnie, and it was always thus, is that you simply don't understand the ways of the world."

"The ways of your world I don't want to understand."

"Whatever system there is in control of our lives, and there will always be a system of control, the systems always need functionaries like me, we make it all go tick tock, tick tock. I do the smelly jobs, and we do them without question because someone has to take the shit out. I'm necessary, more necessary than some painter or poet."

"You believe that?" I asked, "Of course I believe that, don't get me wrong, I was never a Nazi, not really. Oh of course they did some things right as history will prove, but some of their ideas were plain stupid. But I had a great war and I have a lot to be grateful to them for. But I will serve the Communists or the Allies just as well. Make no mistake, they all have their little Ratwerllers, just like me."

Before I could respond to his cynicism he swerved the car off the centre of the road as bullets tore into the car's windscreen. I looked up as we crashed into the bushes and trees and caught a swift glimpse of a lone British Spitfire fighter plane as it swept past our position and banked steeply preparing to attack us again.

As we smashed into the trees I could see that Ratwerller had been wounded in the arm and was unable to steer, I sat helplessly as we hit the trees and although I braced myself with both my legs there was nothing I could do as the Rat's head and shoulders smashed through the car windscreen.

The doors of the car were forced open as we hit a huge tree and seeing this opportunity for escape I leapt from the car. As I lay on my back looking up and panting from the effort I saw through the canopy of trees as the RAF plane completed it turn and came in for the kill. I braced myself to die, convinced that this was it, my time to die. I saw Ratwerller stir and instinctively I jumped to my feet and back into the car, Now I was operating on adrenaline as I raced against the aircraft as it swooped towards us and I tried to brace my back against the leather seat and use my legs to kick Ratwerller sideways from the car. Somehow his body began to slide half out of the car but it was so difficult.

I looked up and the fighter plane seemed to fill the sky above me, I could see the pilots face as he pressed the firing button of his guns and the bullets tore into the car, tracing their way up the bonnet of the car just as Ratwerller's body fell from his side of the car and I jerked in the opposite direction from it. The bullets tore the car apart but I hadn't been hit. The Spitfire flew away, its engine noise reducing as it departed. Ratwerller was standing and shaking his fist, "British bastards!" he screamed, and then realizing the danger we were still in he rushed around the car and dragged me away as it's petrol tank exploded in a ball of flame.

For a long while we lay exhausted on the ground, unable to get up. We looked at each other and I wondered why we were like cats. Why did fate want the two of us to live?

Later, the wreckage smoldered but the flames had burnt out an American army Jeep screeched to a halt. The two soldiers in it got out of their vehicle, pointing their weapons in our direction, suspicious of the circumstances. "Help me please, I'm trapped over here." I called, in my best English. The older man, an officer approached me slowly, he looked like he would have been happier driving a taxi in New York. "Bill," he called to his colleague, "Check the Nazi bastard out, any funny stuff and you shoot his head off, shoot first answer questions later, got it?"

I lay very still, and hoped for the best. Bill called back to his officer, "Can't we shoot the bastards anyhow, and no one'll know the difference?"

The officer ignored Bill and moved closer to the inert body of Ratwerller. He nudged him with his boot and Ratwerller grunted in agony. Meanwhile Bill knelt by me. "You look OK, kind of, but I think I'd best shoot you anyhow." "What did I do to you?" I asked him, "Let's show the bastard!" the officer shouted back. He dragged Ratwerller to his feet, and I was roughly manhandled and handcuffed my wrist to the Rat despite my trying to explain that I couldn't use my arms. We were shoved into their Jeep and we rapidly drove off.

The vehicle forced its way through an ever-increasing flood of hapless and ragged refugees. Signs of a recent bloody battle were all about us. Burnt out tanks and half tracks and unattended German corpses littered the roads. "Will you let me explain, I am not a Nazi!"? I tried again to tell the Officer. "Sure you're not. You're just out joyriding with your Gestapo pal here."

Ratwerller smiled, "I told you Arnie, every system has their own Ratwerller," "And you can keep your smart mouth shut!" said the officer to Ratwerller.

We were silent in the Jeep as we drove into a camp. It seemed innocuous enough and the only thing that struck me as strange was the wording of the slogan set above the gates, "Work will set you free." We drove past two American guards. Large bonfires lit the area, casting weird shadows. It was then that we began to see and understand where we were.

Emaciated men, women and children sat in small groups. They are skeletal; their eyes appeared huge in contrast to their sunken faces. Behind them, in a huge pile we could see something. At first we thought it might be piles of wood, or discarded clothing but as our eyes adjusted to the gloom we understood that these were thousands of unburied human bodies. We had entered a shadow world that I had dreaded, had partially imagined in my worst nightmares, but couldn't believe was possible. Nothing could prepare a human being for the shocking totality of this.

Medical orderlies were spraying disinfectant over the living and the dead with spray guns. Their masked faces lent an almost science fiction feeling to the scene. The officer turned to us, "Give me one good reason why we shouldn't shoot you Nazi bastards here and now?"

Ratwerller turned to face him, "Because you are a civilized man." He replied. Bill raised his gun and aimed it at Ratwerller, who winced as he thought his life might finally end, "You can't want to be like the people who did this." I said to him.

The American officer forced Bill's gun arm down to the ground, he seemed to realize that I wasn't like the Nazi's he had encountered up to then. "Undo that one's handcuffs." He instructed, which Bill then did. "What's wrong with your arms?" the officer asked, "Why do you ask?" "Because a normal person rubs his wrists when we take the cuffs off, everyone does that."

"I haven't been able to use my arms since I was seven years old. Polio." The officer was baffled, he looked at me thoughtfully, "Why didn't you say something?"

"Would you have believed anything I said?" "No, I guess not, I wasn't in the mood to listen. Come on, follow me." He said to me, and then led me away from the horrific backdrop. "What about me?" called Ratwerller, "I'm bleeding to death!"

The officer looked back over his shoulder at Ratwerller, "Good."

I followed the man into a large prefabricated hut that the Americans had erected inside the camp. It was clean and full of the best American supplies; in fact it was like being in an American microcosm. Everything had been shipped from the USA. We sat on two stools with our backs resting on the bar. The windows were blacked out by closed shades and the walls decorated with posters and pictures depicting American scenes. The officer was soon swigging beer from the bottle and occasionally held another bottle for me to do the same. He gestured to the room and the other men who were also taking some time out to have a drink, "This keeps us sane, this little bit of home."

"It's very nice." I commented, "My name is Hank Aaronson. Henry really, but you can call me Hank." "You come from New York Hank?"

He took another long pull from his bottle and gave me one from the other bottle, "Near enough Arnie, Philadelphia, how about you, where are you from?"

"Darmstadt, it was a little city, but now its gone. Do you think you are going to let me go Hank, I really was one of the good guys?"

He sighed and looked at me intently, as if studying my face would give him some answers. "You know what my job is going to be. I am a combat marine but now they have me sorting through this place to find out who were the Nazis and who were the good guys, someone has to run things in the future, maybe someone like you could help me, maybe I could get a handle on how this all happened."

"You're in intelligence?"

"Well kind of, but you've got nothing to worry about from me have you. I need to talk with you, folks like you anyhow. How could this have happened, you people seem like regular folks back home. You seem normal, a stand up guy. Tell me, did you all just go crazy one day?"

"No," I shook my head, "it happens inch by inch, the madmen take over a place and turn it into an asylum where they, the mad people are in charge. Once you believe that black is white and white is black, then anything begins to seem the wrong way around. It's their big lies. Once the big lies become an accepted fact then everything follows that madness. It's as if the country was a tree and the tree was poisoned, then all the fruit that comes from that tree will also be poisoned."

He looked at me thoughtfully, "What's your story, how did you end up sharing a car with that piece of garbage?"

"Is this an interrogation Hank?" He smiled, and he shook his head, "More like some friendly questions and answers. I can't help it; I was an attorney before this war interrupted my career. Now take another swig of this excellent beer and answer my questions."

I did as he suggested, the beer was cold and although not to my normal taste, it was fine. "It's a very long story," I began, "We've got nothing but time." He encouraged me.

A long time and a great many beers later we were still talking, but we were now both loosened up by the booze. "One thing is for sure Arnie, no two things," he slurred his words slightly, "One is that if you're a woman its really not a great idea to get too close to you, it is dangerous, no question, and two is, you need legal representation. Did I give you my card?"

"I don't need a lawyer right now." Was all I could think of to say. He smiled and continued, "If you're thinking of doing any business in the United States you need a lawyer or you'll be skinned alive."

"Why? I don't need one here unless there's a special contract." He looked at me with pity, "Bubela, you're going to have register as a charity, no tax that way, what a wonderful scam, a business for the handicapped, run by the handicapped, for the benefit of the handicapped, its beautiful. You're going to need headquarters, staffing, expanded funding, political connections, they've got to be vetted, and you've got to be protected."

"Who from?" I asked with a growing sense of exasperation, "From people like me you idiot!"

I could only smile at his honesty about his potential dishonesty. "You're playing games with me?"

"Sure I am. It beats us thinking about that mess outside don't you think?" With that he walked to the door of the hut, somewhat erratically, "I only drunk this much since I got here you know, before I was here it was coffee and a cigarette, now I don't sleep so good. You know what I mean?" I nodded my head. I understood. I wouldn't be able to sleep with those images burnt behind my eyes.

We were both compelled to leave the warmth of the hut to witness the reality of our surroundings, this nightmare, what the Nazi inheritance was going to mean to us all. This was a vision of hell on earth. We walked past people too weak to stand; too scared to sit in case they would simply die unnoticed. Steam seemed to seep from the ground and through these living skeletons, they looked at us with their huge eyes, and we shared the intimate knowledge that they were nearer to their maker than the world we were standing in.

I was too numbed too cry for them, and too inadequate to do anything other than register what I was seeing so that I could paint it later. It was a part of me that I hated, this divorcing of me from my surroundings in order that I could regurgitate the scenes I witnessed to order, even re-inhabiting the moment. This meant I was sometimes present but not there emotionally. Women, especially, hated this part of me, which I could do nothing about.

Hank led me to another American temporary building. We entered. A young soldier was asleep at his desk. The room is plainly some kind of records office. Papers and files are strewn everywhere. Some of the papers are partially burned. Hank spoke to me quietly, anxious not to wake the soldier. "You people kept real fine methodical records didn't you. Seems that some of the high ups weren't so proud and tried to burn them, but a bit too late, we stopped them just before they made a big bonfire of the whole bunch."

"Why did you bring me here?"

"I believed your story. I think maybe you'll find something that leads you to your pal, Helmut in here. It's worth a shot."

I looked at him with new regard, regard and respect. "Maybe I should have one of those business cards of yours." He smiled and placed a card in my jacket pocket. "Sure you do, everyone needs a mouthpiece." We looked at each other, and both of us knew a new friendship had just been struck.

Hank went behind the young sleeping soldier and shouted in his ear, "Wake up soldier, you've got work to do!"

The soldier woke comically, almost falling out of his seat with surprise. He sprung to attention and knocked his chair over.

While I was engaged looking at endless books of photos Ratwerller was seizing the opportunities that fate presented him with. I wasn't aware of it, but he was making sure that our fates would continue to be interwoven.

Several hours later and I was as weary as the young soldier. We had been working together for hours before I decided to leave after finding no leads. Hank entered the hut and asked me if I had made any progress. I shook my head, "So many photographs, so many faces, gone, all of them gone. All of them dead?"

"Yes," he was quiet a moment, thinking about those huge files of lost people, "Anyone whose record is in that hut is past tense. So if your pal was here, and not listed amongst those people he could still be alive."

"How many of these places were there?"

"We're still finding them all over this part of Europe, too many to count. Are you going to keep looking for your pal?"

"What would you do?"

"Same as you, I'd look until I couldn't look no more. That makes us two dumb shmucks. You ready for some more bad news?"

I wasn't sure I was but what could be worse than this place? "Tell me." I said, "Your friend, Ratwerller, he's escaped. He must have got out somehow, security thinks he must have dressed as an inmate after stealing clothes, and possibly the identity from a dead man"

215

"That would be typical of him, what are you going to do about it?" I asked, nonplussed by this turn of events.

"What we call a SNAFU, situation normal, all fucked up, what can I tell you, you know that's how comes you win wars, you fuck up just a little less than the other guy and you win."

"Don't you realize what a dangerous little bastard he is? You have to send men after him."

"What do you want me to do stick a broom up my ass so I can sweep the floor as I'm looking? We're chasing a nation of dangerous little men, he ain't any worse than a whole pile of the bastards, believe me."

I couldn't maintain my anger with him, I found myself smiling, and realized that Ratwerller would have to wait for another day. "At least there is one upside to all this, that creep Ratty or whatever his name is, he won't dare show his face round here again, and that means he won't bother anyone around here again."

"I hope you're right. Hank, can you do me one more favor?"

"Sure thing, name it," he said, "I want to go home."

It wasn't long and Hank, good as his word, had arranged for the American military machine to crank up and transport me back to my home. As the jeep dropped me by the front door of our old Darmstadt Hessel family home I could see it was still shuttered and appeared to be in one piece, if sadly neglected. It looked forlorn somehow. The driver took the key from under the ornate flowerpot to the left of the front doors where we'd left it and opened the house. He stood aside as if it would be inappropriate for him to enter my home before me. He stood awkwardly to one side as I entered. I smiled in his direction, "It's all right, you don't have to worry about me, I can look after myself," I assured him, and hoped it was true as he said goodbye and left me alone with my memories.

After a while it wasn't so bad. I had been able to enlist domestic help from local women only too pleased to be earning something again. I found myself compelled to be in my studio, painting without stop. Compelled to commit to canvas everything I had seen. The scenes I painted were nightmares that occupied my mind, sleeping or awake, I was obsessed with these images, and knew that it was something I had to paint until I could paint no more. Every dead body, every walking skeleton, the chimneys, the pleading eyes, all of it, all had to inhabit my canvases to bear witness forever.

Day followed day for me in a blur that turned into weeks and months as this series of paintings flowed from my brush as if painted by someone who had control over my body.

Eventually the weather started to turn and old habits took over and I found myself continuing my work in the Rose Garden, where I had always found solace painting since I was a boy. It was one day, whilst I was painting one of those terrible camp scenes that I felt a presence behind me. I was nervous but there was nothing I could do to defend myself against the intruder, I slowly turned to face the stranger. As I did so he spoke, "I don't think it will sell very well this Christmas Arnie." It was Helmut, my old friend had returned to life!

He was gaunt and dressed in rags, but it was Helmut, threw the dirt and his beard you could still recognize him. He was smiling and as happy as me. He rushed over and hugged me and we both wept unashamedly. We pulled back after a while and looked at one another.

"I looked for you, I tried so hard, but no one knew where you'd got to, you're OK?" I asked, "Eventually I learned to bend with the wind old friend, it was a tough lesson."

"It's wonderful to see you Hynie. That bastard Ratwerller, he told me you were killed in the bombing."

"Since when did you believe a single word that the Rat said? I heard about Kathrin in town. I'm sorry, you'd grown to love her, yes?"

"Yes," I replied simply, it was the truth; I had grown to care for her very deeply, not in some passionate way, but with a caring and tender emotion that can be just as compelling and perhaps longer lasting. "Yes, I loved her but now she's gone, I'm alone with you my old friend, just like the old days, two boys together, it will be great."

I said it, but neither of us felt like those innocent boys any longer. "What about Marlene and your boys, where are they?"

"She's helping the boys grow up in the only place where this poison won't touch them and the men they'll become."

He didn't ask me any more about this for the moment, waiting for me to continue my explanation as I nodded towards the painting, "How could we ever explain any of this to them?"

"How do you feel about Marlene now?" He recognized my silence as his excuse to change the subject, "Well time is a great healer, so they say."

"Fancy a drink?" I asked, and he smiled his assent and we walked back to the house, "I could drink the entire Rhine if it was made with whisky and beer!"

Over the next hours we tested our drinking capacity to the limit. Eventually we were amiably chatting the kind of semi-inebriated nonsense reserved for such times.

"You know, to be honest, you don't look too bad considering what you've been through. What camps were you in?"

"I was in a transit camp, or was it a prisoner of war camp, and then a de-Nazification thing, and then I was here. I don't bloody know do I. What do you mean?"

"That lying bastard Ratwerller said you were in the cellar of the building when it went bang, said you were buried there, said you had to be dead, lying little Rat, how comes God doesn't kill the little shit and do the world a favor, if there's a bloody God how does he let that Rat get away with what he's done?"

"Let's have another drink, fuck the little shit Rat, he'll get his, eventually the world moves in mysterious ways, and it all gets leveled out, and he'll get his."

"Do you think so, do you really think so?" I asked, and that was the last thing I remember of our drunken reunion.

Chapter Twenty

New York, USA
July 1956

We were sitting outside an elegant art gallery opposite Central Park West. The display window contained an oversize self-portrait of me in it. Self-promotion had never embarrassed me but New York took it to extremes that I enjoyed hugely. There was a sign by the painting that read, "Tonite the Gallery On The Park is proud to present the first American Gala Exhibition of the Works of Arnulf Hessel."

A long black limousine swept up to the curb as I enjoyed the summer warmth on my face. Helmut jumped out of the back seat of the long vehicle, "Well," he said, "What do you think?"

"I still don't see the point of all of this." I nodded toward the gallery, I admit in retrospect, being somewhat tetchy, perhaps I was just tired. "We've discussed this a thousand time Arnie, you need an up market image. You need critical acceptance in America if we're ever going to break this market big time."

I shrugged, "I don't know what's so special about America, their art is shit, and this country is shit. Everything here is so complicated." It was a cry from my heart; I had enjoyed life so much more when it was simple. We entered the building with Helmut fussing about like a mother hen, hugely excited by the whole American experience.

The Gallery interior was one of polish and moneyed restraint, We walked into the middle of a row between my American mouthpiece, Hank, now thicker set and suited in the best that Saville Row could offer, and an elegant younger woman. They both turned to face us as we entered. "Hello you two. Meet Susie Robarts, and don't let her southern country girl accent fool you, she's harder than nails." I looked at the woman and imagined what it would feel like to know her more intimately. I wished I was more mature, but my penis had no conscience, and it was with my penis that I thought. Susie and I exchanged smiles, and there was a moment when I realized Susie and I could be more than business associates. I caught Hank and Helmut exchange weary and knowing looks, "Do you like our gallery mister Hessel?"

"Call me Arnie, please," I looked around the gallery and noticed the exquisite and beautiful décor, "Well what do you think, we just did the facelift."

I tried to be polite, "It's very nice, indeed it's more than pleasant." But I thought that it was like her, a bit uptight, too much hidden, not enough revealed, you need a little taster to anticipate the culmination with more relish.

Susie wasn't happy with my response, "That's a bit worse than telling me its unique, do you like it or don't you?" She was very intense when she was angry, I couldn't help notice that her titian hair was her real color, her natural alabaster white skin was now reddening as her anger deepened. I loved her passion. Both of us lost sight of the fact that Hank and Helmut had wondered off, knowing that anything they had to say at this moment would be ignored by both of us. I also noticed that the little part of her cleavage visible above her one open blouse button blushed as only a red haired woman can. It was very appealing and I wanted to see more of the woman concealed under her buttoned down appearance. I was sure there was a tigress smoldering just below her controlled surface.

"What do you want me to say Susie, that it is awful?"

She nodded her head in agreement, but was unable to stop herself pointing her finger at me in accusation, to punctuate her words, "If you think its awful then tell me its awful!"

"But I don't think it's awful, it just isn't what I would have done with it."

"Oh," she said, "What would the great artiste have done with it?"

I smiled to try and lighten her mood, "Less."

This made her think for a moment, and she looked around, and then nodded. "Why are you so angry?" she asked, and I thought about her question and understood why she asked it, I had become a grouchy middle-aged man without noticing it. My edges had been chipped, rubbed and burnished until they no longer existed and what was left was a ball of anger and frustration. I saw all this reflected in the eyes of this young, perceptive woman who had seen right through my hard carapace to where I was still soft and vulnerable, and I liked her for that. We both saw through each other, and it was refreshing.

"You know what your New York clients want, I have no idea, I only know what appeals to me."

"Oh," she said, a smile playing at the corner of her glossy crimson lipstick mouth, "and do you see anything that appeals to you?" the double entendre was obvious, but none the less appealing; I returned the smile, "I don't like exhibitions; the nerves make me physically sick; do you know anywhere else to go and spend time more creatively?"

She knew what I meant, but she wasn't going to make it that easy for me, "You have to be kidding, you've had exhibitions all over Europe and South America already."

"And I've been sick an awful lot lately."

"I'm trying to keep this conversation above the belt, let's keep this professional, at least in the gallery, tell me what you think about the exhibition I've mounted for your work?"

"You have adorable eyes." I answered, and it was true, they were stunning, the fleck of another, deeper color highlighted the green, in her now angry eyes, "Why do men like you put women down that way?"

I'd paid her a compliment and couldn't understand what I'd done to make her angry, "But your eyes are beautiful, and I, as an artiste and a man want to tell you I had noticed and appreciated them, and I could add your skin is perfect, you would make a wonderful model for me to capture on canvas."

Her irritation was now almost uncontainable, "My exhibition must be truly tragic if you want even comment on it."

"And your lips are like petals that just need water to make them bear fruit." I was enjoying myself, and she was trying hard to deal with me on two levels, "And you just happen to have some water available to do the job right?"

"I want to kiss you, everywhere, but first I want to trace your body with my tongue, tasting you, my tongue being my fingers, but much more sensitive."

I saw the flush in her cheek, and I knew my sensual thoughts were beginning to register with her imagination, "I've heard some good pick up lines in my time, but you must think I'm a real sucker."

"Because I want to share myself with you?" I asked with feigned innocence, "What is it, do you have a bet on with your friends over there, whoever lays the chick wins a free dinner?" she asked.

"Do you dislike my work that much?" I responded, throwing her momentarily off balance with my change of tack, "What are you talking about?"

"You're the curator here lady, you arranged this exhibition of my work, you're supposed to be an expert, and you don't understand that I'm about passion, and commitment. Do you really believe I would compromise these beliefs with something as sordid as you are suggesting?"

Susie was contrite, "I'm sorry, I don't mean to put you down, but you have to admit you do come on pretty strong, and we hardly know one another."

"I'm an artiste, is it wrong for me to express my honest passion, is it wrong, can it be wrong, when two people meet under especially intimate circumstances, to find release for our fleeting, but nevertheless true and intense needs and loves of each other. I want us to know one another, to experience everything, to have and to let go, to take every opportunity to live life to the full, to create memories that we will share forever, just you and me?"

She giggled almost coquettishly, something this sophisticated woman probably hadn't done since she was fifteen years old, "Stop it, this is embarrassing," she said, but her eyes said carry on, I'm enjoying this flirtation, I leaned towards her so that only she could hear my whisper, "I want to be inside you, I want you to feel me, to share our rhythm, and I want you to know what a special experience it is to share love with a man who can only use his mouth and his manhood." She didn't pull away, and I know I had her; all that remained was to reel her in without panicking her. "Is this something you always do you naughty man?" she whispered back to me. I smiled and so did she, "Follow me," she instructed and I did so, willingly. I was mesmerized by the sway of her wonderful posterior as she sashayed down the wide corridor, I had no eyes for anything but her derriere, what a lovely ass that woman had. She swept into her private office and after I had followed her in she closed and locked the door.

"I won't run away, promise," I assured her. She smiled and swept her desk clear, knocking everything to the floor. "You aren't going anywhere just yet mister Hessel."

She took off her street clothes and I was delighted to notice that she wore sheer black stockings and suspenders, a lacy bra and sexy black silk knickers. She closed the distance between us like a big cat and I could smell her soft perfume and the beginning of her arousal. I let her lips touch mine, and our tongues swirled in each other's mouths. She reached down and felt me and made a small noise of satisfaction, "I can see why the girls like you mister Hessel, little Arnie's a big boy isn't he, and he wants to come out to play." We both grinned as with one hand she took my penis from my trousers and stroked me. After a little while she removed her bra and I saw her firm breasts, they had the most tasty nipples that stood up, waiting to be kissed, sucked and licked, and she allowed me to worship them, first one then the other, until she began to moan with pleasure. "Eat me." She implored, removing her knickers. I looked at her shaven mound and I had a feast.

Eventually we both felt the moment had arrived and she stood back from me, a vision of pleasure and unselfish giving, a gorgeous mature woman, who wanted the ultimate intimacy, "I want you inside me, now." She instructed, and this was one instruction that it is always advisable for a man to follow, the rewards are perfect.

We had built to such a pitch of mutual hunger that there was nothing that could delay us, she threw her coat on the floor and lay on it, she spread her legs and we found each other. She was loud and unrestrained, and I remember wondering what the other staff going past her office would make of the noises. But I couldn't care less as we moved together, and reached a crescendo of repeated mutual satisfaction.

"Don't you ever stop?" she shouted in my ear, "No, don't stop!"

I heard someone rattle the door, but fortunately the lock held, it was Hank, "Everything all right in there?" he called. This brought us back to earth. It took us a few minutes to get dressed, me being helped by Susie, who couldn't keep the smile off her face. She patted me on the cheek; "I should bottle you and keep you in my purse." She finished straightening herself up and I waited while she left the room past the seemingly unfazed Hank. I came out a moment or two later, he stuffed a one hundred dollar bill in my jacket pocket.

"You screwed the ice lady, that is truly amazing, no one has even got to first base with her before, everyone thinks she's a lesbian. How do you do it?"

I smiled, "I don't think she's a practicing lesbian any more and you don't have to pay me on the bet, it was a pleasure."

"Amazing," he repeated, "come on dish the dirt, what was she like, what's the secret?"

"We're both grown ups and a gentleman never tells. But as I have never been a gentleman I can tell you she is a real fire cracker." I continued, "And all you have to do with her or any other available woman is say what she wants to hear and do what women love to do."

"Sure, like I never did that." he said, "I've done that three times and all I got were three sets of alimony payments I have to make."

He led me into the crowd who had gathered with the opening of the exhibition. At least Susie had taken my mind of this aspect of my profession, which I genuinely loathed.

Strangers, critics, friends and enemies swirled up to me and spoke, but I found it hard to concentrate on anything they said. My life at this point was empty and vacuous, I lived to screw around and party, to be a money making machine. I didn't care or feel, all I could do was count the unending tide of money as it enveloped me and all those around me.

I reacted to the strangers who swirled around me but I didn't think about what they were saying and I followed my newly acquired habit of being flippant and ridiculous, seeking to outrage and gain notoriety in the easiest way I could.

A huge black man blocked my path, "I'm Washington Abercrombie, Rutgers University." He boomed, "And I am Arnie Hessel, Darmstadt, Germany." I responded with my usual cynicism, "Your art is simplistic, without a pattern, and your attitude is paternalistic and your subject matter is overly schmaltzy."

I laughed in his face, "And you're here why?"

"To tell you what I think." I felt the presence of Hank and Susie who had overheard this exchange and were immediately seeking a blocking position between Washington Abercrombie and me. "It's OK," I said, "So why does your university purchase my work?" I asked him, "I don't rightly know Hessel; I'm from the math department, I just wanted you to know that some of us believe you are costing our university money it can ill afford."

A familiar voice interrupted him, "And you are a rude and ignorant man who should go back to counting!" I turned and there was that familiar smile, Marlene, who never failed to surprise me had done so again. Abercrombie was not so easily deterred, "And what right do you have to dismiss like that?" he asked her. Marlene, who looked great, looked at him steadily, "Go away you silly man, I have a lifetimes to catch up on with my man." Abercrombie looked between us and walked away as Marlene closed the distance between us and hugged me. It was so wonderful to feel her arms around me, "It's been too long." I said, and for once I meant it, she took half a step back, looked into my eyes, and nodded her head. "You're still a devastating old goat." "You never fail to astonish me, and talk about devastating, you look wonderful!"

Marlene smoothed her hair and turned to Helmut, "Where can I take this man for a drink and to catch up?" He opened the back door of the limousine and ushered us both in, "Your carriage awaits my prince and princess. It's all set up for you, just relax and enjoy."

The driver, a laconic New Yorker spoke to us, "Don't worry, I ain't about to turn into no pumpkin!" and drove us gently into the night.

We sat back after Marlene put up the partition between the driver and us. She looked around the back of the almost palatial car. It was great to see Marlene again. She found a bottle of brandy in the bar between our seats and poured us both a drink. She took a swig and gave me one also. "It's been a long time Arnie." "Too long." I agreed, "Why didn't you come back for me?"

She took another swallow, "You didn't really want me, you wanted a memory, a dead memory." Marlene gave me another pull on the drink, "Why does everyone have to make things so complicated all the time? We were happy once, we could be happy again."

"Aren't you happy?" she asked, looking me directly in the eye, "No, no I'm not, I got everything I ever wanted and in the end I realized it was all nothing."

"I'm sorry for you, I really am." She stroked my hand with her own. "Don't feel pity for me, you know I can't deal with people pitying me. Let's change the subject. What about you, what have you been doing, where have you been?"

"Oh you know, here and there, this and that, learning to live again. After I got your mother and the boys to Israel I went to Tel Aviv and." She paused, and it was significant, "And?" I asked, "You can't leave it like that, and what?"

"I met a man, Yigal, and we were married, he is a very kind man, a strong man, solid, dependable."

I tried not to let her see my hurt, but it was like a dagger between my ribs, it took the breath out of me. "Say something, be happy for me," She implored. "You found happiness with this man, with Yigal?"

"He has given me a home, and peace, security and hugs, sometimes these are the best things in the world. And I have this with him."

"But do you love him?" I persisted, "Yes, I love him, with all my heart." She was crying for what might have been, for us, and for all that had been lost. I found myself crying also; "I'm happy for you Marlene, I will always love you and I want the best for you, you deserve nothing but the best. But why didn't you let me know, at least I could have sent you something nice as a present."

"I wasn't sure how you would react. Neither was your mother. She told me I had to kiss you for her." Marlene kissed me, and I don't know if I was hoping for something different, but there was no passion, just a quiet echo of love.

"Ah, so the plot thickens, my mother has sent you to me, what does she want?"

"No, not really, Yigal is in Washington with the trade delegation. But your mother is concerned about you. Why don't you telephone her or the boys, or at least dictate some letters?"

"They don't even know me, what would be the point? It would just confuse them."

"You're their father. See if from their point of view, stop being so bloody self centered. To them it must feel as if they must have done something wrong. You just cut them out of your life."

"I send money, they have their own lives, and it's not a life spoilt by all my rubbish. I check regularly that they need for nothing."

Marlene slapped my face, hard. "That went with the kiss from your mother. She thinks you deserve that slap, and so do I."

She knocked on the glass partition and it lowered electrically. The driver, who had clearly seen the slap in his driving mirror, was respectful, almost comically deferential to the feisty lady, "Yes ma'am!"

"Let me out at the next subway station we come to."

Before he could respond I intervened, "You came all this way to slap my face and tell me you were married?" The car pulled to a halt outside the 81st. Street station and Marlene stepped out. But before she walked away she turned to face me, there were tears in her eyes, "I don't know what's made you so selfish, but the world doesn't revolve around you just because you're talented or because you can't use your arms or because you screw every woman you can get your cock into. It all doesn't matter to your kids, not your money, or the houses, or the toys. To them its you who counts. I don't know why but they still idolize you, and you, you sod, you have two gorgeous sons and you don't even know them. Those boys don't understand why their daddy never sees them, and nor do I. Goodbye." She slammed the door and ran to the subway steps without looking back.

Initially I was too stunned to react, and then I said to the driver, "Driver, can you take me back to the gallery please."

The driver got out of the car and walked around to my door, which he opened, "I ain't driving you nowhere mister, you're walking."

I had no alternative but to do as he instructed and the long walk gave me time to think.

Chapter Twenty-One

Los Angeles, California
1963

Hank's office on Wilshire Boulevard was that of a hugely rich, nationally famous attorney, it was sumptuous and huge. He liked to boast it was the size of a tennis court, and he wasn't exaggerating, much. Hank had finally gained some weight, but had kept his hair dyed jet black, even though it wasn't quite so thick and lustrous any more. We were facing each other at either end of a long oval redwood table, with Helmut in one of the numerous empty leather chairs running each side. As ever at our seemingly endless charitable trust executive meetings Hank was reading from reams of account statements, cash flows, turnover, and net profits, until both Helmut and I were finding it difficult to stay awake. I couldn't have been more bored.

Hank droned on, "Our English operation has been particularly successful for the last tax year the British foundation will clear a surplus of approximately nine hundred thousand pounds sterling and as for Latin America the figures are even more."

I cut in, "The Tax Authorities are a whole lot more interested than I am. Can't you just share this with Hynie, I want to slash my throat, but you'd have to stop reading to help me." I pleaded, "It's you duty to know everything that the Foundation does, you're President for life, and you need to know the income and expenditure, how many people are being helped, everything."

"That's all very German of you Helmut, but I'm supposed to be a bloody artiste, not a book-keeper. And don't tell me you actually believe our own propaganda. It's all down to the bottom line and that's how much money we have in our bank account.

230

Hank understands all that, don't you Hank?" Hank didn't reply, but Helmut did, "You're drunk, its not even lunch time and you're drunk."

"That isn't true, I am high, I am not drunk, I just smoked some weed that my nice model gave to me, delightful girl." I laughed, but both my friends looked at me with something bordering on contempt.

"How long has it been since you actually painted a picture of your model instead of screwing with her?" Helmut insisted on asking me, "I haven't painted a decent picture in years, but who cares as long as we have a thriving business. What do I do I go on fucking lecture tours and I find other bloody cripples who can be taught to hold a bloody paint brush with some part of their anatomy, we pay them a lousy salary and that makes us respectable, bring in more bloody money, so that you can find ways of paying no tax. It's a treadmill, what does it have to do with art? Nothing, none of it has anything whatsoever to do with art, or creativity. I've had enough of this shit, I'm finished, and it's over!"

Helmut sighed, "You just need a vacation, somewhere to come down of all these drugs, get your head together, this isn't you talking, it's the drugs."

"Yes'" Hank agreed, "A nice vacation someplace, we can fix it up for you, then you'll be back on form, the Arnie we all know."

"You can't quit Arnie, too many people depend on you for their living." Helmut finished, "None of you have needed me for years, and you know it, I've become just a figurehead, someone to wheel out for the interview, I'm an irrelevance."

"This is such shit Arnie," Helmut insisted, "You're the inspiration for thousands of people, and yes, your role is different now, its become that of a leader, you can't do this as a one man show any longer, it's a team, and there are a lot of people, handicapped and otherwise in that team, depending on it. They're all over the world, all kinds of people. Stop feeling so sorry for yourself and help them."

"I've done enough, haven't I. let someone else do it. I'm so tired. How much can one person give?"

Helmut stood up, clearly angry with me; "I never thought I'd hear this from you. Let me ask you a better question. How much can one person take?"

"Who do you think you're kidding? This was always just a great big scam, a business like any other, to make us all rich." I was disappointed with myself as soon as I said it, and I could see how I had upset both my friends. "Of course it was, to begin with," said Helmut before continuing, "then we had to survive the war. These things happen piece by piece, you can't divorce our reality from the rest of the world. After the war it had become something else, we really did a lot of good for thousands of people who otherwise would have starved. It's a force for good, surely you know that about this business, after all you were its father."

"If you really believe that garbage you should be sitting in my chair, I don't believe it any more."

"It's not garbage Arnie, its what makes us come in every morning. It's a pity if you're so confused that you don't believe it any more, but we can't let you pull the whole temple down just because you've lost faith." Hank finished and sighed heavily, he closed the folders he had been reading from.

"You can talk, how rich have you become Hank from your work with my Foundation?" I wanted to hurt him, and to punish him for making me look inwards. It was sheer spite and looking back I could only hate myself for it. Hank was looking at me sorrowfully. "Arnie, you'd better go take a risk someplace because I am not going to take that kind of abuse from anyone."

Before I could anything further Helmut leant forward in my direction, "You apologize to Hank, he hasn't taken a cent from the Foundation in fees for the last ten years and while we're on this matter neither have I. And if you had ever listened to these meetings, or read any of the papers we sent you would have known all this you sad fool!"

I was stunned, "I didn't know, I promise you I didn't know, so how did you two live, how do you afford the houses and the cars and everything else?"

"We'd already made enough for the rest of our lives five or ten years back, and we own enough assets to keep us in luxury for the rest of our lives." Helmut answered. "Why didn't you tell me?"

"We did you idiot, you just forgot how to listen to anything or anyone but yourself." This time it was Hank who nailed me. I knew it was time for Arnie Hessel to do what he was told for once, it was time for me to find myself, to do what everyone else was doing, drop out and turn on.

Chapter Twenty-Two

London
July 1967

I was sitting in a café on the Kings Road in London's Chelsea. I was part of the flower power generation, even if they thought I was too old for anything but a bus pass and a pension. I watched the dolly birds stroll past in their micro mini skirts from Biba's, their hair cut by the style gurus at Vidal Sassoon, they were accompanied by their peacock boyfriends, and I understood what it was to be almost invisible to the young and attractive. They only had eyes for each other, not an old fool like me. But I could still look and dream. As ever I was surrounded by a bunch of fashionable but poor freeloaders, always glad to join my table as long as I kept on picking up the check.

I looked at my companions through my ever-present cocktail of drink and drugs. My pals were preening themselves, sprouting their usual nonsense. Looking at myself wouldn't have been pleasant, I was described in the newspaper gossip columns as dissolute and louche, and I took this as a compliment.

The passing of the years had eviscerated my emotions; I imagine what it was like to be gutted like a fish. Maybe I looked like the old Arnie but my warmth and humanity had fled me and been replaced by a void. I felt nothing. "Same again waiter, for me and all my friends!" I called to the young fellow who rushed to fill the order, knowing me as his biggest giver of tips.

The buxom blond girl next to me stroked my leg under the table, and I can't even remember her name, or sadly even her face. I'm sure she meant well. "I'm your number one girl ain't I Arnie, your special model, but we ain't getting much painting done are we Fritz?" she made sure all of her friends heard her.

The crowd of youngsters all laughed, "You call me Fritz and I shall call you all Tommy?"

The black girl seated to the other side of me took a drag on whatever she was smoking, "From what she tells me darling we should be calling you bloody King Dong!"

"You English girls, so shy and reserved, that's why I've always loved you." The black girls boyfriend raised his glass in my direction, "Hey Fritz, leave some of our crumpet to us will you."

The waiter began to serve the round of drinks but before he does so he gave an envelope to my blond companion. It was addressed to me so I nodded for her to open and read it. "It's only a telegram from New York, New York, from a bloke called Hynie," I was instantly sober; Hynie didn't bother with me unless it was something serious these days.

"What does it say?"

Something about the tone of my voice made the whole group become silent as we all waited for her to continue reading from the note, "Bertha Hessel gravely ill STOP Flight booked today to Tel Aviv on El Al Heathrow Terminal 3 at 15.30 hours STOP Medics strongly suggest you go. STOP Regards Hynie MESSAGE ENDS Hey, I didn't know you was married."

I didn't bother to respond, I was already whistling for a taxi to the airport.

Chapter Twenty-Three

Israel
July 1967

The airport was a madhouse. The air conditioning was winning the necessary and unceasing summer battle with the overwhelming heat. I felt so totally alien but impressed with this, my first look at the rapid progression of this country. I couldn't quite grasp that almost everyone I saw was Jewish, be they bus driver or orthodox, soldier or prostitute. Everyone was here because they felt driven to be here, except for me, I was there, I hoped, in time to say farewell to my mother. Every fiber of this small country was buoyant and almost exultant after their recent triumphant war that had lasted just six days. The victory had been almost biblical in its margin of triumph but no one had any idea of what to do next.

A pretty, slim raven-haired El Al stewardess helped me pass through customs and immigration before all the other passengers. Someone had been very efficient, I thought appreciatively. We rushed through the busy security area until we reached the outer door, which opened automatically. The harsh sunlight blinded me for a moment, but the stewardess noticed that my sunglasses were in my jacket pocket, "Would you like me to put those on for you?" she asked, and I nodded. As she put them on the bridge of my noise I could suddenly see through the Polarized lenses. The crowd seemed to be full of young men, and I studied them, looking for someone that might appear familiar. The stewardess said her farewells and I grunted in response, still looking intently in the buzzing crowd.

Then I saw them, two handsome young men in military uniform. They are dark I thought, burnt brown by the never-ending sun. They were hard from their training, and suspicious of me because I had given them a lifetime of reasons.

One is dark, dark brown eyed and almost swarthy, the other is taller, blonde and blue eyed. The perfect Aryan I thought. The two young men moved towards me, but they left a little island of space between us.

"My sons?"

The blond boy answered, "They call me Ben, and this is Ezra."

"They aren't the names we gave you."

"They're the names Israel gave us, they're our names now." Said Ben, and there was another moment of silence broken when I smiled and Ezra spoke, " Have you got any bags?"

"I came as soon as I heard, in what I was wearing."

Ben, who I began to realize, was the softer of the two, spoke again, "We'll fix you up. Come on the Jeep is over there."

He pointed to a Jeep illegally parked amongst the taxicabs but the boys didn't take any notice of the hooting horns of the cab drivers.

Ezra drove with controlled aggression through the growing pandemonium of the late rush hour traffic. He made no effort to conceal his resentment of me and I didn't know what to say, or whether this was the right time. I realized that these two men were strangers, and one might be interested in me, but the other just seemed to hate me.

"How is your grandmother""?

"She's asking for you." Said Ben, "She's dying." Added Ezra.

"You don't have to be so cruel." Ben said quietly to his brother.

"It's OK Ben, I understand." I tried to bring down the emotional temperature.

We were at the traffic lights and Ezra turned to face me, "I don't want you to understand me. I don't want anything from you at all. Why change the habits of a lifetime. Ben the only thing he has in common with us is his blood."

"Would it help if I admitted I was wrong, if I said I was sorry?" I asked him.

"Now isn't the time." Ben insisted, do you follow football. Dad?"

"Call me Arnie, both of you please, you'll be more comfortable with that."

"No, dad is better for me," said Ben, I've always wanted to call someone dad, and it might as well be you, as you are my father. I thought I might understand you, but I don't. Do I? No, I don't. But Ezra is right, none of this is OK, none of it ever made sense."

"Will the two of you really say what you feel."? Said Ezra, "Everyone is dancing around the real issues, and who knows it might be twenty years or never before we get another chance to talk. Why did you abandon us?"

He drove the car fast through the traffic, making spaces where there weren't any, weaving in and out, ignoring the honking horns of the other angry drivers. I had no idea what to say to these two strangers, these handsome, tough young men, my boys.

We pulled up outside the Hadassah hospital in Jerusalem, a vast modern complex. We got out of the car and hurried in through the entrance, which was more like an American hotel than a European hospital.

I followed my sons as they rushed into the first elevator and made space for me. The crush of the other passengers forced us into proximity, and almost touching. It was uncomfortable for all of us. The elevator stopped, the doors opened and we got out. Again I followed Ezra and Ben as they hurried through the broad corridor. We arrived outside a room with the name Bertha Hessel on the space for the patient's name. "We put this on your tab, we thought you wouldn't mind." Ezra said pointedly to me, "Of course its all right." I started to say more, but I was more intent on going into the room, "Prepare yourself dad, she isn't like she used to be." Ben told me. I nodded as they opened the door and I followed them in.

There was a crowd of men gathered around the bed, so many I couldn't even see what had happened to my mother. Ben and Ezra understood better than me, they looked at each other and donned their army berets. I didn't immediately comprehend the situation. The men in the room felt our presence and turned, seeing us they parted to let us through. My mother, Bertha, was lying there, dead.

A heavily bearded man turned and smiled kindly, his face benign but sad. He was clearly a rabbi, about my age; his hair completely white, and he was dressed in the formal black clothes of the ultra orthodox Jew; he gripped my shoulder. His face was familiar but I didn't know any orthodox Jewish men. Instead I noticed that he had a skullcap under his broad fur trimmed hat and wondered why a person needed two head coverings. Something about him was familiar, but I still couldn't see past my tears and shock, he patted his face with a large white handkerchief, it was very warm. Then he embraced me in a brotherly fashion, his fine silk coat felt cool against my cheek. He even smelt familiar. He sighed and then talked to me. His English was heavily accented, but had a European edge, his first language wasn't Hebrew I thought. He patted his face with the large handkerchief again; it was very hot in the crowded room.

"I wish you a long life. Your mother had a good heart." He said to me. "I was too late." It was the only thing I could think of to say at that moment. "Can you read Hebrew?" the rabbi asked me. I shook my head, "I'm sorry, no I don't." I didn't understand why he asked.

"Kaddish, the prayer for the dead. Don't worry, I can say the words, and you just repeat them after me." He was very kind.

The next thing I clearly remembered was standing in the prayer chapel at the graveyard; friends and relatives of Bertha, none of whom I knew, surrounded us. I was standing alone at the end of the small sunlit hall next to my mother's plain pine coffin. I hadn't remembered the Jewish ways and tradition, no flowers, no fuss. You come into the world with nothing and you go out the same way.

Ben and Ezra moved silently so that they stood either side of me, each with an arm placed protectively around my shoulders. At that moment I understood a little bit about being a part of a family for the first time. The Rabbi uttered the ancient words praising God in the prayer for the dead and I quietly repeated them, finding comfort in them as I looked at my mother, who was at peace at last.

"I want to say a few words for Bertha Hessel;" the rabbi said, "Who can find a woman of worth? For her price is far above rubies. She stretches her hands out to the poor and needy. She is clothed in strength and majesty and she laughs at the times to come. She speaks with wisdom and the law of love and kindness is on her tongue. Give her the fruit of her own goodness and let her works be remembered. The Lord repays you for your efforts and a full reward will now be given to you by the Lord God of Israel."

For the first time I could remember I began to sob uncontrollably for someone other than myself. My sons embraced and supported me from each side. I was distraught; the rabbi smiled kindly towards me. As he turned to speak to one of those attending something about the way he stood struck me, but I couldn't think what it was.

Later, after the coffin had been interred we returned to my mother's house. I spent days there for the Shiva, the seven days of mourning customary for all Jews when someone in the family dies. The mirrors were covered, the pictures put in drawers, the principal mourners sitting on low uncomfortable chairs. Family and friends came every day to say prayers, share some refreshment and to reminisce.

Because there were no mirrors I didn't see how unkempt and disheveled I was becoming. The Rabbi had me sit on one of the small wooden chairs and then instructed me, "Please stand up

Mister Hessel." I did so and he showed me the razor in his hand, "This must be done." He deftly hacked at the lapel of my jacket, splitting the fine material and then he cut and pulled at my shirt collar and tie. I didn't react.

Something made me look into the eyes of the rabbi, and I knew who it was. Standing in front of me was Ratwerller, now disguised as a rabbi.

"You!" I said, inches from his face, he tried to smile at me, and my two sons realized something was happening between me and the rabbi who still had the razor inches from me. How ironic, I thought in that moment, that a rabbi was going to take my life.

Ezra approached as Ratwerller nodded his head. I saw Ben pull his Uzi sub machine gun from the cupboard in which it had been stored. Ratwerller concentrated on me, "It started as a clever disguise." He said, "Where better to hide, who would look for me dressed as a Jew, among so many others?"

I snorted with derision, "You don't expect mercy do you, we don't turn the other cheek any more, us Jews, we fight back. You deserve whatever you get."

"So you're Jewish now, me as well, I really am, I became Jewish, what do you think of that?" He asked me, "I wish you death so you can meet your maker and let him decide." I replied.

Ratwerller nodded and looked at me with curiosity, "Why did you have to come here, I was a good rabbi you know. This is a fine country, fine young men, you should be proud of it, of them."

I was about to tell him that we needed nothing from him when he raised his razor, I thought I was about to die. But instead Ratwerller smiled at me, in the most-friendly way, and suddenly, in one sweeping motion he slit his own throat.

A great gush of Ratwerller's life-blood flew in my face and he slumped to the floor at my feet. I was too shocked to move.

Ben and Ezra tried to revive him but it was hopeless. "He's a murderer and a Nazi torturer!" I told them, hoping they wouldn't try, "We're not like them." Said Ezra, "Bastards like this we want to stand trial, to be punished." But, as Ben said as the last breath juddered through Ratwerller's torn throat, "What better punishment could there be for him than to live as a Jew?"

It delayed the Shiva that day as the authorities descended on the scene, determined to investigate with forensic thoroughness the strange death of the Nazi rabbi. But this is Israel where family and tradition comes before everything. They soon cleaned up the bloodstains on the floor and removed all the physical traces of the incident. They had rapidly decided that the best thing was to let the Shiva proceed. They would deal with the implications of this messy suicide after dealing with the immediate needs of the living.

The following day I sat on the same little stool in the same small room, the object of much curiosity from the seemingly never ending crowd of well wishers, all of whom wanted to wish me a long life. They talked to me about my mother, with endless anecdotes extolling her virtues in every conceivable way. I found myself surrounded by this strange, unruly but loving mass of humanity. Although I knew she wasn't perfect I was thrilled that her life had so obviously been blessed with love and warmth. Finally I had found a place, which felt like it was my home.

Ben came over to me with an attractive, vibrant girl in tow, "Father this is Michal." She smiled, and the room seemed to light up, "I'm sorry to meet you in such circumstances Mister Hessel."

"It's funny you know, I'm not really Jewish. I had never prayed a Jewish prayer until yesterday, I don't understand any of it." I smiled.

"You know your mother was Jewish, but my mother wasn't." Ben answered, "So under Jewish law that makes you more Jewish than me. We follow the mother's line, not the father's. Anyhow, all of this is what nana wanted, it isn't for you or me."

I smiled at him, "Your mother taught you well; and you're right, I shouldn't always think of myself at the centre of every story, but it's a hard habit to break when you've been the hero in your own mind for all your life."

He looked at me and paused, then he smiled, "I guess not, but time passes, and we have to let go, move forward. Today we sit Shiva for nana, just for this last day with the High Holy Days coming tomorrow. Meantime Ezra and Ben are kidnapping you so that you can all get to know each other."

"It sounds good to me, is Ezra OK with it?"

Michal smiled then, "It was his idea, and he doesn't usually take any prisoners so I'd say yes if I was you. Besides, a bit of our country air will do you all good."

On the other side of the room, out of my earshot, Ben and Ezra were arguing with each other. "I don't want any part of that man," said Ezra to his exasperated brother, "I can't stop you wasting your time if that's what you want to do."

"Give him a chance." Ben said, "He's still our dad, we don't know what went on in his life. It's time to find out for ourselves, we're grown up now; we need to hear this directly."

Ezra pointed his finger at Ben, jabbing it at him to emphasize every point, "He had his chances, a million of them, we're twenty-one years old. He is a selfish old bastard!"

"So you know all his problems do you?" Ben challenged Ezra.

"I don't care about his problems. Are you like everybody else, blinded by his talent, by the fact that he overcame his handicap? Hoo-bloody-ray! Can't you see he only cares for one person, himself!"

I could see the boys were arguing, but I preferred not to hear so I was talking as loudly as I could with whoever would listen. I just wanted to love my boys and I hoped it wasn't too late, and I didn't know how to ask for help any more.

Ben looked over at my anxious face and turned back to his twin, "Look at him, he needs our help, now he needs us. Are you going to be like him in order to punish him?"

Thank the Lord, I thought. The next day we were in Michal's house in the hills near an artist colony called Safed, a beautiful little town. We had driven there first thing in the morning. The atmosphere hadn't been easy in the car, but it eased as the scenery improved.

I was seated on the verandah of Michal's house overlooking the beautiful scenery. Michal was painting a candid portrait of Ben and Ezra who lay sleeping on adjoining recliner chairs dressed only in swimming trunks, their taut, lean muscled bodies being fed from the sun.

She leaned back from her work, "Don't they look sweet, your boys."

"They look dangerous to me. Excuse me for being abrupt, but I'm getting too old for being patient. Are you and Ben going to marry?"

She laughed again, she was very attractive in the sunlight dappling her face, her thick hair framing her wide set and penetrating eyes, "I think you had better ask me that again after he pops the question."

"I'm sorry, I took it for granted. You paint well, when we drove through this town it looks like its full of artists."

She nodded, "Yes, it was for a very long time, hundreds, maybe thousands of years, a centre for theological study and now it's the art capital of Israel. Do you like my town?"

"Yes I do, its warm and comfortable, like you."

"You know how to pay a pretty compliment mister Hessel."

"One of my few real gifts."

"Why don't you stay in Israel, live here, in this town, you'd love it I'm sure, this is your real home?"

I shook my head, "I'm more German than Jewish in my ways. I'm used to my wife of life, for whatever its worth. It's too late to change now."

"What kind of life is it?" she persisted, "Women and money are that much more important to you than your sons?"

I winced from the direct hit, "They might have been in the past, but not now. I know my reputation is pathetic, I'm sorry for what I did, or didn't do, but I can't remake my past."

She came over to my seat and knelt next to my chair, "I'm so sorry, I didn't think."

"Why apologize, he's famous for his boozing and whoring?" Ezra had woken up and this had also woken Ben. "And for his wonderful talent."

"Look," I said, "My talent was never an excuse for my behavior, but I don't want you to argue about me. This isn't right, I don't want you to fight ever, especially about me, I'm not worth it. I'll go back to London, today."

Michal, who had now stood turned to my sons, "Can't you stupid men kiss and make up. This is your father. You only ever get one. I wish my daddy was still here for me to cuddle right now. Don't let your daddy slip through your fingers, love him today and every other day God gives you!"

We all went silent for a few moments as she walked into the house and left us all facing one another.

"She's right." I said, "Not about me being worth anything, I'm probably not worth one minute of your time. But haven't we hurt each other enough now?"

Ben got up from his chair and walked over to me, he kissed me on the cheek and it felt good. "She's right, I love you dad, whatever you did or didn't do."

Ezra also rose from his chair, "I can't just forget all those years. All we ever got from you was money, never anything but money. And that meant nothing to you. I used to dream about you when I was a child. I used to pretend that when I got home from school you'd be there, waiting for us. I used to hope you'd die so that I could stop hoping you'd come. Do you know how many times I cried?"

Ben went to his brother and hugged him. My tears fell as I watched my boys, thinking what had I done to deserve to be in the lives of these two magnificent young men.

"I can't do anything about what's past, but I can promise that it won't ever be like that again. What do you say, will you give me one last chance, I know I don't deserve it, but I'm asking?"

"Tell me one good reason why we should." Ezra demanded of me.

"Because one day I am going to die, and it won't be so long and I don't want to be alone. I want my sons to say the prayers for me that I just said for my mother. I'm too old to fight any more, too old and too tired. I can even forgive the bastards who did such terrible things in the war; so, I'm asking you to forgive me. I know I'm not a good man, and I've been a total mess as a father, so I deserve your contempt; but I want your love. Please, I'm begging you."

There was a long pause while we all looked at each other, then my sons came to me, one on each side, and they hugged me, and my life was complete.

"Now can I go home?"

"How can you want to go home when we've finally found each other?" asked Ben, "He's right." Ezra suggested, "Stay with us here. This is your home. What's there in Europe so special?"

"I'm a painter, and that's where I can paint, and it has been too long since I saw my home. But there's no big rush."

We embraced again, understanding one another, and all of our needs, for the first time. Now I could look in the mirror again, and like what I saw.

Chapter Twenty-Four

The Hessel House, The Rose Garden, Darmstadt, Germany
Spring 1986

My life had, by now, become mellow, the pace gentle, even the air felt mild. The colors were pastel, not so vibrant. I was aware that I now looked the part of the patriarch, the great white haired old artiste. Some things never changed I thought and chuckled quietly as I painted. My model was a young nubile blond, she was nearly naked, and was standing at almost exactly the same spot where Marlene had stood so many years before.

The blond spoke to me, I would tell you her name if I could remember, she was very beautiful, in a hurry like all young people. I do recall she had a broad American accent, from the Deep South, somewhere like Georgia. "I'm really an actress you know maestro. I'm only doing this kind of thing because you're so famous, for the painting without the arms and all. This is kind of like a classier version of me posing for Playboy. And I get to make postcards of the painting to send to all the talent agents like you promised, that's class, pure class man."

"Keep still please." I told her, she kept fidgeting.

She couldn't maintain her position for more than a few moments, and I was thinking that she was more trouble than she was worth however beautiful she was.

"Wait until I tell all the gang that my painting is hanging in some old European gallery." She turned to smile in my direction, breaking the pose yet again. I let the brush fall out of my mouth in exasperation.

"You can put your robe on for now. Thank you." I told her.

"Maybe you want to get to know me a little better. I don't mind that you're old and wrinkly because you're really famous."

She moved so her lovely breast was just inches from my mouth. I could feel her heat.

"Come on old guy, you still got what it takes? Let's party!"

I tried to stand up, and back away a little, but she moved closer again. Our bodies were touching and despite myself I began to get excited. This is ridiculous, I thought.

"No, I'm too old and too tired, you should be with a young man."

But she had her hand on me, and my penis never had any sense or emotion, it responded for the first time in a long while. She kissed me and I began to feel the blood pump within me. She kissed me passionately and it was then that I felt the first stab of intense pain hit my chest. It was like a huge hammer hit me. I fell to my knees. My breath came in huge gulps. I struggled to find air.

Through a fog I saw the blond girl panic, "Stop it, stop it, you're really freaking me Arnie!" she shouted at me, but although I tried to smile to reassure her I couldn't control myself. I slumped to the floor. Prostrate. I saw the blond move away from me, repelled by my battle.

Strangely, through that pain there was an oasis I reached, a moment when I could remember everything, and I saw, clearly my mother, she was smiling at me, "Mama," I said, "Is it a good picture, did I do it well?"

I returned her smile, and then was no more.

Chapter Twenty-Five

The Jewish Cemetery, Frankfurt
1986

As the many cars pulled into the ground of the cemetery the media were fighting hard to gain a good view of the private proceedings. Ben and Ezra stood next to their father's coffin as an old man walks over to each of them and shakes them by the hand. "I am Helmut, we never met but your father was a very special man." Before they could respond the rabbi started the service.

The prayer hall was crowded with dignitaries, but Ben leaned to his brother and whispered, "Dad would have been happy, look at how many friends he had." Ezra looked at the chapel, full to capacity, and then noticed through the windows, that there were hundreds, possibly thousands more outside in the grounds of the cemetery.

A very old man with a stick went to the lectern when asked by the rabbi, "Hi," he said, "My name is Hank, and I'm here just to say a few words for my dear friend Arnie Hessel. He was an extraordinary man born in the most extraordinary of times."

Before he could continue Hank began to cry. He was unable to speak further but Ezra took his place.

The eulogy he delivered would have made his father happy and content. He talked of the last twenty years, when the family grew to include his marriage and children, and those of his brother, now the tribe was bigger, but they were all so proud of all the people that their father had helped around the world, helped to help themselves. The fact that Arnie Hessel had given away his entire fortune to his trust, and that this had now grown to encompass every continent. He was a diamond, perhaps a rough diamond, but their diamond nevertheless. "I am proud that this man was my father." He concluded.

Shortly after the coffin was gently lowered into the ground. The rabbi led Ben and Ezra in the rituals and they recited the Kaddish for their daddy, just like he had wanted. As is the tradition the gravediggers gave each of his sons a shovel and they dug into the loose earth around the grave and poured it onto the coffin, it made a very final sound as it hit the wood. When they had started the process each man present took their turn to do the same thing, and very soon the grave was full of earth.

Despite it not being part of the Jewish tradition hundreds of young artists each dropped a flower onto Arnie's grave and the colors were joyous, just like one of his paintings, and when no one was left at the graveside, a number of butterflies settled on the flowers, they formed a rainbow as they beat their wings, as if in tribute.

THE END

Epilogue

Some facts about Poliomyelitis. It is, or rather was, a very cruel but widespread illness, and remains a deadly part of our world in many regions of the planet. Polio was first recognized as a distinct condition by Jakob Heine in 1840; Its causative agent, poliovirus, was identified in 1908 by Karl Landsteiner. Although major polio epidemics were unknown before the late 19th century, polio was one of the most dreaded childhood diseases of the 20th century. Polio epidemics have crippled thousands of people, mostly young children; the disease has caused paralysis and death for much of human history. Polio had existed for thousands of years quietly as an endemic pathogen until the 1880s, when major epidemics began to occur in Europe; soon after, widespread epidemics appeared in the United States. By 1910, much of the world experienced a dramatic increase in polio cases and frequent epidemics became regular events, primarily in cities during the summer months.

In order to make a polio diagnosis, the doctor will order certain tests that will look for the virus or antibodies the body has made against the poliovirus. In order to perform these polio tests, a stool sample or a throat swab may be taken.

There are a number of diseases and conditions that are similar to polio in signs and symptoms: Bite from a snake (such as a cobra) Poisoning Diphtheria, Myasthenia gravis, Guillain-Barre syndrome, Transverse myelitis, Tick paralysis, Rabies Botulism.

When a person is infected with poliovirus, the virus resides in the intestinal tract and mucus in the nose and throat. Poliovirus transmission most often occurs through contact with stool of this infected person (known as fecal-oral transmission). Less frequently, polio transmission can occur through contact with infected respiratory secretions or saliva (oral-oral transmission).

Common signs and symptoms of polio symptoms include fever, sore throat, and nausea. Symptoms usually appear 7 to 14 days after a person becomes infected with the poliovirus. Up to 95 percent of people who are infected with poliovirus will have no symptoms. However, people who are infected and do not have symptoms can still spread the poliovirus and cause others to develop polio.

When a person becomes infected with poliovirus, the virus begins to multiply within the cells that line the back of the throat, nose, and intestines. Polio symptoms usually appear 7 to 14 days after a person becomes infected with the poliovirus. This period between polio transmission and the start of symptoms is called the "polio incubation period." The incubation period for polio can be as short as 4 days or as long as 35 days.

Between 1 to 2 percent of infected people develop aseptic meningitis from poliovirus. For these people, early symptoms can be similar to minor polio symptoms. Then aseptic meningitis symptoms can develop, including stiffness of the back or legs and increased or abnormal sensations. These symptoms improve rapidly, usually within a couple of days (2-10 days) with complete recovery.

With Paralytic Poliomyelitis less than 1 percent of cases will result in paralysis. In these severe cases, symptoms begin with fever, muscle aches, loss of reflexes, and other "minor illness" symptoms.

These early symptoms improve after several days. However, 5 to 10 days later, the fever returns and paralysis begins. Paralysis progresses for two to three days. Once the temperature returns to normal, there is usually no further paralysis. Along with paralysis, other polio symptoms with paralytic poliomyelitis can include painful muscle cramps and muscle twitching.

The risk of paralysis from polio increases with age. In children under the age of five, paralysis of one leg is common. In adults, paralysis of both arms and legs is common. Muscles controlling urination and breathing might also be affected.

Many people with paralytic poliomyelitis recover completely, and muscle function returns to some degree. However, paralysis after six months is usually permanent.

People who develop serious symptoms (including paralysis) may experience complications. Polio complications in severe cases can include: Inflammation of the heart muscle (myocarditis) High blood pressure (hypertension) Fluid in the lungs (pulmonary edema) Pneumonia Urinary tract infections (UTIs).

Approximately 2 to 5 percent of children and 15 to 30 percent of adults with paralytic polio die from the poliovirus infection.

Fortunately, widespread and effective vaccination to protect the young was developed and distributed globally after the Second World War and this dreadful disease was all but eliminated in the industrialized world. In 1988, when the Global Polio Eradication Initiative began, polio paralyzed more than 1000 children worldwide every day. Since then, over 2.5 billion children have been immunized thanks to the cooperation of more than 200 countries and 20 million volunteers, backed by an international investment exceeding US$ 8 billion.

Today, polio has been eliminated from most of the world and only four countries remain endemic. In 2009, fewer than 2000 cases were reported for the entire year. Charitable groups such as the Bill and Melinda Gates Foundation work tirelessly to eliminate this disease.